Mutts and Mistletoe

Mutts and Mistletoe

NATALIE COX

G. P. PUTNAM'S SONS

New York

PUTNAM

G. P. Putnam's Sons
Publishers Since 1838
An imprint of Penguin Random House LLC
375 Hudson Street
New York, New York 10014

ISBN 9780525539193

Printed in the United States of America
1 3 5 7 9 10 8 6 4 2

Book design by Laura K. Corless

This book is dedicated to the memory of Tally the chocolate Lab, my trusty fireside companion and canine muse these last fifteen years, and to Grace the Great Dane puppy, who already exasperates and inspires in equal measure.

Mutts and Mistletoe

chapter 1

T. S. Eliot was wrong. December is the cruelest month. If the rampant commercialism of Christmas doesn't get you down, the dreary London weather will. This morning, on the way to work, when it was bucketing with rain and I should have been answering e-mails, I got to thinking about everything that was wrong with the holiday season. And almost without trying, I came up with a list of *Ten Things I Hate About Christmas*:

1. The phrase *Happy Holidays,* which is meant as a greeting, but feels more like a command: one that instantly makes me want to disobey.

2. Ditto foreign language salutations: *Feliz Navidad, Joyeux Noel, Yuletide Greetings.* If I don't want them in English, I don't want them in French or Spanish.

3. Office Christmas parties, which are really just a pathetic excuse for married coworkers to drink too much and take liberties with each other. (Unless it's Sean from finance, who is free to liberate himself with me anytime.)

4. Drunken revelers on the tube, aka the bloated guy wearing a tissue-paper crown who fell asleep next to me last night on the Northern line and drooled on my coat. To be fair, my late-night rendition of "Santa Baby" on the Jubilee line last Thursday did draw some aggrieved looks. But I was egged on by my companions. Who were even drunker than I was.

5. Stupidly large wheels of cheddar cheese in lieu of proper food at parties. Partial though I am to cheese, I need some sausage rolls, too.

6. Mulled wine: Why does everyone get so excited about bottom-of-the-bin Bulgarian red, heavily laced with sugar and spice? Especially since it leaves you with a monstrous hangover the next morning. Which I now have.

7. Chocolate advent calendars. This is just marketing run amok. Scarf a large bar of Cadbury's on the first day of December and be done with it.

8. Disney-themed holiday decorations, especially those along Oxford Street. When it comes to Hollywood at Christmas, we should emulate Nancy Reagan and *just say no*.

9. Greeting cards bearing photos of offspring that lurk like land mines in my postbox, reminding me that I am thirty-one and have not yet spawned.

10. Elves. The annoying kind. Which is pretty much all of them.

In the spirit of fairness, I decide to compose a rival list of what I *do* like about the holidays:

1. Mince pies.

2. Real Christmas trees (the kind that smell nice and will cause untold misery for future generations by contributing to global warming).

3. Time off work.

Obviously 10:3 is not a great ratio, so I guess I'll have to work on that second list. But right now, as I elbow my way along Oxford Street, I am struggling to understand the appeal. These days Christmas is little more than a parody of itself: any vestige of Victorian charm has long since been quashed by Black Friday and the Top Gear Christmas Special. At Bond Street I'm forced to shoulder my way through a flock of excited Japanese tourists taking photos of a neon orange Christmas tree (whatever happened to silver and gold?). I then sidestep a portly older woman garlanded with bright red tinsel who rattles a tin aggressively in my face, like some sort of charitable assault. It's not that I don't believe in being generous during the Christmas season, but I honestly don't think Jesus intended donkey sanctuaries to be the beneficiary of all that goodwill. Even if they *were* present at his birth.

I dash down a side street and reach my favorite Italian café, pushing open the door with relief. Inside, people are huddled up to cappuccinos, their overstuffed shopping bags nestled like loyal spaniels against their feet. On the far side of the room I spy my friend Sian, her cheeks flushed pink and her ash-blonde hair swept atop her head in a ratty mess. I pick my way across the restaurant and sink into the chair opposite. "Aw," I say with a grin. "You did your hair just for me."

"Never let it be said that I don't make an effort," Sian replies, patting the unruly tangle. As always, Sian makes zero concessions to femininity while still being every inch her own woman. "Here." She slides her mug of cocoa over and I take a restorative slug.

"Bring on the New Year," I say. "I'm fed up with Christmas and it's only the second week of December."

"Season's Greetings to you, too."

"I should warn you that I'm not in a particularly festive mood."

"Was that meant to be some sort of spoiler?" Sian raises an eyebrow.

Suddenly I lean forward, eyeing her clothes suspiciously. "Please tell me that's not a Christmas jumper."

Sian opens her coat and proudly flashes a bright red sweater with a reindeer's head emblazoned across her chest. Each antler sports a tiny bell at its tip. "Owen chose it," she says proudly.

"Since when do you take fashion advice from a three-year-old?"

"He has surprisingly good taste. He talked me out of a purple velvet onesie the other day that would have been a terrible mistake."

"Are those real bells?"

In answer, she jiggles up and down in her seat and I hear a vague tinkling. I shake my head.

"Don't be such a grump," says Sian. "I love Christmas."

"Not me. I'm opting out this year. So don't expect a present."

"You can't opt out of Christmas."

"Watch me."

Sian narrows her eyes suspiciously. "What brought all this on?"

"Capital Radio," I say. "This morning I woke to the sound of aging rock stars desperately trying to salvage their careers by exhorting me to feed the world yet again. They should know by now that I can't even feed myself."

"I don't believe you."

"It's true." I shrug. "I've never been much of a fan. And this year I'm not only a Scrooge, but a newly single Scrooge. So I've decided to indulge my inner killjoy."

"What about your mum? Won't she be counting on you for carols at the Ark?"

My redoubtable mother and her fifth husband, Richie, sold up and retired a few years ago to a houseboat in Little Venice, which Sian promptly dubbed the Ark. They're forever dropping in on me when the plumbing goes wrong on the boat, which happens frequently, especially during cold weather. Thankfully, this year they decided to put the boat in dry storage and decamp to warmer climates for the winter.

I shake my head. "Not this year. They're off to Melbourne to see my stepbrother and his sprogs."

"Then you should definitely come to our place for the holiday."

"No, thanks."

"Why not? It'll be grand! You can stuff sausage meat up a turkey's arse while I ply my elderly aunties with prosecco until they collapse in a drunken stupor on the sofa."

"It goes in the neck cavity."

"What?"

"The sausage meat." I might not be a gourmet chef, but even I know that.

Sian frowns. "I knew that," she says.

"As tempting as it sounds, I'll pass."

"Listen, Charlie. I'm not about to let you spend the holidays moping over He-Who-Must-Not-Be-Named."

"Lionel. His name is Lionel. And I'm not moping."

"Good. Because he doesn't deserve it."

"But I'm still not coming for Christmas."

t takes most of my lunch hour to persuade Sian that I am serious. The truth is that I have no intention of spending the holiday with *anyone*. I plan to hole up in my flat in Nunhead with a six-pack of chardonnay and watch old black-and-white Audrey Hepburn movies back to back. Lionel always hated watching movies on TV, so I'm relishing the opportunity to indulge myself now that he's moved out. I also intend to binge on gummy bears, anchovy pizza, and barbecue-flavor crisps, all of which he also abhorred. In fact, I realize now that I abandoned great swathes of myself during the four years we lived together: reading in bed (he hated the light), crossword puzzles (he found them tedious), tinned chicken noodle soup (he pronounced it full of additives), and singing in the shower (it was Lionel who first told me I couldn't carry a tune). There are loads of upsides to single life, I tell Sian: more wardrobe space, fewer dirty dishes, and the freedom to wear whatever I like in bed.

Eventually, I manage to convince Sian that I am *fine*, but back in my flat that night I feel the familiar creep of doubt. The truth is that my seemingly stable life had capsized in an instant and I'm still floundering to make sense of what happened. Bizarrely, my breakup with Lionel was prompted by an anonymous e-mail. I might never have opened the attachment if the tagline hadn't caught my eye: *The camera doesn't lie*. And it was true: the photo of Lionel having sex with a fleshy brunette on a rowing machine appeared entirely legitimate, his hair darkly matted with sweat, her breasts splayed outward like badly inflated balloons.

When I showed it to him, Lionel confessed that he'd been sleeping with his personal trainer for more than a year. Relationships, he told me earnestly, weren't meant to last. They were fragile, fleeting constructs propped up by society's expectations and by the outdated institution of marriage. Looking around the kitchen, his eyes alighted on the kettle, and he held it up as if to underscore its relevance. What happened to us was inevitable, he said. Relationships ran smoothly at first, then deteriorated over time, until they finally broke down and you replaced them. Like a kettle.

So I'd been traded in for a younger appliance. Initially, I'd been devastated. I'd noted with bewilderment that my replacement was not as conventionally pretty as I would have expected, and I had no idea whether I should feel relieved or angered by that fact. Lionel and I had been together four years. And, for the first few, I'd been crazy about him; indeed, we'd been crazy about each other. But over time our relationship had slowly soured. And while four years wasn't an eternity, I quickly calculated that it amounted to more than a hundred million seconds of my life. Lionel had stolen that time from me—or maybe I'd given it away. Either way, there was no getting it back. More than a hundred million seconds of me were gone forever. I would have to make the most of what remained.

The night Lionel left me, it took only a few hours (maybe ten thousand seconds) for my anguish to be replaced by anger. But after several days, even that had faded to resignation. It occurred to me that maybe Lionel had been right; maybe romance *is* a modern fiction. Maybe it has been conjured out of the barest ingredients to satisfy our cravings, and maybe love itself really is as flimsy as a kettle. The more I thought about it, the more I questioned whether what I'd felt for Lionel really *was* love, or whether it was something else altogether. What exactly had we experienced all those years? Familiarity? Comfort? Security? Convenience? Perhaps all of these things. Did they add up to love? Or did they just equal expedience?

Over the years I'd watched countless female friends slide into relationships with partners who fell short of their expectations. Perhaps, unwittingly, I had done the same. In the future, I resolve that I will not make the same mistake twice: I would rather be alone than settle for an impostor. And when I crawl into bed, wearing jogging bottoms, a flannel shirt, and oversized socks, I know that if I can just get through the next few weeks, January will bring a fresh outlook. This thought is still circling my head like a lazy fly when the explosion tears through my flat.

chapter

2

Apparently, I am *extremely* lucky. Or so the stout Nigerian nurse in the emergency room tells me the next morning, while carefully cleansing my wounds with iodine. A concussion, bruised ribs, and a random smattering of abrasions are nothing compared to what might have happened when my upstairs neighbor's gas oven exploded. Someone was watching over me, to be sure, she declares, yanking open the curtain that surrounds my bed with a startling ferocity.

I bite my tongue in response: my own definition of luck does not involve ambulances, bedpans, or a prolonged risk of exposure to deadly airborne pathogens. In the next moment I catch a glimpse of two orderlies on the far side of the room restraining a drunk. The blurry-faced man lurches sideways, skittering a wheeled bedside table into the wall with a clatter, before he is unceremoniously removed from my line of sight, thereby depriving me of my only form of entertainment. The nurse disappears and I lie back with a sigh.

Someone has strung two spindly strands of silver across the ceiling, like aimless tinsel snakes, and a 1950s-style poster of a Santa has been taped to the wall. But instead of smiling, retro Santa wears a grimace on his face: red-cheeked and grumpy, he looks as if he's about to be wheeled down the hall for gastric surgery. On the far side of the room a half dozen handmade snowflakes have been stuck to a window; and across the corridor a tiny, crooked tree perches atop the nurses' counter. The combined effect of all these efforts is almost tragically heroic. It is virtually impossible to kindle the spirit of Christmas on a National Health Service ward, but God bless them for trying.

As luck would have it, the explosion tore a hole right through my bedroom ceiling and I was hit by flying debris. A jagged chunk of pipe had impaled itself on my pillow, missing my forehead by millimeters, but a vast hunk of ceiling *had* landed squarely on top of me, and now I feel as if I've ingested a lorryload of plaster dust. My head throbs and my breasts feel as if they've been fed through a meat grinder. At some point in the early hours of the morning I tried ringing my father to let him know what happened. My father has long been my go-to parent: while he isn't very practical, he's always sympathetic. But when he failed to pick up, I texted my mother with a carefully edited account of the night's events, downplaying their severity.

I should have known better; within minutes I received a distraught phone call from Melbourne. She was already in full crisis mode, demanding details of the incident, consultants' names, work contacts, etc. At the time I was feeling too crappy to fend her off, but now I regret that I hadn't had more presence of mind. Especially since she ended up berating me for living in substandard accommodations (somewhat unfairly, I thought, given her own aquatic living quarters—not to mention how often she's turned up at my flat for a shower) and chastising me for my failure to have private health insurance.

Now I hear an insistent buzzing in my bag. I reach down and pull out my phone. "Hi, Mum."

"How are you? Has there been any change?"

"I'm fine."

"No double vision or nausea?"

"Honestly, it's just a few bruises. I'll be right as rain in a day or two."

"Don't be ridiculous, Charlie. You're obviously in shock. You shouldn't be left on your own. Your cousin Jez is driving to London as we speak. She's taking you back with her to Devon."

"Mum, I can't go to Devon! I've got to work."

"Not anymore. I spoke to your boss, and he's giving you the rest of the week off."

"He *agreed* to that?" Frankly, I'm amazed. My insufferable boss, Carl, is the most unsympathetic person on the face of the planet, especially when it comes to illness. You'd have to be stricken with Ebola before he'd grant you sick leave.

"He was a little grudging at first, but I reminded him of his statutory responsibilities as an employer."

Crap! He'll make me redundant in a flash. The thought of my mother ringing Carl and making imperious demands suddenly makes my head throb even more. On top of that, since last June there have been whisperings in the corridors about a restructuring.

I need to get back to work as soon as possible; otherwise I'll be out of a job before you can say *layoff*.

"And the consultant said no LCD screens for at least a week."

"I'm sure she was just being overcautious, Mum."

"Don't be ridiculous. Concussions can be very serious. It's absolutely imperative that you rest and recover." My mother has always thrived on calamity and at the moment she sounds utterly exhilarated. I sigh, knowing it's useless to protest.

"Fine. I'll go to Devon for a few days. But only until my flat is sorted." Which will be as soon as possible, as far as I'm concerned.

"The fresh air will do you good, Charlotte. And the animals will be positively therapeutic."

Crap. I'd completely forgotten about the dogs. My cousin Jez runs an upmarket kennel that is billed as a sort of luxury pet hotel. It's called Cozy Canine Cottages and instead of cages or pens, the dogs are kept in individual "suites." There are clubhouse suites, executive suites, and a penthouse suite that's bigger than my entire flat. Each suite has a miniature bed (complete with duvet and pillows) and a window overlooking the paddock. There's even a pool for hydrotherapy, and a chauffeur service to collect and deliver the dogs to and from their homes. My mother is perfectly aware that I'm not a dog person (a euphemism for "failed human," in her view), so this last comment from her seems almost spiteful. And while I've always liked my cousin Jez (and admired her entrepreneurial spirit, even though it means toadying to the rich), the thought of spending Christmas at Cozy Canine Cottages surrounded by a bunch of yappy, overfed terriers, rather than at home on my sofa cuddled up with my extensive DVD collection, makes me want to weep.

After my mother rings off, I lie in bed contemplating how quickly my life has unraveled. Not two weeks ago I was happily ensconced in a relationship (albeit with an unfaithful man), employed in a reasonably well-paid IT job (with a loathsome boss), and living in an affordable (if barely habitable) flat. Now I'm temporarily homeless, single, and quite likely to be sacked. How had all this happened so quickly? And what did I do to deserve it? I'm not a religious person, but I've always subscribed to a vaguely Buddhist way of looking at things, which is effectively summed up by the what-goes-around-comes-around school of thought. Have I unwittingly brought all this adversity on myself? I rack my memory, considering my actions over the past few months. OK, I behaved a little peevishly in the staff meeting last week, when Carl announced that everyone might have to share desks in the future, owing to cuts in overheads. I merely pointed out that seniority should entitle me at least to my own drawer space, whereupon the ever-annoying Carl responded that *seniority* meant leading by example. And I hadn't exactly been kindhearted to the vagrant who'd accosted me outside Tesco's the other night. But he'd stepped out of the shadows and frightened me witless, and I don't think that sort of approach should be rewarded, should it? Though . . . the old man had seemed harmless enough. Perhaps if I went back to the shop, he'd still be there? Or was it too late to make amends? Was karma even retroactive?

Now Lionel's words from the night he confessed drift back to me. "Sometimes you can be so glib, Charlie. I honestly thought you might not even *care*," he'd said. I did care, but possibly not for the right reasons. I woke up the morning after he left expecting to feel heartsick, but what I felt instead was something closer to heartburn. Indeed, I felt scorched: angry with love, angry with Lionel, and most of all angry with myself, for allowing my life to be yanked out from under me. At the end of the day, I, too, had been untruthful—in a way. I'd gone through the motions of leading a happy life, but hadn't truly lived it.

Suddenly the nurse appears, drawing back the bed curtain. "Rise and shine," she says briskly. "You've got a visitor." She steps aside and I see Jez lurking behind her wearing a faded green Barbour jacket and a flat wool cap, the sort that Welsh sheep farmers favor. Her dark brown hair is bunched in thick wodges on either side of her head, and her heavy eyebrows are arched upward, almost disappearing under her hat.

Jez nods to the nurse as the latter departs, then steps forward to my bedside. "Ouch," she says sympathetically, looking me over.

I give a small, sheepish wave. "Thanks for coming. You really didn't have to." In fact, it's a relief to see her, and I am suddenly hugely grateful that she has driven all this way.

Jez smiles. "I thought your mum was exaggerating. But I gotta say you look like shit."

"Great to see you, too."

"Couldn't you have . . . rolled out of the way or something?"

"I'll make sure I practice for next time."

Jez looks over her shoulder, then drops her voice. "What's that awful smell?"

"Blood, maybe? Death? It's a hospital."

Jez shakes her head, wrinkling her nose. "It's more like disinfectant."

"I'll ask them not to clean."

"Don't bother. I'm not planning to hang around. Are you finished?"

"I think they have a few more humiliating things to do to me."

Jez frowns slightly. "The thing is . . . I'm in kind of a rush."

"Oh."

"Can you walk?"

"How far?"

"I'm double-parked just outside."

"In Chelsea? Are you mad? You'll get towed!"

"Not if you hurry."

Miraculously, when we emerge blinking into the daylight a few minutes later, Jez's battered Land Rover is still sitting right where she left it. As I struggle into the front passenger seat, Jez grabs a disabled parking permit off the dashboard and leaps inside. "Who's that for?" I ask.

"Margot."

"Who's Margot?"

"An aging Weimaraner who sometimes stays with me."

"You have a disabled parking permit for a dog?"

"She's got hip dysplasia. It can be very serious."

"But she's not in the car."

"She could have been," says Jez defensively.

Jez drives the massive Land Rover like it's a tanker, barreling through amber lights at junctions and blaring the horn at seemingly random intervals. All around us I notice drivers and pedestrians veering out of the way like panicked rabbits. I briefly think about asking if we can swing by my flat to pick up some things, but then I remember that my bedroom is virtually a bombsite, and my clothes are unlikely to be wearable—that is, if I *have* any clothes left. Owing to a very thoughtful fireman, I have my coat, my phone, and my purse with me, and that's about it, apart from what I was wearing at the time of the explosion.

In the end, we had had to sneak out of the ER without being properly discharged, as Jez had been really fidgety. "What if I need more treatment?" I protest as I climb into the car.

"The vet's due in the morning. He can give you a once-over," says Jez.

"Great. I'll be given drugs intended for canines."

"Actually, he's a bovine specialist."

"'Bovine' as in . . . ?"

"Cows."

"Perfect."

"Strongest painkillers on the market," says Jez with a grin. "And that's speaking from experience."

Once on the motorway, Jez turns on the radio and I close my eyes. It had been a long night. Apart from the belligerent drunk in the cubicle across from me, there was a crying toddler somewhere off to the left and a confused elderly woman just beside me who kept drawing back the curtain and asking for water. "I'm sorry, do I look like a nurse?" I had finally replied, holding up my bandaged arm.

The old woman blinked several times, then nodded.

"Actually, I work in computers," I said. The old woman continued to stare at me beseechingly. "It's not usually regarded as one of the caring professions," I muttered, craning my neck around the ward to see if I could find a nurse. But the staff had all vanished mysteriously and for once the ward was oddly quiet. Finally, I rolled off my bed and limped across to a sink in the far corner, filling a plastic beaker I found in a cupboard. I returned and placed the beaker gingerly in the old woman's hands, prying her swollen knuckles apart, and she stared down at the beaker as if she had no clue what it was for.

"It's water," I explained. "You asked for it."

The old woman regarded the beaker for a moment, then handed it back to me, and for the briefest instant I considered tipping it over her. Then I set it down on the table and crawled back to my own bed, closing the curtain firmly behind me.

Now I doze off to the sound of *Gardener's Question Time* on Radio 4, dreaming of cubicles and snarling drunks and aging, watery eyes, which are somehow all mixed up with giant slugs and blighted potato plants. Sometime later I wake and see that the Land Rover is bumping up the Cozy Canine driveway. I sit up slowly, rubbing my face, and Jez smiles over at me.

"I was just beginning to wonder if you were comatose."

"Thanks for your concern."

"How you feeling?"

Truthfully? I think I should probably be in hospital. But compassion isn't Jez's strong suit. "I've been better," I say.

"Come on," she says, pulling up beside the house and turning the car off. "What you need is breakfast. I'll make you the house special."

The house special turns out to be two fried eggs atop a bed of whatever leftovers are lurking in the fridge, which in this case is chili con carne. While Jez sets about reheating the chili and frying the eggs, I waft around her farmhouse kitchen. It's just the right side of messy, with a sagging dark blue sofa; a heavily ringed wooden table surrounded by mismatched chairs; a wall of old cookbooks with fraying covers, and a massive pinboard layered with photos, old notices, dog show certificates, Christmas cards, and old party invitations. The stove is an ancient dark green Rayburn, which Jez loads up with coal from a tarnished copper bucket as soon as we come in, and within a few minutes the room feels surprisingly snug. While the eggs fry, Jez heats milk and makes lethally strong coffee in a French press. When I sink back into the sofa with a steaming-hot mug, I decide that maybe my mum was right. A few days in the country might be exactly what I need right now.

Then I hear the patter of tiny claws on linoleum. *Ah. Just when things were starting to look up,* I think wistfully. A fat, coffee-colored beagle waddles into the room, pausing to greet Jez at the stove.

"Hey. I wondered where you were," says Jez, leaning down to pat the dog's head fondly. "What happened to the usual meet 'n' greet?" The beagle ambles over to sniff at my shoes, then stares up at me. I'm no expert, but I could swear this one is frowning at me.

"That's Peggy. I'm afraid you're in her spot," says Jez.

"Sorry, Peggy." Out of politeness I reach down to give the beagle a perfunctory pat on the head, a gesture it seems to only barely tolerate. In fact, the dog almost seems to recoil from my touch. "Except I'm not *really* sorry, am I?" I whisper loudly. "Since sofas are for *humans.*"

Jez laughs. "Don't worry. Peggy's the only house dog. And she's too fat to get up there now, anyway."

"Guess you don't believe in doggy diets."

"She's up the duff," explains Jez. "Her litter's due in January."

"Oh. Wow. Sorry, Peggy, I hadn't realized. I guess congratulations are in order."

"Actually, she got out by accident. I'm not even sure who she mated with."

I look down at the beagle, who is collapsed heavily on one side and is now licking her pendulous teats. "Bit of a slutty pup then, are we, Peg?"

"The vet reckons the litter's massive. I'll be lucky to find homes for them all," says Jez. "And they won't be pedigree, so I'll practically have to *give* them away. You don't want a mutt, do you? Or three?"

"No, thanks. Though, in principle, I'm all for mixed marriages."

"Who said anything about marriage?" says Jez with a grin. "This was a quick shag behind the woodshed." She places two heaping plates of food on the table and I haul myself off the sofa and sit down, eyeing the concoction in front of me. Jez has slopped salsa, grated cheese, sour cream, and what looks like paprika onto the eggs and chili and the result looks like a Jackson Pollock painting.

"Um . . . what exactly do you call this?" I ask tentatively, picking up my fork.

"Cozy Canine Huevos," says Jez, already digging in. "And if you don't eat it, Peggy will."

chapter
3

I sleep the rest of the day, rising only briefly in the evening for a bowl of carrot soup and a hot bath before dragging myself back to the overstuffed bed in Jez's guest room. When I eventually wake the next morning, I feel as if my body has been run through the tough-stain cycle on the washing machine: clean but pummeled. I lie in bed, sunlight flickering through the faded yellow curtains, and road test each of my appendages. My ribs are tender, but my limbs and digits all appear to be in good working order, and the thundering headache that was with me most of yesterday seems to have mercifully abated. Perhaps I really am lucky, after all.

I rise and gingerly pull on my tracksuit bottoms and flannel shirt, deciding that a change of clothes will be necessary before much longer. I wonder where the nearest H&M is? Hours away, if memory serves me right. Jez lives on the outskirts of Cross Bottomley, a small village on the edge of Dartmoor. The nearest town is Plymouth, some forty minutes' drive away, and I know that Jez rarely makes the journey if she can help it, preferring to make do with whatever she can source locally. Cross Bottomley is the sort of place where the village's only newsagent doubles as the post office, launderette, and barber shop. The village also boasts a church, a pub, a small but reasonably well-stocked food shop, and a hardware store. Aside from that, there isn't much to recommend it apart from the scenery, which is often described as "rugged" in brochures, but on a bad-weather day it's just the wrong side of desolate.

When I get downstairs, I find Peggy sacked out on the kitchen sofa, her bloated teats drooping over the edge. *Too fat my arse,* I think, making a mental note to get up earlier so I can bag the sofa first from now on. Apart from the beagle, the kitchen is deserted, though there's fresh coffee in the French press and I can hear voices out in the yard. I pour myself a mug, eat a slice of buttered toast, then decide to ring Sian to let her know I'm still alive. She picks up almost instantly.

"Where *are* you?" she demands. "I must have rung you fifty times last night! Owen *refused* to poop just to spite me. I practically had to give him an enema in the end." I glance at my missed calls and see that there are a few dozen from her. Sian is a single mum with an adorable three-year-old son. Owen is cuteness incarnate, but he can also be the spawn of the devil when he wants to be. She loves him to distraction, but sometimes they're like the odd couple; my chief role as his only godparent is to talk her down during such moments.

"Sorry," I say. When I tell her about the gas explosion, she's incredulous.

"Good grief. I thought gas explosions were an urban myth."

"Um . . . definitely not. I have the bruises to prove it."

"Are you sure it wasn't a terrorist attack? London has been on stage 4 alert for like . . . years." Sian has an overactive imagination, possibly stoked by playing the Lion King for literally hours on end, long past the stage when I would find crawling around on the floor impersonating Mufasa crushingly dull.

"It wasn't a terrorist attack. Why would anyone want to attack Nunhead anyway? No one's ever even heard of it," I say.

"Fair point. I guess even ISIS can't object to nuns," she admits. "Still, it's a shame. We could have launched your social media campaign off the back of it."

"But I don't want a social media campaign."

"It could get you a rich boyfriend. Maybe even a Calvin Klein model."

"I don't want a rich boyfriend. Or a Calvin Klein model," I tell her.

"Are you mad? Why not?" Sian has basically given up on finding a partner for herself, at least in the short-term; in truth, although she complains about raising Owen on her own, I don't think she's prepared to share his childhood with anyone. But she still has high hopes for me. When we both became addicted to *Love Island* last summer, she immediately applied for the next season—using my details but lowering my age by five years. Her application was rejected with the speed of light. Apparently, even a much younger me is not sufficiently attractive, thin, or vacuous enough to lounge around a pool surrounded by muscular hair-dressers from Essex.

"OK, maybe a rich boyfriend would be fine," I concede. "But not if I have to share my life with a hundred thousand followers on Instagram."

"Fine. You'd be crap at it anyway. And false eyelashes would look like spider's legs on you," she concedes.

"Thanks. I'll remember that."

"So how long are you planning to stay there?"

"Hopefully only a few days. Until my flat is habitable again. I'm sure that my landlord is arguing with the insurance company as we speak."

"So that'll be like . . . a few years."

"God, no. I hope not."

"Does your cousin know you hate dogs?"

"Um . . . I've yet to share that with her."

"I'll bet the dogs know. Animals can be very intuitive."

"Well, they don't seem very keen on me, either."

"No wonder. Still, maybe you'll have a change of heart while you're there."

I glance over at Peggy, who is busy burrowing into her private parts with the enthusiasm of a truffle hunter.

"Unlikely."

t's true. I do hate dogs. Which is not something I often admit to in public. Among the British, it's a little like saying you hate chocolate. Or sunshine. Or world peace. In a roundabout way, I blame my mother. For a brief period when I was six years old, not long after she'd ditched my father, she was married to a short, balding guy from the Midlands called Russell, whom she met and married in less time than it takes to grow salad cress. Hamlet would have been appalled. I know I was, although she pretended not to notice at the time.

Russell owned his own bathroom fittings company, which meant that he was basically a glorified plumber, though my mother insisted on referring to him in company as an *entrepreneur*. He also owned two sexually deranged pugs, Pickle and Pepper, who would hump anything that remained stationary for more than three seconds, including me.

I'd had no prior experience with dogs and at the age of six I was fairly indifferent to them. Sure, I'd read about them in books, seen them on TV, even owned a few cuddly toy versions, but to my six-year-old mind, they were mythic rather than real—like dragons or unicorns. None of our neighbors had one and none of my school friends and no one in our extended family were dog owners. When we passed people walking their dogs on the street, my mother refused to stop, pulling me sharply to one side until they passed. And any suggestion of a pet in our house was swiftly and comprehensively curtailed.

So I was a little taken aback when Russell and his canine wards came to live with us. Russell, too, had been married once before, but, unlike my mother, he had no children. Instead, he had Pickle and Pepper. Not surprisingly, he was granted full custody; apparently his ex-wife got the Jacuzzi, and he got the dogs. Each time he pulled up outside our flat in his white van, I saw them perched on the dashboard like oversized hood ornaments, their dark eyes bulging, their tiny pink tongues flapping in the wind. They were stubby, black, and barrel-shaped, because he insisted on overfeeding them, and they actually had to be lifted in and out of the van.

For about a nanosecond they were interesting. At first, I tried playing with them, but they showed no interest in or facility with balls, ropes, or even squeaky toys. Their chief hobbies appeared to be eating, sneezing, gagging, and sleeping. Russell was their deity, and on the rare occasions when he left them behind, you could see the terror in their mashed little faces. They would spin round and round with anxiety, sometimes making themselves sick in the process. Often, he would be forced to relent and scoop them up, carrying one under each arm like a rugby player as he left the house.

I tolerated them for the first few weeks until their almost-continuous wheezing, together with the annoying scrabble of their claws on the lino, the scratchy bristle of their fur against my bare shins, and their vaguely rancid smell, put me off. Unaccountably, Russell adored them. And for a brief period, my mother, too, became dog-obsessed—though, really, I think it was the accessories she fell in love with. She went through a phase of acquiring ludicrous canine fashion items (plaid coats, rhinestone collars, fur-lined mitts for their paws) not to mention pug-themed homewares (mugs, cushions, tea towels). She also urged me to bond with my new stepsiblings, even though they were asthmatic and offered zero play value. She even tried to persuade me to let them sleep on my bed, which I point-blank refused, on the grounds that they snored.

But it wasn't until the pugs chewed the limbs off my doll collection that I really began to hate them. After a few months I ended up with a ragged assortment of quadriplegic Barbies and headless Kens. My mother was unsympathetic. "You can still play with them, darling," she insisted when I complained. "Use your imagination: *pretend* they still have arms and legs." That night I stole her favorite cashmere sweater and lined their dog bed with it and in the morning they'd gnawed off part of the sleeves. *You can still wear it*, I thought with satisfaction. *Pretend it still has sleeves.*

She was speechless with anger, and I like to think this small act of defiance spelt the beginning of the end for Russell and his four-footed offspring. Somehow it destabilized the household. Not long afterward, I heard my mother berating Russell through the bedroom door for failing to clean up after them and within a month she'd ejected both Russell and his dogs from the conjugal bed. They were the first and last pets we ever had.

After I hang up from Sian I realize I need to find Jez, so I pull on my coat and some old wellies and wander outside. The yard is quiet, though the Land Rover is still there, and next to it is parked an old dark blue Volvo station wagon. I call out for Jez but there's no answer, so I poke my head into the first outbuilding, a large, modern, corrugated iron barn.

Inside there's a bare cement floor, several breezeblock stalls, and a half dozen large metal crates along the wall. An elaborate black hose with a complicated pistol-shaped nozzle dangles like a deadly anaconda from a hook near the stalls. Beneath it, a series of circular metal drains studs the floor. I walk over to the snake contraption, which appears to be some kind of high-powered doggy hygiene unit, and can't resist grabbing the nozzle off the hook. It really does look like a semiautomatic weapon, and I take aim at a nearby wall. A powerful jet of water shoots out and the nozzle flies out of my hands, coiling back on me like an angry serpent, splattering me with ice-cold water.

I emerge damp from the barn and walk across the yard toward the kennels. They're housed in a long, low bungalow lined with a series of doors, each with a square glass window. I peek inside the first window and see a miniature four-poster bed complete with a ruffled canopy in a pale, insipid blue. A sign on the wall reads COZY CANINE ROYAL SUITE and I snort. The area around the bed is carpeted with bright green artificial turf, and a plastic hatch on the opposite wall leads to a paddock outside. I peer around, but the suite appears to be empty. Maybe corgis are in short supply these days. I try the door handle and it's open, so I step inside. The suite may be intended for royalty, but it still smells of wet dog. I test the mattress and am relieved to find that it is nothing more than plastic-covered hard foam. Maybe Jez isn't bonkers, after all.

I leave the row of suites and circle back to another outbuilding, located behind the first, stepping through a large open door. The floor inside is covered with straw and the room is strewn with brightly colored canine exercise equipment. There's a cloth tunnel, a small stepladder, a seesaw, a long wooden plank, and a series of balls in various sizes, all painted in primary colors. Aren't dogs supposed to be color blind? In one corner sits a rectangular plastic Jacuzzi, and in the other is a giant metal exercise wheel. *Oh please*, I think, walking over to it. The wheel is taller than I am and sits squarely on an enormous triangular steel frame, like a massive industrial fan without blades. Inside it's lined with thick, black rubber matting. I peer at a small plastic sign embedded in the frame: *Caution! Not suitable for large breeds over 70 kg!* What sort of giant mutant dog weighs more than 70 kg, I wonder.

Do I qualify as a large breed? Surely not. So I place one foot tentatively on the black rubber mat and step inside. The structure seems to hold my weight and the mat feels vaguely springy underfoot. With one hand I grab on to the central axle of the frame, then take a tentative step. The wheel slides easily beneath me and I pitch forward. I steady myself and take a few more steps, the wheel moving smoothly under my feet. I relax and begin walking at a normal pace, deciding that the wheel is really rather pleasant; it almost makes me envy hamsters. As I carry on walking, the wheel seems to stealthily gather speed, and soon I'm forced to quicken my pace. The problem is that, apart from jumping off—which I really don't fancy while the thing is moving—I don't quite know how to make it stop. I look around for a brake of some sort, but there's nothing obvious, and the faster I walk, the faster the wheel turns. I'm quickly forced into a sort of slow jog, my hands thrust out in front of me to keep my balance. I'm just beginning to contemplate a sideways lunge when suddenly I stumble, my feet flying out behind me and my hands splaying against the mat in front. The wheel carries on spinning and I brace myself, my entire body tipping upside down. I scream, and my arms give way; in the next instant I tumble sideways onto the floor, banging the side of my head hard on the wheel's edge.

I land facedown on the floor, the consultant's words ringing in my ears: *No contact sports, no dangerous activities, nothing that will put you at risk of a further fall.* Next to me the empty wheel carries on spinning happily. Slowly, I roll over with a groan.

Clearly, it's an instrument of torture. And, clearly, I'm an idiot for getting on it in the first place. I reach up to my ear, which stings like hell, and feel something wet. *Oops.*

"The thing is, it's not really designed for bipeds," says a male voice behind me. I turn my head to see a tall, thirtysomething, dark-haired man wearing faded jeans, a plaid shirt, and a burgundy-colored down vest standing in the doorway, his arms crossed against his chest. His expression is one of mild bemusement, but his tone is vaguely patronizing. Even sideways I can see that he is fetching in a rough-shaven sort of way: wavy hair, strong jawline, nice forearms. Not perfect by any means, but definitely what Sian would call *man candy.*

"You need four legs," he says. "Otherwise the centrifugal force tends to work against you."

I stand up sheepishly, dusting bits of hay off my clothes, and glance at my fingertips, where two tiny spots of blood have bloomed from my ear. "Physics was never my best subject at school," I say, curling my hand into a fist so the blood doesn't show. The man candy walks over to me. He has a backpack slung over one shoulder.

"Presumably Health and Safety wasn't your forte, either," he says. "Or maybe you just missed the class on common sense?"

Whoa. The guy is practically radiating scorn. I lift my chin stubbornly. "I had *no* idea it wasn't intended for humans," I say a little defensively.

"Really," he remarks. "Were you planning to try those next?" He nods toward a series of giant plastic hoops mounted on elevated wooden stands. I give him my coolest smile.

"I never jump through hoops." We have a sort of standoff, during which I can't help noticing that his eyes are a ridiculous shade of blue.

"You're lucky you didn't crack your skull open," he says.

Me and my darn luck!

"Aren't I, though." Actually, I suspect I *have* cracked my ear open and it hurts like hell. Hopefully my hair covers it.

"You better let me take a look." He slings the backpack to the ground and steps forward suddenly. Before I can object he reaches for my chin, turning it slightly and frowning at the bruises from the explosion. "Wow," he says. "Are these new?" He is clearly more than a little puzzled.

"Um . . . no. I had those already. I'm sure I'm fine," I say, just as he lifts my hair.

"Ah," he says. "You've lacerated your ear. It's not deep, but it'll need to be dressed," he goes on in a manner that seems overly competent. He bends down and unzips the backpack, rummages around inside, then withdraws a couple of plastic packages and a small bottle of saline solution. He stands up again and reaches for my chin, tilting my head sharply to one side.

"You're not in one of the caring professions, are you?" I mumble a little suspiciously.

"As a matter of fact, I am," he says quietly. His fingertips lightly brush my neck and I feel a small stir of warmth from his breath, which is like a cattle prod to my nervous system. But in the next instant I feel the cold jet of saline solution on the cut, which burns like mad.

"Ouch!" I say, pulling away slightly. The liquid dribbles across my cheek and down my chin. He frowns and tilts my head again.

"Hold still for a second," he says. "I need to clean the wound."

It's not a request; more like an order. He dabs at my ear repeatedly with a bit of cotton wool, then breaks open a package of sterile strips and applies them to the cut. "I'm not going to ask how you got those earlier contusions," he murmurs while he does this, his tone just this side of schoolmaster.

Then don't! Because I have no intention of explaining. But he is clearly expecting some sort of answer, and the silence stretches awkwardly between us. "Just a small household accident," I say.

"Huh." I can tell from his tone that man candy doesn't believe me.

Who is he anyway?

"I'm Cal, by the way," he says. "I'm the vet."

Good grief. I'd forgotten about the vet's visit. "So . . . you must be *Bovine* Cal." He frowns.

"That's not what it says on my business card." He finishes and stuffs his kit back into the backpack, shouldering it.

"Sorry. It's just that Jez told me you were into cows."

"I *treat* cows. If that's what you mean. Along with many other types of animals." Maybe it's my imagination but Bovine Cal seems a little peeved.

"A Cal who treats cows," I say, trying to lighten the moment. "Nice alliteration." He gives me a look.

"It's not why I chose my profession."

Yeesh, I think. Bovine Cal isn't even smiling. "I'm Charlie, Jez's cousin," I say. "I'm just visiting for a few days."

"From?"

"London."

He nods—a little too knowingly, I think. As if he's already got me typecast as some gormless urbanite. "Come to experience the delights of the countryside?" he asks in a vaguely mocking tone. I briefly consider telling him about the explosion, then decide I do not want his sympathy.

"Something like that." It sounds pathetic, but I'm really not inclined to explain.

"Well, don't overdo it," he says, glancing around. "The countryside is full of hidden dangers." Now he is definitely mocking me.

"I'm sure I'll manage," I say. "We city types are very resourceful."

"So they say," he replies. "I guess I should let you get on with it," he adds, glancing over at the wheel.

I feel my cheeks redden. What am I supposed to say? *It looked like fun?* "Actually, I was just looking for Jez."

"She's out in the paddock," says Cal.

Then he turns and walks out of the barn, leaving me to stare after him.

chapter
4

wait a few moments, gathering myself, then follow him outside.
By then he's already started the Volvo and is backing out of the
yard. I watch as he drives off without so much as a wave, and I
realize that Bovine Cal is definitely not a fresh prospect. Most
likely he's married. Or gay. Or both. More to the point, he isn't
exactly what Jane Austen would call amiable. Who needs a man
who can't be bothered with the barest of civilities, such as waving
good-bye? I hear footsteps and turn to see Jez coming around the
corner carrying a small, gray poodle. "Sorry, I meant to introduce
you to him before he left," Jez says, nodding after the departed car.

"We met."

"Did you ask him to look you over?"

"Um. Sort of."

"And?"

"All good."

"Excellent. Then you can help me with the chores," Jez says.

"Sure," I reply a little half-heartedly. *Aren't I meant to be convalescing?* "Who's this?" I ask, nodding at the poodle.

"This is Sebastian. But I call him Slab."

I look at her askance and Jez shrugs.

"Well, he's basically immobile." She sets the poodle down very gingerly on the ground, as if it were a china statue, and I realize that the dog is so old it can barely stand. Both its legs are bandy with age, and one eye is almost entirely clouded over with cataracts. The poodle stares up at Jez anxiously with his one good eye, as if being required to stand is more than should be expected of him. After a moment his legs begin to quiver slightly.

"Wow. He looks a little past it."

"Yeah. He's hanging in there. Sixteen and counting. Aren't you, Slab?"

"Wouldn't it be kinder to just . . . put him out of his misery?"

"Oh, he's got some life in him yet. Besides, Slab likes it here. We spoil him rotten. And to be honest, he's a bit of a cash cow."

"How long's he here for?"

"Well, he's sort of permanent. His owners boarded him about a year ago for a fortnight, and they just keep extending. I don't think they plan to have him back." Jez shrugs.

"That's heartless."

"It would be, if they weren't so good about paying their bills." Jez grins.

"What sort of people name a dog Sebastian, anyway?"

"Posh people."

"Really? What's wrong with Rover? Or Spike?"

"It's a time-honored tradition: posh people name their children after their dogs, and their dogs after their children."

"That's just disrespectful," I say. "To the dogs."

"Yep," says Jez, scooping up the poodle. "But it makes the children easier to remember." She carries Slab over to one of the smaller suites, deposits him inside, then closes the door. "Right," she says, turning back to me. "Ready for some chores?'

"What sort of chores?"

"Don't worry. Nothing too strenuous."

The way she says *strenuous* makes me suspicious.

As it turns out, flea combing isn't strenuous. It's even sort of satisfying. For a hefty fee, Cozy Canine offers an *organic* flea treatment service, which basically means that Jez eschews napalm in favor of traditional household remedies and old-fashioned elbow grease: hand-culling the nasty little blighters with a long-tooth comb. Only this morning an elderly client dropped off a two-year-old Pomeranian for the holidays and the dog is basically a giant hairball.

"The thing about fleas," says Jez, "is that they're surprisingly clever. It's like they can sense the comb coming, and when they do, they scamper. So you need to comb in all the out-of-the-way places because that's where they'll be hiding. They're agile little buggers. If humans had the jumping power of fleas, someone your size could clear the height of that barn," she says, indicating the building behind us.

"So we should show some respect," I say, nodding thoughtfully.

"Exactly," says Jez, handing me the comb and the dog. "They're a worthy opponent."

I sit on a stool with the Pomeranian balanced on my thighs. The dog looks at me with startled, pink-rimmed eyes. In spite of what amounts to a ludicrous amount of hair, the dog's body is no bigger than a small grapefruit, and considerably less solid. It's an ideal tossing weight, really, what Sian would call a *dropkick dog*. And it is so docile I begin to wonder if it hasn't been doped by the owner, though tranquilizers don't strike me as very organic. The more obvious explanation is that it actually *likes* being groomed, a suspicion that is confirmed a moment later when the Pomeranian seems to almost shiver with pleasure.

"Hey, what's this one called, anyway?" I shout over to Jez. She sticks her head out of the barn door.

"Hermione."

"Figures."

"But I call her Hulk."

I t takes nearly two hours of combing before Hulk is given the all clear by Jez. I set her down on the ground and she minces away daintily, as if a shampoo and set were all that was necessary. I stand up and groan, rubbing my lower back. Dog-grooming is far harder on your muscles than being hunched over a computer screen all day, I decide. I turn to see Jez lifting an enormous sack of dry dog food from the back of the Land Rover. "Need help with that?" I ask a little unenthusiastically.

"No, thanks, I can manage." Jez hoists the sack up onto her shoulder with a grunt and disappears into the barn, and I follow. I know it's unwise, but I've spent a considerable part of the last couple of hours replaying the conversation with Bovine Cal in my mind.

"So, how come the vet was here?" I ask as casually as I can. Jez is busy decanting the dry dog food into an enormous trash can.

"Slab's been really constipated. It happens to old dogs. It can be quite painful if you don't treat it."

I nod, not really wanting the details. "Have you known him long?"

Jez stops and sets the bag down, one eyebrow raised. "Slab?" she asks.

I color. "Bovine Cal."

"Bovine Cal? Did you call him that to his face?"

"No!" I say hotly. "Well, sort of," I admit.

Jez laughs, then lifts the bag again to finish the pouring. "Bet he *loved* that," she says.

"What's with him, anyway? He was a bit . . ." I pause.

"Grumpy?" asks Jez with a grin.

"I was going to say patronizing."

She finishes emptying the bag and puts it down.

"I've known Cal forever. He's really not that bad once you get to know him. Sometimes his manner can be a little off-putting. To humans, at least. I don't think the animals notice," she adds with a grin.

"Great," I say.

"He's been in a bit of a rut lately. Think he's found it hard to shake off."

Join the club. At least we have that much in common.

"How lately?"

She stops and thinks. "A year or so? Maybe longer." I frown.

"That's not a rut," I say. "That's more like . . . a gorge." Jez shrugs.

"Well, you know vets. Most of them prefer animals to people."

Really? "So he hates bipeds?" I say.

"Oh, I wouldn't say *that*," says Jez, dragging the bin back to the corner.

I look up at her hopefully.

"He's crazy about birds."

Fine. Bird-and-Bovine Cal is clearly a nonstarter. Who needs hunky medical guys anyway? Especially ones with complicated backstories. Anyway, it's far too early to be on the prowl. I've only been single for two weeks. I should still be in my post-breakup fasting period: no dates, no flirtations, definitely no random hook-ups with strangers in bars or kennels. Love-lite is going to be my maxim for the holidays.

"So, are you ready for your next chore?" Jez asks.

"Sure," I say. *Because what could be worse than slaughtering vermin with your bare hands?* She picks up an odd-looking tool with the handle of a spade and a pair of metal jaws at its base.

"What's that?" I ask suspiciously.

"Pooper-scooper."

"Seriously?"

Jez grins and holds it out to me. "All part of the glamour."

chapter
5

Ah, the countryside! There must be a thousand things to occupy myself with here. But apart from the dogs, I am genuinely hard-pressed to think what they would be. I'm sure Devon has all kinds of diversions, which I am bound to discover in due course. And in the meantime, the fresh air will do me good.

So, if nothing else, I can while away the hours *breathing*.

As long as I don't mind sharing the air with dogs.

Jez has five "clients" boarding with her at the moment, though she's due to lose three over the course of the next few days. Christmas is traditionally a slow time of year for dog kennels, she explains over lunch. Pet owners go all warm and fuzzy around this time: they want to bond with their animals over the holiday period, even if they're happy to pack them off to boarding school for the rest of the year. Except, of course, for those who have holiday homes in far-flung places, like Antigua or Cape Town: those pets are booked in annually and come fully prepared with Christmas stockings lovingly assembled by their owners. Jez will be expected to parcel these out on Christmas morning and, in the more extreme cases, take videos of the dog unwrapping its gifts.

"Seriously?" I ask. "But *I* don't even get a Christmas stocking. Come to think of it, I haven't had a Christmas stocking in *years*." Somewhere around my twelfth birthday, my mother had announced in her brook-no-opposition voice that since Father Christmas was a thing of the past, so, too, were stockings. My mum always resented the extra work Christmas involved, and made no secret of that fact, often referring to it as "Mother's Festival."

"You can share with Slab," says Jez with a grin.

"Clearly I was born into the wrong family," I muse.

"Or the wrong species," says Jez.

The next morning I wake feeling almost normal. When I look in the mirror I'm pleased to see that my right cheek is no longer swollen, though my temple has developed a rather fetching lurid yellow bruise. Last night, Jez dug out some spare clothes for me: faded dungarees, a few T-shirts, and an old wool cardigan that had probably been a nice shade of burgundy at one time but now reminded me of the remnants at the bottom of a glass.

When I go downstairs to breakfast, Jez already has her coat on and is pulling on her boots. She casts her eyes over my outfit with approval. "Farm-chic suits you."

"Who knew?" I reply, heading for the coffee. "Where you off to?"

"*We.* Bring your coffee in the car," she says, holding out my coat. "We've got a date."

I frown. "With who?"

"An old friend. Who's dying to meet you."

"Fine," I say, shrugging on my coat. "But just so you know, I don't do threesomes."

I assumed we were off to meet one of Jez's school friends, but when we walk into the post office ten minutes later, I find myself face-to-face with a tiny, birdlike woman with honey-brown skin and snow-white hair piled atop her head in a delicately spun nest. "Geraldine, this is my cousin Charlie," announces Jez. "Charlie, this is Geraldine, postmistress extraordinaire."

"Call me Gerry." The woman smiles. "No one but Jezebel here calls me Geraldine." She wipes her hands on a cream-colored apron printed with faded songbirds and sticks out her hand. Her grip is surprisingly strong; I look down and see that her knuckles bulge like burnished walnuts.

"Very good to meet you," says Gerry.

"Charlie's visiting. From London," Jez tells her.

Gerry tips her head to the side and appraises me. "Ah. The siren call of the countryside," she says. "We all hear it, sooner or later."

Do we? I shoot Jez a look and she shrugs, as if to say: *Don't go there.*

"Are you staying for the pageant?" asks Gerry.

Once again I turn to Jez with raised eyebrows. "Um . . . What pageant is that?" To me the word *pageant* immediately conjures a long line of toothy blondes wearing matching tiaras and identical swimsuits.

"The Christmas pageant," says Gerry.

Ah. That sort of pageant. The blondes instantly morph into a row of weeping Virgin Marys. "I'm afraid not," I say apologetically.

And in the exact same instant Jez says: "Definitely."

There's an awkward beat while Jez and I exchange glances, but Gerry blasts right through it. "Cross Bottomley hosts the most marvelous Christmas pageant," she tells me. "You'll love it. Everyone does. It's the highlight of the year."

I give her a frozen smile. *Christmas!* Inescapable, inviolable, unbeatable.

"She wouldn't miss it for the world," says Jez smoothly.

"Of course she wouldn't," says Gerry with a wave, as if this is a foregone conclusion. "Hang on a minute. I nearly forgot why you've come." She turns away and spends a minute poking among a long series of wooden cubbyholes behind her. "Ah. Here we are," she says finally, pulling out a small parcel from one of the cubbyholes. She turns around and hands it to Jez, who looks at it with a frown. The parcel is about the size of a box of tea and is wrapped in plain brown paper.

"What is it?" asks Jez, staring down at the parcel and turning it over.

"Why not open it and find out?" suggests Gerry.

Jez hesitates. "The postmark is from Finland," she says. I can just make out the tiniest of tremors hidden inside her voice.

"So it is," murmurs Gerry.

Jez looks up at her, and the older woman raises an eyebrow. Suddenly it's like they're speaking some private language that is completely incomprehensible to me. Jez slowly unwraps the paper, picking at each end cautiously, as if the parcel itself might protest.

Eventually the paper slides free to reveal a plain white cardboard box. Jez lifts the lid and all three of us crane forward to see inside. Nestled in a bed of cotton wool is a tiny object made of what looks like bleached white bone. "Oh my God," whispers Jez.

"What is it?" I ask.

"If it's what I think it is, then it's a bloody miracle," Jez says under her breath. She carefully lifts it out of the box and holds it up. It takes me a few seconds to work out what it is.

"Is that . . . a miniature sledge?" I ask, puzzled. Jez nods, beaming.

The sledge is a perfectly carved replica made of worn wood and what looks like bleached ivory. The runners resemble long, thin tusks and the tiny, upright staves are delicately turned with round finials. A series of thin slats is intricately lashed to the runners with pale brown sinew, and a tiny ivory clover is suspended between the staves as a simple ornament.

"I've been searching for one of these for ages," says Jez. "It's taken me almost three years to find!"

"It was worth the wait," says Gerry admiringly, casting an appraising eye over the sledge. "How old is it?"

"This is probably nineteenth century," says Jez, turning the sledge over and peering at the bottom.

"Where did it come from?" I ask.

"Greenland, probably. The Inuit used to carve them and give them as gifts at Christmas."

"But . . . who sent it to you?"

Jez hesitates. "I'm not completely sure," she says slowly, in a way that suggests precisely the opposite.

She lifts the remains of the cotton wool and peers at the bottom of the box, then carefully lays the sledge back in the wool. She starts to replace the lid, then notices a small square of paper fixed to the inside. "Hang on," she says. "There's something taped to the lid." Jez pries the paper off and unfolds it, her eyes scanning the length of the page.

"What does it say?" asks Gerry.

Jez takes a deep breath. "It's an invitation," she says, staring at the paper.

"From who?" I ask.

Jez shoots a look at Gerry.

"Father Christmas," says Gerry with a smile.

Five minutes later Jez and I are back in the Land Rover, barreling down the road, and I am none the wiser. The white cardboard box sits on the seat between us like an incendiary device, and if anything, Jez's driving is even more erratic than usual. She keeps flexing her grip on the steering wheel and her jaw is working overtime, the muscles clamping and unclamping in rhythmic spasms. She comes to a sharp bend and downshifts, the car lurching heavily to one side. I grab the dashboard to steady myself and decide that if we're going to die because of the contents of that damn box, then I reckon I have a right to know why.

"I'm afraid I still don't understand. Who *exactly* are you going to visit?"

Jez hesitates. "A friend," she says eventually. It's the way she says *friend*, drawing the word out into two syllables, that makes me realize . . .

"What sort of friend?" I ask cautiously.

"It's complicated."

"So are algorithms. Try me."

"The thing is, we've never actually—" Jez starts to speak, but then her voice breaks off. "Not face-to-face, at any rate. We've only just . . ." Jez pauses again, flushing. It's like she's carrying on a conversation with herself.

"Only *what?* C'mon, Jez. Don't be so obtuse!"

Jez sneaks a quick glance over at me, then looks back at the road. "We've only Vibered."

"'Vibered'?"

"We speak on Viber every day. Sometimes twice a day. Or even three times," she admits a little sheepishly.

"Where does your . . . friend live?"

"In northern Finland. Lapland, actually. She's doing a PhD in anthropology at the Arctic Research Institute."

Lapland? Arctic research? Man, have I had Jez pegged wrong!

"How did you meet?" I ask.

"On a dogsledding website."

At this I burst out laughing. "Are you serious?"

"It's not as strange as it sounds. Eloise is an enthusiast, too. And we started corresponding. And one thing led to another."

"To . . . *what,* exactly?"

Jez shrugs. "You know . . . a *thing*."

"What sort of thing. And how long has it been going on?"

"Awhile," Jez admits. She glances over at me. "Nearly two years," she confesses.

"You've been having a phone romance for *two* years?" I cannot conceal my amazement.

"It doesn't feel like that long."

"And you've never met?"

Jez hesitates. "Well, we were both busy. And it was going so well. And we didn't want to . . . spoil it."

By *meeting*? But then, who am I to criticize? I'd been living cheek by jowl with my boyfriend and I had managed to spoil *that* easily enough.

"Viber," I say, frowning slightly. "Does that mean just talking? Or do you . . . do other stuff?" Jez laughs.

"None of your business," she says. She downshifts again and pulls into the Cozy Canine driveway, grinding the car to a halt. Once the engine is off, she turns to me with an arch look. "The thing about Viber is, it's very versatile."

"Never mind. I don't want to know."

"Don't be such a prude."

"I am *not* a prude," I say, affronted.

Am I a prude? Maybe I'm a little bit of a prude.

"So . . . you really don't mind if I go?" she asks.

"To Lapland? Why should I mind?"

"Because it means being on your own for a few days. Actually, a couple of *weeks*. And I promised your mum I'd look after you."

"Jez! I'm not a five-year-old. I don't need looking after. Irrespective of what my mother says. Anyway, I'm only here for a couple of days. As soon as I get the all clear from the insurance company, I'll be straight back to London."

Jez smiles. "Thanks, cuz. You're the best."

"What will you do about the dogs?"

"I'll get someone in. There are loads of people around who need work."

Thank Christ for that! I'd been terrified she was going to ask me to help out, and as much as I love Jez, I have absolutely no intention of spending Christmas with quadrupeds. Anyway, I have a date with Audrey.

We might even Viber.

chapter
6

A techno romance! I think that night in bed. Something I have never in my wildest dreams considered. Maybe I really *am* a prude. The irony is this: as fond as I am of Jez, I've always secretly regarded her as something of a country bumpkin. It was *me* who was the urbane Londoner with the übercool job in the cutting-edge industry; Jez was the wool-clad animal-lover, scraping together a living in the countryside. But now I'm single and Jez is having a thoroughly twenty-first-century romance with an academic on the outer reaches of the Arctic Circle. It is all rather glamorous and bewildering. And, I have to admit, a little bit thrilling.

But not for me, I think, rolling over with a sigh. I came of age in the era of Internet dating, and I decided years ago that online chat rooms were not my scene. During the past few years my single friends in the city have all become obsessed with Tinder and Grindr, but the whole idea of casually swiping left or right like

St. Gabriel strikes me as just plain ill-mannered. When you meet someone for the first time in person, you're forced to engage in social pleasantries out of politeness. You smile and nod and maybe write them off in your head, but you don't banish them with the flick of a finger. I find it all so calculating. Not to mention callous. Maybe I'm a twenty-first-century coward, but I don't have the stomach for it. It doesn't stop me envying Jez, though.

The next morning, when I get downstairs, Jez is in full throttle, sorting out travel plans and making arrangements for the dogs. She has some errands to run, so I offer to exercise Slab, Hulk, and Peggy in the paddock. I find an old tennis ball in the boot room, but after a few minutes I realize I needn't have bothered. I'm fairly positive Slab cannot see or smell the ball, much less retrieve it. And when I throw the ball for Peggy, the beagle simply collapses onto her stomach with a loud grunt, as if the effort of watching me throw it has been too much for her. Finally, I turn to Hulk, holding out the ball. "What do you reckon?" I ask. Hulk tiptoes forward, sniffs the ball, then sneezes. I toss it a few yards away, and the Pomeranian looks at me as if I'm out of my mind.

When we come in from the paddock, Peggy heads straight to the sofa and resumes her customary spot, making it obvious that she's done me a massive favor by accompanying me on the walk. I'm just filling the kettle when I hear a knock at the kitchen door. I turn to see Bovine Cal and his ridiculously blue eyes at the back-door wearing a brown-plaid flannel shirt. I cross to the door and open it. Irritatingly, he is more good-looking than I'd remembered. Cal nods at the side of my head.

"How's the battle scar?"

I raise my hand to my ear. "Fine, I think. I'm not really sure. But I can definitely still hear you. So that's something."

"I should probably take a look. As your attending physician." He nods at me expectantly, as if awaiting my permission.

Seriously?

"Um. OK." I step a little closer and turn to one side, raising a hand to lift my hair out of the way. Cal leans forward until he is only an inch or so away; with one hand he reaches up to gently pull the outer rim of my ear forward, peering at it intently.

Is this really necessary?

For a moment he doesn't say anything, but I can feel his breath stirring the hair on the back of my neck.

"How is it?" I ask.

"Fine," he murmurs. "But I'm not really an expert. Funnily enough, dog ears are quite different from a human's," he remarks, bending my ear forward slightly. "They're softer, for one thing," he says. "And more flexible. Not to mention furry. Plus, they hear much better than we do."

"So what you're saying is that my ears are pretty crap by comparison?"

"Yep."

"I wouldn't object to dog ears," I say. "Think I'd go for . . . basset hound."

He pulls back and regards me with surprise. "Basset hound?"

"Why have little tiny Chihuahua ears when you could have great big lovely droopy ones?"

He looks at me doubtfully. Clearly, he thinks I'm mad. "Your ear looks fine," he says.

"No permanent scarring?"

"Unlikely."

"Thank you, Doctor."

"Vets don't really get called 'doctor' around here. We don't go in for fancy titles in the country."

"OK," I say. "What should I call you?" *Bovine Cal?* I think. He hesitates, as if he can hear what I'm thinking.

"Just Cal is fine."

"OK. Cal."

"So, I see you haven't fled back to the great metropolis," he says.

"Nope. I'm still here," I say breezily. "Haven't experienced all the delights that rural Devon has to offer," I add.

"And what would those be?" He leans against the doorway and raises a quizzical eyebrow, forcing me to enumerate.

"Oh, you know. Clotted cream, scrumpy . . ." I hesitate, desperately trying to remember what else Devon is famous for.

"Red Rubies?" he offers.

"Those, too," I nod. I have no idea whether you eat Red Rubies or wear them, but I'm not averse to the color.

"Don't try them raw," he advises.

"I like mine deep-fried," I say a little rashly. Bovine Cal gives a smug smile, as if to say: *Is that so?* I feel the color rise in my face and instantly regret my comment. Cal peers over my shoulder.

"Where's Jez, anyway?"

"She's out."

"I promised to stop by with these." He hands me a small brown bag. "Tell her to keep them in the fridge."

I peer inside the bag, thinking it might be food. Inside are a dozen tiny white plastic rockets. I look up at him.

"Suppositories," he says.

"Ah." I must look a little perplexed.

"They're for the *dogs*."

"I knew that," I say.

"Of course you did," he says. "So, how long you here for?"

"Not sure. A few more days?"

He nods. "Maybe see you around."

I watch as Bovine Cal gets in his car and drives off, once again without a wave. His manners are truly lamentable, I decide. And I'd be better off if I never saw him again.

"W as that Cal's car?" asks Jez a few minutes later when she comes in.

"Yep." I hand her the bag. "He left these—said to keep them in the fridge."

Jez peers inside and nods.

"By the way, what are Red Rubies?" I ask.

Jez looks up. "Why?"

"He warned me not to eat them raw."

"Red Rubies are cows, Charlie."

I give a rictus smile. "Of course they are."

settle myself on the kitchen sofa with an Agatha Christie novel for the afternoon, resisting the temptation to watch *MasterChef* on my phone. I discover, to my horror, that Jez does not even *own* a television. Though she does have a fairly up-to-date computer in the office. But I've promised my mum that I'll avoid LCD screens at least for a few days, so I'll have to seek old-fashioned solace in the printed word. I doze off after two chapters (who knew reading real paper books was so tiring?). When I wake I hear Jez remonstrating on the phone in the office, the tone of her voice becoming increasingly more pleading and insistent. Eventually, I hear the receiver slam down and, after a moment, Jez appears in the doorway looking sheepish.

"Did you just hang up on someone?"

Jez runs her fingers through her hair. "I'm not sure. Maybe?" She flings herself down in a chair with a sigh.

"What's wrong?"

"I had five different people in mind to look after the kennels. But not a single one of them can do it! It turns out that everyone on the planet already has plans over the holidays. Where are all the cash-strapped millennials when you need them?"

Uh-oh, I think. A loud siren starts to blare at the back of my brain.

"Christ! It's not as if it's difficult! A five-year-old could manage it," Jez mutters to herself. Suddenly she looks up at me with a frown. "How long did you say you were staying?"

I stare at her. "Not long enough," I reply.

"But I'll only be gone twelve days."

"Jez, I've got to work. Remember?"

"But it's the holidays! Everyone takes time off over the holidays!"

"Not me." Technically speaking, this is a lie: I am currently booked in for a week's holiday between Christmas and New Year's. Which I am determined to spend in my flat curled up with Audrey Hepburn, Gregory Peck, and Rock Hudson. Is that selfish? Then call me selfish.

"Tell your boss you're having headaches!"

"He won't care. Besides, I'm a terrible liar," I lie. A terrible, selfish liar. *Surely she can find someone else?*

"What if we got you signed off by a doctor?"

"Are you mad? Look at me. I'm perfectly fine. No doctor in their right mind would sign me off! Because I'm not *unwell*," I point out.

Jez frowns. "Someone who owes me a big favor might sign you off," she says slowly. I look at her askance.

"Jez, no one owes you *that* big a favor."

She smiles. "You might be surprised."

" A bsolutely not!" Bovine Cal has the look of a raging bull. I honestly think that steam might come out of his ears. It is the next morning and we are standing in the examination room of his small surgery. In order to gain access we have had to ever so slightly bully his receptionist: a plump, middle-aged woman wearing red-and-green earrings in the shape of Christmas wreaths that were obviously homemade. *Perhaps this is what people do for fun in the country?*

Cal is tightly holding on to a tabby cat being prepped for surgery. The cat has already had its abdomen shaved, leaving a loose sack of wrinkled pale pink skin horribly exposed; not surprisingly, it looks suitably mortified. I'm not a big fan of cats, either, but can't help throwing it a sympathetic glance.

Hairless isn't a good look for any of us, honey.

"Come on, Cal, you *owe* me," says Jez pleadingly.

"Not that much," says Cal. "Besides, it wouldn't work."

"Why not? You're a physician, aren't you? You write notes, don't you?" says Jez. "How difficult can it be to write a letter to someone two hundred miles away whom you will never, ever meet?"

Cal turns and thrusts the cat into a small crate in the corner, then goes to the sink to wash his hands, lathering them aggressively with antibacterial soap, which he punches out from a dispenser hanging on the wall. Once again, I can't help noticing his ridiculously muscular forearms. When did I develop such a thing for forearms? He finishes drying his hands and turns back to us.

"Look, the point is it's fraudulent and unethical. Remember a little something called the Hippocratic Oath? Once upon a time I took the veterinary equivalent of it."

Absolutely, I think. *Bovine Cal would never break an oath.* In fact, I only agreed to come along on this lark because I was positive he'd refuse. And because I wanted to see his forearms.

"Besides," he says. "Leaving the dogs with someone like her is just . . . irresponsible."

"Don't be ridiculous," says Jez. "Charlie's perfectly capable."

"With all due respect, your cousin doesn't have a clue about animals. And on top of that she's—" He breaks off suddenly and shoots me a look.

What? I think, aggrieved. *I'm what?*

"Reckless," he says. For an instant his eyes lock onto mine and an image of the dog wheel flies into my head. *Fair point.*

"Cal, you don't even know her!" Jez is clearly offended on my behalf.

Cal flashes me a look that says: *Do you want to tell her or shall I?*

"I know that she's not qualified to look after the kennels," he says instead. "Come on, Jez, the dogs deserve better."

Hang on! The dogs deserve better? I may be reckless and clueless and unqualified, but I know an insult when I hear one. I draw myself up, affronted.

"For God's sake," says Jez. "They're *dogs*, not prizewinning Thoroughbreds. They eat, they sleep, they crap. I think she can handle it."

Cal crosses his muscular forearms and turns to me expectantly.

"Well?" he says in a belligerent tone. "Can you?"

For the briefest instant I do not answer. Not because I don't think I'm equal to the task, but because I suddenly see my extended holiday with Audrey evaporating before my eyes. And while I definitely do not want to spend Christmas scooping dog shit, Bovine Cal has just thrown down the biggest, fattest gauntlet I have ever seen.

"I expect I can manage," I say coolly.

"Fine," he says. "But don't come running to me if you can't."

chapter
7

My loathsome boss is not pleased. Once back at Cozy Canine I ring Carl and tell him that I cannot possibly return to work until after the holidays.

"Seriously, Charlie? What about the deadline on the Acorn contract?" He sounds deeply irritated. And not a little suspicious. Acorn is a six-month contract for the London council of Bromley, and from the outset the job has been beleaguered by politics and infighting: it is underfunded, understaffed, and well-nigh impossible to achieve in the time frame and we all know it. Last month I suggested that the project moniker be changed from Acorn to Hemlock; Carl was not amused.

"I've just come from the doctor's office," I say. "He's worried I may be developing PCS."

"Which is . . . ?"

"Post-concussion syndrome. It's a chemical imbalance triggered by the injury," I say, reading from the paper in front of me. "If I'm not careful now, the symptoms can linger for months." After all his complaining, Bovine Cal went a bit overboard on the letter—I think he was overcompensating. It runs to nearly two pages and details, among other things, the symptoms, likely causes, and long-term risks of PCS. I had to resist the urge to compliment him when he finally handed it over: *Fraudulence suits you!*

Now Carl sighs dramatically on the other end of the line.

"Fine," he snaps. "But I'll need a doctor's note."

"I've got one," I say quickly. "I'll e-mail it to you."

"And if your condition improves, I want you straight back here. We are truly up a creek with this contract, Charlie. And your absence has not been helpful."

"I know that, Carl. And I really am sorry."

Which is true, I decide after I hang up. I really *am* sorry. Because owing to my stupid pride, I've now forfeited any chance of spending Christmas the way I'd planned. More fool me.

But then I hear Jez talking on the phone in the office and this time her tone is so delighted I start to relent. She is obviously speaking to Eloise and they are both so utterly over the moon at her impending visit that I cannot begrudge them a little happiness. Jez deserves her romantic moment in the tundra, I think. And like it or not, I will spend Christmas shacked up with Peggy.

A few minutes later, I'm reading the newspaper at the kitchen table when Jez comes back into the kitchen and settles herself opposite me. "By the way, Eloise sends her thanks," she says.

"My pleasure," I say. *Munificence suits me.*

"And I've managed to persuade the owner of the third dog that was due in for the holidays to use a rival outfit."

"Great," I say, not really paying attention. One dog or four, I think. They all have bad breath and poor table manners.

"So that only leaves Hulk and Slab in the kennels," says Jez. "And Peggy in the house." She pauses for a few moments. "Oh, and the twins, of course," she adds. I'm engrossed in a newspaper item about how selfie accidents kill more people now than sharks, when her words slowly filter through to me. Actually, it isn't her words really—it's her tone, which is decidedly off-key.

I look up and Jez flashes me a mollifying smile.

Once again, alarm bells begin to toll.

"What twins?" I ask.

t turns out they are housed in a special run of their own behind the barn. This smacks to me of concealment, though Jez assures me it's not. As we round the corner, I stop short, my feet rooted to the ground. Behind the house there is a fifty-foot-long wire cage that has been festooned with tiny white outdoor Christmas lights. These do not even begin to conceal the run's occupants, who lounge casually, as if taking in the evening air.

"Jesus, Jez! You didn't tell me you kept wolves!"

Jez laughs a little awkwardly. "Relax. They're only a teeny-weeny bit wolf."

"How teeny? And which bit?" I ask.

"Um. Not really sure. But what I *can* tell you is: these dogs are about as much wolf as a Chihuahua is."

"They bloody well don't look like Chihuahuas."

As we approach the cage, both dogs leap to their feet and fix us with an intense stare. They are starkly beautiful, in a feral canine sort of way, with almond-shaped eyes, dense charcoal coats, and snow-white tails that curve up and over their bodies in luxurious plumes. On top of that, they have perfect posture, I think. But then, so do wolves.

"The thing is, *all* dogs are almost indistinguishable from wolves genetically. But these two are no more wolf than Peggy is, if that makes you feel any better."

"It really doesn't."

"Although they *are* a little bit feral," admits Jez with a laugh. "Aren't you, boys?" Both dogs continue to stare in silence as we approach the cage.

"What are they?"

"Alaskan malamutes. Sled dogs. Bred for strength and endurance."

"No kidding." The dogs stand tall and broad, with deep chests and muscular shoulders: the canine equivalent of small JCBs.

"Hello, you two," says Jez affectionately. She unlatches the cage and I feel my mouth go dry.

"Are they safe?"

"Safe as houses."

"Then how come you don't let them *in* the house?"

"They prefer the outside. Plus, they take up a lot of space. And they smell. Anyway, three dogs in the house would make me the canine equivalent of one of those crazy cat ladies." Jez grins.

"News flash: you already *are* a crazy cat lady."

Jez shrugs. "Maybe so. This one's Romulus." One of the dogs comes up and rubs against her legs and Jez kneels down, stroking him fondly. The other approaches and, after the briefest hesitation, comes forward and nudges her for attention. "Hello, Remus," says Jez.

"Seriously?" I raise a brow at her.

Jez shrugs. "I thought it suited them. They're survivors. Cal found them on his doorstep one night in the dead of winter. They were only four weeks old. It was a miracle they didn't freeze to death. He hand-reared them, then passed them on to me."

I take a step forward and lower myself to the ground beside Jez. Tentatively, I put out a hand and touch the plush carpet of fur along Remus's back. These two couldn't be further from Pickle and Pepper, I grudgingly admit to myself. "So Bovine Cal rescued you, huh?" I murmur. The dog turns and pierces me with ice-blue eyes. I glance at Jez. "He seems so . . . self-possessed."

"Malamutes are bred partly for confidence. They don't see themselves as inferior to humans. They regard themselves as our equals."

"I didn't even know they were out here. When do you exercise them?"

"Early in the morning. Before you get up." Jez nods over to a fancy two-wheeled contraption housed in a shed behind the cage.

"Is that a trap?"

"It's called a sulky—it's a kind of sled. They love it. They can pull it for miles. That's how I exercise them."

The sulky has two enormous wheels on either side of a low, padded seat. A curved metal bar extends out the front, attached to a sort of axle, and there is a small, metal hitching bar at its front.

Two diamond-shaped harnesses hang next to the sulky on wooden pegs. "Is it difficult?"

"Well, it's not for the uninitiated. It can be hard to control. Though admittedly, once you're hitched up, the dogs do most the work. But don't be fooled: the sulky can be dangerous if you don't know how to use it, so just leave it alone while I'm gone."

"What happens if you don't exercise them?"

She grins. "They can get a little tetchy."

"Like eat-their-carer tetchy?"

"Nah," she says. "They'll be fine if you just let them out into the paddock for a run a few times a day."

I carry on stroking Remus. Unlike Peggy and Hulk, there's something mesmerizing about him, and vaguely comforting. *Truly, he would make a fabulous rug.* I almost want to burrow down inside his fur and hide there. When Jez eventually stands up, I'm a little reluctant to follow.

"So, what do you say?" Jez asks a little nervously, nodding toward them. "Are you up for looking after them?" I look down at Remus and, once again, he fixes me with his glacial stare.

"Sure," I say with a shrug.

How hard can it be?

On our way back to the house Jez explains that she'll leave for London in the morning, just as soon as she's fed and exercised the dogs. She's booked a flight from Heathrow to Helsinki the next evening, with a connecting flight through to Lapland, which gives her a few hours in town to sort out her Christmas shopping and buy a killer dress.

"What does one wear to impress an Arctic scientist?" I ask.

"Clothes. Lots of them. Apparently, the temperature can drop as low as minus-thirty at this time of year."

"Better pack your wool knickers, then."

"Who has wool knickers?"

"Sheep."

When we get to the kitchen, Jez reaches in the fridge and pulls out the small brown bag. "Um. About these," she says tentatively, holding them up.

I narrow my eyes suspiciously. "*What* about those?"

"Cal prescribed them for Slab."

"Of course he did. Just to spite me."

"Honestly, there's nothing to it."

"Forget it. Not a chance."

"Just a quick shove up the bum and Bob's your uncle."

"Can I remind you that your dad is called Archie? And I'm not going anywhere near a dog's bum."

"Please?"

"Oh, come on, Jez. Can't I just feed him some prunes?"

She shakes her head no, then sighs. "Fine," she offers. "I'll pay you."

I hesitate. "How much?"

"Slab's fee for the fortnight. It'll be the easiest two hundred quid you ever made."

"Did I just hear you say three hundred?"

"No, you did not."

"Two fifty?"

"Two hundred. Take it or leave it. Valko would do it for free, so count your blessings."

"What sort of person would do that for free?"

"A desperate person."

"*I'm* desperate. And I wouldn't do that for free. Who is Valko, anyway? And why didn't you get *him* to look after the dogs?"

Jez sighs. "Valko is my Bulgarian neighbor. And he's not really capable of looking after anyone. Least of all himself."

"Why? What's wrong with him?"

"He's depressed. His mail-order bride ran off with another man and he hasn't really recovered."

"People in England use mail-order brides? From where? America?"

"Moldova. Anyway, he's been struggling to get over it."

"When did she leave?"

"Oh Lord. Maybe three months ago?"

"What's a Bulgarian doing in Cross Bottomley anyway?"

"Who knows? Valko pitched up here last February. He's been working odd jobs around the area ever since. He lives in a trailer owned by a friend of mine. That's how I met him. He helped me to install some new fencing last spring." Jez holds up the brown bag again and gives it a little shake. "So, do we have a deal?"

I sigh. "Fine. But don't expect me to groom them for that price. I don't intend to groom *myself* over the holidays. Let alone them."

"OK by me. And in spite of what he says, if you really have a problem, you can always ring Cal."

"Right. I'm sure he'd be thrilled to get that call."

"Trust me, his bark is worse than his bite."

don't want to think about his bite. In fact, I don't want to think about Bovine Cal at all. The man is infuriating. And I am perfectly capable of restraining myself from the province of male allure for two blessed weeks! I am not some hormonal-hyped fifteen-year-old. I'm thirty-one years old, single, and thoroughly self-sufficient. I do not need men, and I especially do not need veterinary man candy. What I really need right now is a distraction: a focus for all my energy. And the obvious one is right under my nose. Canines! While Jez is away, I will reverse the habit of a lifetime and bond with the animal kingdom. Instead of battling Peggy for the sofa each morning, I will get in touch with my inner beast.

Apparently, I'm not the first to have this idea. When I google it on my phone later that evening I find hundreds of sites devoted to the topic. Apparently, there are myriad of ways you can foster your inner animal: going barefoot, sleeping on the ground, embracing the sun (which means, among other things, eschewing sunscreen), and rolling and crawling on the floor are all on the list. I don't really fancy the first two, at least not in the dead of winter, but I reckon I can manage rolling and crawling if the spirit moves me, though these strike me as rather closer to toddler than animal behavior. And I'm not sure rolling and crawling will bring me any closer to Peggy, who at the moment is snoring loudly on the sofa, apparently getting in touch with her inner human.

"Valko's offered to help exercise the dogs," says Jez, coming into the kitchen.

"I thought you said he wasn't trustworthy?"

Jez shrugs. "Well, he's capable of taking them into the paddock. And he wants to help. So I think you should let him."

"Do I have to?"

"Yes. He's lonely, Charlie."

I sigh. "Fine. Hang on, you're not trying to set me up with him, are you?" I ask suspiciously.

"Hell, no!"

"Good."

"He's not that bad. Anyway, he's part of the Cozy Canine package." She disappears into the office—and sirens start up in my head again.

What else is part of the package?

A few minutes later I hear a car pull up outside. Jez pokes her head out of the office and peers out the back door. She frowns, pulls on a coat, and goes outside to investigate. A moment later I glimpse her talking to a sandy-haired man in an open-topped dark green sports car. And while I'm not an expert, the car looks like it might be worth more than my flat. It's a sunny day, but it is still the dead of winter, so I wonder what sort of nutcase would drive with the top down in December? I crane my neck to get a better view and just then the man shifts to one side to reveal an enormous white dog, the size of a small pony, seated in the front passenger seat of the car. I watch as the man points to the dog, and then I see Jez shake her head. Clearly, whatever he's selling she isn't buying, or vice versa. I pull on my coat and step outside just in time to hear her reiterate her refusal.

"I'm sorry, sir, but we are absolutely full to capacity this Christmas."

At the sound of my approach the man turns to me with a plaintive look that would melt an iceberg, though clearly not Jez. In that moment, I see that he is not only desperate, but desperately *beautiful*: high cheekbones, Roman nose, golden blond hair. To compound the effect, he is impeccably dressed in a handsome dark blue peacoat and a plaid cashmere scarf that almost screams of wealth and breeding.

Heigh-ho!

But Jez is not just immune: she's annoyingly resolute. She apologizes and shakes her head again. I glance over at the giant dog, who is seated ramrod straight, staring at us with enormous, unblinking hazel eyes, in a manner that could almost be described as *august*.

"I promise you, he's really no trouble at all," insists the man, running a hand through his hair. "He's an absolute prince of a dog."

"Yes, sir, they all are," says Jez, smiling.

But they don't all have owners like this one! I squint at the dog and decide there may well be something vaguely noble about him. *And, anyway, what's one more quadruped when you already have-five?*

"Hello," I say, giving a cheery wave. "I'm Charlie."

The man turns to me with a perplexed but hopeful smile. And lo! He has dimples! Two perfect adorable thumbprint indentations on each side of his square-cut jaw. He thrusts a hand out toward me like he's reaching for a lifeline. "I'm Hugo. And this is Malcolm." He motions toward the dog. "And we really are desperate. You would be doing us the most tremendous favor."

I turn to Jez with a hopeful look and am just about to insist it's no bother when she shakes her head once more. "Any other time we'd be absolutely delighted," she says firmly. "Please do think of us again." And with that she guides poor, handsome Hugo back into his car with a helpful arm, shuts the door, steps back, and waves him off. With no alternative, handsome Hugo starts the engine and pulls out, driving off with a forlorn wave. Such nice manners, even in the teeth of disappointment, I think. Even my mother would approve.

After he's gone, Jez turns to me and shakes her head. "Dane owners! They act as if they're bloody entitled."

"Was he Danish? I swear he sounded English."

"The dog. Great Dane."

"Oh. But the owner seemed nice," I suggest tentatively.

"They all seem nice. Until they aren't."

And he looks *even nicer,* I think wistfully, watching the convertible disappear down the lane.

Jez walks back into the house, leaving me to wonder whether it is something in the water that explains the magnetism of Devon men.

chapter
8

When I go downstairs the next morning, I spot a bright red wheelie bag packed and waiting beside the back door. I can hear Jez talking on the phone in the office. "Sorry, we're absolutely jammed," she says vehemently. "Afraid we're booked solid over the holiday." I hear her put the phone down and a moment later she practically comes skipping into the kitchen.

"Funny, you don't *look* sorry," I say with a grin.

"She's called *three times* now. I'm sure she disguised her voice the third time, but it was definitely the same woman."

"Persistence pays."

"Not this time! She can bloody well look after her own dog! This Christmas, it's *my* turn to go on holiday."

"If a trip to the North Pole in the dead of winter constitutes a holiday."

"Lapland!"

"Same difference."

"Not to me, it isn't," says Jez with a sly smile.

"Enough with the smut! I haven't even had my coffee." I pour myself a mug and sit down at the table, picking up the newspaper. Jez is an absolute dervish of activity: she whirls around the house for another twenty minutes before eventually throwing a plastic folder and a set of keys down in front of me.

"Right! Here's everything you need! The keys to the house, the kennels, and the Škoda, and a sheet of emergency contacts— owners' details, Cal's number, doctor, hospital, boiler guy, Gerry, and Valko. Keep an eye out for him. He may come by later."

"Thanks," I say, turning to the crossword. "I'll be sure to memorize them all," I add, picking up a pencil.

"And here's a list of what everyone eats," says Jez. "Just in case you forget." She hands me a typed page and I scan it quickly before looking up at her.

"My name's not here."

"You're not a dog," says Jez.

"I still have to eat, don't I?"

"Help yourself to the contents of the fridge and freezer," says Jez. She turns and grabs her coat off the hook and picks up her bag, before turning back to face me, her eyes blazing with excitement. "Well? Aren't you going to wish me luck?"

I stand up and give her a hug. "Of course I am," I say. "And let luck be a lady," I add with a grin.

Jez laughs. "But not *too* much of a lady," she says.

"Enough! Get out of here before I change my mind about the suppositories."

"Happy Christmas," says Jez.

"Just go."

After she's gone, I sit back down and glance over at Peggy, who's asleep in her usual spot on the sofa. "Hey," I say. "Guess it's just you and me now."

The beagle opens one eye, regards me for a second, then shuts it.

"So, what you do you reckon? Should we hang out?"

The beagle shifts her massive bulk beneath her, stretching her forepaws out.

"What's a four-letter word beginning with *J* that means reject?"

Peggy takes a deep breath and sighs.

"If this relationship is going to work, you're going to need to put a bit more welly into it," I say. Peggy's eyes remain firmly shut.

I look back down at the crossword, and suddenly the answer bites me like a snake. It's a verb I'm looking for—not a noun.

And the answer is *jilt*.

Later that morning I drive the Škoda into the village to stock up on food. The plan is to lay in a fortnight's worth of snacks, chocolate, booze, and frozen meals, then hunker down in front of the telly until Christmas is no more than a distant memory. The only hiccup is the telly, or lack thereof. I have no intention of spending the holidays watching seasonal repeats on my phone. So, after some prevaricating, I decide to spend all of my earnings from Slab's bottom-maintenance on a new telly, which I order for over-night delivery. Who knew that you could get a twenty-two-inch flat-screen full-HD Slim Smart LED television with built-in Wi-Fi and Freeview delivered to your door in less time than it takes to finish the *Sunday Times* crossword? We live in a miracle age.

Once my online shopping spree is over, I drive to the village shop and park right in front, nodding to the teenage girl behind the till as I go in. With relief I note that eyebrow piercings and purple hair have finally managed to find their way to rural Devon, even if they are a few decades late. I grab a wire basket and roam the aisles, loading it with crisps, sweets, and various types of choc-olate; the selection is a bit thin, and the shop is missing some of my favorites (how do these people *survive* without Ferrero Rocher?) but I manage to fill the basket in no time. Depositing it by the till, I grab a second and fill it with Chilean chardonnay, frozen pep-peroni pizzas, and some random meat pies for variety. On my way back down the aisle I spy a rack of chocolate reindeer lollies on sale and on impulse I grab a handful. *Who says I don't have the spirit of Christmas?*

When I'm finished, I hoist both baskets onto the counter with a grunt and survey my haul, deciding that I've done a fine morn-ing's work. Even Carl would be proud, I think. But the purple-haired cashier seems unimpressed. "Do you need bags?" she asks, barely managing to conceal her boredom.

"That depends on whether you'll let me borrow the baskets." I flash my most winning smile, but the girl merely reaches under the counter and pulls out a handful of eco-unfriendly blue plastic bags.

"They're twenty pence each," she says, which is practically extortion, but I nod and begin to unload the baskets. After a moment I hear a car outside and look up to see a battered blue Volvo pull up and park. *Uh-oh.* My insides lurch as Bovine Cal gets out and heads into the shop. I look down at my purchases: they aren't exactly an advertisement for healthy living. I frantically begin stuffing items into the bags as fast as the cashier can ring them through. I grab a large package of gummy bears and suddenly the girl reaches out and snatches it off me.

"Hang on," she says, "I need to check the price on that one." She turns and walks down the aisle just as Cal enters the shop. I instantly drop down behind the till, pretending to fiddle with my shoelace as Cal strides past and disappears up the dairy aisle. A moment later the girl returns to the counter and holds up the gummy bears.

"They're £1.99," she says. "Is that OK?"

"Fine," I say, stuffing the gummy bears into the plastic bag. Then I turn to see Cal heading toward me with a liter of milk. He is glancing down at his phone and still hasn't seen me, but when he reaches the till he looks up and, for the briefest instant, I see something flash across his face. I cannot tell whether it is surprise or irritation or a mixture of both.

"How's the PCS?" he asks after a moment's hesitation.

"Fine," I say. At once I color. "Well, *not* fine, in fact. Still suffering headaches. And dizziness. And all that."

"I'm sure," he says. He looks around. "Where's Jez?"

"Already off."

"Leaving you in charge."

"That would be correct," I say.

He sucks in his breath, glances down at the array of snacks and wine laid out before me, then looks up at me with surprise. "Throwing a party?"

"No." I shake my head emphatically. "No. Not at all. Just . . . laying in some supplies."

"Right." Cal raises a skeptical eyebrow, and I give a nervous laugh.

"You know," I explain. "For the holidays. Thought the dogs deserved a few treats."

Now he really is frowning. "You *do* know that chocolate is dangerous for dogs?" Once again his tone is just this side of schoolmaster.

Seriously? How could chocolate be bad for anyone? "Of course," I say, stuffing the chocolates into a bag. "The dogs can have the crisps."

He crosses his arms, clearly trying to work out if I'm serious, and I cannot help but stare at them. Who the hell has forearms that practically sizzle?

"Actually, salt isn't brilliant for them, either," he says. "Especially Slab. He's got high blood pressure." I drag my gaze back to his face and give him my coolest smile.

"I was joking," I say. *God, he's irritating!*

"Excuse me," interjects the cashier just then. We both turn to look at her. She holds up a fistful of reindeer lollies. "These are on sale," she says pointedly. "Five for five pounds?"

"Um . . . OK."

"But you've got six," she adds accusingly, as if I have deliberately tried to cheat her. The reindeers stare at me with bulging cartoon eyes.

"That's fine," I say crisply.

"Well, I'll have to charge you £1.49 for this one," she adds, holding up the sixth.

I hesitate, then snatch it from her hand and stalk over to the display, placing it back among the others, before returning to the till, my face newly alight. The young woman may have saved me a few pennies, but she has cost me my dignity.

Cal nods at the lollies. "Guess you're all sorted," he says.

"Guess I am," I reply.

He fishes some coins out of his pocket, places them on the counter, and nods to the girl with purple hair. "Happy Holidays," he says, raising the milk in a salute and walking out of the shop. I watch him climb into his car and drive off.

"You, too," I mutter.

A few hours later I'm sprawled across the kitchen sofa reading Agatha Christie when I hear a rustling sound outside. In the next instant the door opens and a tall, thin-faced man sporting a scrubby beard walks straight into the kitchen without so much as a how-de-do. I bolt up off the sofa, dislodging Peggy, who gives an unhappy grunt, and position myself in a sort of tae kwon do stance facing him. The man has the look of a vagrant: sparse hair, sallow cheeks, an oversized coat, and scuffed shoes. He blinks at me with surprise.

"Can I help you?" I ask.

"I am Valko," he says.

I relax. "Right. Of course you are." I've managed to forget all about Valko in the intervening hours since Jez has left. "I'm Charlie. Jez's cousin."

The man bows formally, somewhat to my alarm.

"So . . . um, you're here to walk the dogs? Right?"

He nods, as if to say *naturally*.

"OK! Well, Slab, Hulk, and the twins are outside in the pens, and Peggy's right here," I say, pointing to the beagle.

Valko looks doubtfully at Peggy, who is now splayed across the bottom half of the sofa with her overstuffed belly bared to the world.

"Though I should warn you, she's not much for exercise," I add. Valko frowns.

"Dog will have baby, yes?" He bends down to the beagle and gently splays his hand across her abdomen like a midwife, while Peggy opens one eye and regards him with something akin to alarm. *What the hell is he doing?*

"Yes. Dog will have puppies," I say, lapsing into Euro-speak.

Valko stands up and turns to me with a shrug. "So I take others." I look at Peggy and she almost seems to grin: clearly, she cut a deal with him earlier.

"Sure," I say. "That would be grand. Thank you."

"For . . ." He glances down at his watch. "Maybe half hour."

"Fine. See you in a half hour."

"Then we drink tea."

I stare at him. *I knew there'd be a catch.* But he hasn't exactly phrased it as a question.

"Tea," I say, nodding. "Absolutely."

Whatever else I think of him, I discover over tea that Valko's manners are impeccable. He is polite and solicitous, enquiring in his fractured English about my family and my job and my reasons for coming to Devon, in that order. I parry his questions as best I can, not wanting to let him delve too deeply into my personal life, and ask a few of my own, though I am careful to steer clear of any M-words: marriage, Moldova, misery.

"You like to live in city?" he asks.

I nod. "Yes," I say. I love the ceaseless hum of activity, the sense of perpetual movement and energy, the knowledge that one is surrounded, at all times, by a throbbing mass of humanity. London is a rapidly beating heart that never stops. For a split second I consider articulating all of this to Valko, in pidgin English. But then decide I can't be bothered.

Valko is frowning. He runs a hand through his hair, takes a deep breath. "When I am in city, I cannot . . ." He places a hand on his chest and presses down, mimes being unable to breathe.

I shrug. "Yeah, the air isn't so good."

"No." He shakes his head dismissively. "Not air. In city, it is like . . . I am in box. I am in box that is too small for me. And other people? They are in box, too. All around. I see them. In box." He mimes peering over the edge of his box to look into the other people's boxes. "I see them. But I cannot . . . be with them. It is only me . . . in box."

I stare at him and an image forms in my mind: of my much-loved dark brown sofa, cushions sunk into the corners, an old plaid blanket my mum gave me coiled like a lumpy serpent on one end;

beside it, the coffee table strewn with old newspapers, magazines, empty plates, dead mugs, and discarded tissues; behind the sofa a window, looking out onto other windows. And now it's me who's frowning.

"How long you stay here?" Valko asks.

"Until Jez gets back from holiday."

Valko nods. "I see," he says, pouring himself more tea from the pot, then carefully ladling two spoons of sugar into his cup, stirring slowly until it dissolves. "This is question."

"What is question?" I ask, puzzled.

"Is this holiday?" he asks.

I frown. "Of course it's a holiday," I say. And for the first time I wonder: *Is it?*

"Maybe yes. Maybe no," he says cryptically, his voice trailing off. What is he talking about? The man is like some sort of Eastern European sphinx. And I'm beginning to wonder if his broken English is an affectation. Valko looks up at me and shrugs, as if to say: *Who knows what the future will bring?*

have always disliked Ferris wheels. On the face of it, they appear
to be the most well-mannered of fairground attractions: sturdy,
sedate, benign, *boring* even. They do not produce screams nor
shrieks of laughter from their occupants; they are not replete with
offensive bells or whistles or sirens, nor are they garlanded with
obnoxious flashing lights. But there is always that moment when
you reach the highest point and the mechanism suddenly judders
to a halt with an eerie *clang*, followed by a vast, creeping silence
with only the wind to remind you of your folly; that's when the seat
begins to swing maniacally and your stomach plummets as you
contemplate life far below. Ferris wheels are billed as genteel entertainment, but really they're an elaborate form of mechanical
chicanery: they lull you into a false sense of security, then leave
you stranded high in the sky, with only regret for company.

That is *exactly* how I feel after Valko leaves. Stranded. Anxious. Regretful.

Everything had been going just fine: me, Peggy, the fridge full of pizzas, the flat-screen delivery just around the corner. Now as I look around at Jez's kitchen, the thought that runs through my head is: *What am I doing here?* I should be at home in my flat in Nunhead, nursing my wounded pride, not shacked up with a pregnant beagle in a ramshackle farmhouse on the edge of a desolate moor with my least favorite religious festival looming on the horizon. I take a deep breath and tell myself to calm down. Jez will be home in twelve days' time, and I will scurry back to my bombed-out flat, my loathsome boss, and my disheveled private life.

Maybe yes. Maybe no.

Later that night, Jez rings me from the plane. "We're about to take off," she says excitedly. "Thought I'd better make sure you aren't freaking out."

"Nope, everything's fine," I say in my most reassuring tone. *Of course I'm freaking out.*

"Any last-minute questions?"

"No, all good here." *You're definitely coming back, right?*

"Can I bring you anything from Lapland? A souvenir?"

"No, thanks," I say. *Only yourself!*

"OK. Well, if there's anything else . . . ?" she asks tentatively.

"Jez?"

"Yeah?"

Come back! Please!

"Have a great trip," I say.

"I'll do my best," she says gleefully.

In the morning I am woken by sunshine streaming through the window. Outside a robin twitters and the sky is a reassuring robin's-egg blue. I take a deep breath and last night's fears melt away. Devon is charming, the dogs are delightful, and this is definitely the easiest two hundred pounds I will ever make. Even if I have already spent it.

I rise and dress and after a quick breakfast I square up to my responsibilities as sole operator of Cozy Canine Cottages. First up should be the paying customers: Slab and Hulk will be my top priorities this morning. Then I remember the bag of little white rockets in the fridge and the thought of Remus and his lustrous fur beckons. Maybe Slab and his bottom can wait, I decide, pulling on my boots and coat.

I walk back behind the house toward the run where the twins are kept and as I approach, both dogs rise from where they've been sitting and stand to attention like canine drill sergeants. "At ease, boys," I say a little nervously.

Remus cocks one ear ever so slightly toward me, but apart from that, neither dog moves a muscle. They look like tightly wound giant toys ready to spring, and something deep inside me seizes up with fear. Slab's bottom rockets start to seem preferable and I almost turn straight round. But then I catch a glint of interest in Remus's eye. He is watching me with extreme intensity: in fact, I would say he is *scrutinizing* me. I stand a little taller and lift my chin, looking him in the eye, then step toward the run and lift the latch. *Exude confidence.* I enter the run and turn toward them.

"Good morning," I say in as cheery a voice as I can muster. Then I force myself to kneel down on one leg, my thigh juddering. In an instant both dogs break formation and come toward me, rubbing up against me repeatedly in a curious sort of greeting dance that practically knocks me to the ground.

I stroke them both for a moment, then Remus stops and stares at me expectantly, as if to say, *What next?*

I stand and attach each of them to their leads and let them out of the run, intending to take them to the paddock. But both dogs calmly pull me over to a stretch of grass behind the sulky shed and almost in unison, lift their legs against the fence to pee. *Such gentlemen!* They both squat and do their other business, finishing up almost simultaneously with twin-sized poops, then watch patiently as I dispose of the evidence. When I've finished I take up their leads again but both dogs pull me straight to the sulky shed and sit down next to it obediently.

"I don't think so, guys," I say, shaking my head.

No contact sports, no dangerous activities, nothing that will put you at risk of a further fall.

Remus looks at me and his forehead seems to furrow with dismay.

"It's not that I don't trust you," I say.

Remus blinks, all innocence and disappointment, then gives a small hopeful wag of his tail. I turn to look at the sulky and harnesses. In spite of her warnings, Jez did say it was easy. Perhaps we could manage a quick run.

"Well, maybe just a few times round the yard," I say finally.

The diamond-shaped harnesses are actually quite simple. There's a small opening for the collar, which each dog thoughtfully dips its head for, then a crosshatched section that runs down their back. As I slide it onto Remus he helpfully raises a paw and I realize that the bottom quadrants go around their shoulders and under their chest. Within a minute both dogs stand patiently, kitted out like little gladiators. "Right," I say, standing. "That wasn't so difficult." I pull the sulky out of the shed and position it several feet behind the dogs, lowering the bar in between them, clipping each of their harnesses to the crossbar. As soon as I do I feel the dogs bristle with excitement. Their eyes shine, their mouths loll open and their chests seem to expand like inflated balloons. Romulus begins to paw the ground in a way that seems alarmingly eager, and for an instant my confidence falters. But then I think: *How hard can it be? I sit. They pull.*

"OK, guys," I say. I lower myself gingerly onto the seat and set my feet in the braces that extend on either side, then take up the reins. "And off we go." The twins turn and look at me expectantly. Clearly I have not said the magic word. I look down at the sulky and realize there's a brake mechanism on the left wheel, which I now release. I feel both wheels bounce slightly as they spring into action, and before I can say *mush* the dogs are off at a run, pitching me sideways and almost hurling me right out of the damn thing. With one hand I grab the edge of the seat and with the other I pull back on the reins, shouting, *"Whoa!"* The dogs slow almost imperceptibly but do not break stride. They pull me the length of the yard and head round the corner of the house toward the front drive. I am thinking that if I can just steer them toward the paddock we can do a quick loop around then back again, when out of the corner of my eye I spy a dark blue Volvo station wagon coming round the bend of the road. I jerk the reins as hard as I can toward the paddock but the twins have other ideas, and are now pulling the sulky right out onto the lane; clearly they know exactly where their morning route takes them. I tug hard on the reins and start shouting when the Volvo comes up behind us, then slowly pulls alongside and I glance over to see Bovine Cal gesticulating furiously through the window, just as the twins pull me, bouncing off down a farm track on the left and we disappear round a bend girded by a small copse of trees.

I am still shouting at the twins to stop when I remember the brake. I reach down and grab the lever, pulling it hard, and the sulky bucks wildly, nearly flinging me like a slingshot right onto the twins' backs. It skids on the dirt track, veers to one side, then grinds to a halt. Ahead of me the twins twist round, panting hard. Their chests heave and their tongues loll and Remus has a wildly confused look in his eye, as if to say: *Did we do something wrong?*

For a moment I cannot breathe. I think I have just seen my entire life flash before me: childhood, adolescence, adulthood. I am pretty sure I saw my own funeral. And not enough people were in attendance.

"OK," I gasp, holding tightly to the reins. *We are here. We are whole. And for this we must be thankful.* Behind me I hear a car come around the copse of trees and the blue Volvo pulls up, grinding to a halt, twenty feet behind me. Cal turns off the engine and jumps out.

"Are you insane?" he shouts as he storms over to me. I compose myself and turn to him.

"Is something wrong?" I ask.

"Can you be any *more* irresponsible? You could have been killed back there! *They* could have been killed back there," he says, motioning to the twins. "Frankly, we *all* could have been killed back there!"

"Don't be dramatic. You were never in danger," I say huffily. *Which is true.* "Anyway, I was in complete control," I add. *Which is not true.*

"Bollocks!"

"There's no need to be . . . vulgar."

Cal is literally *heaving* with anger. He shakes his head, runs a hand through his hair, then gesticulates back toward the road. "You have absolutely no business taking that thing out on a public highway."

"It's a country lane!"

"It's an A road!"

"Is it really?" I say, surprised. "Anyway, we were only on it for a minute." *Which is true.*

"A minute that could have ended in disaster."

"But it didn't."

Cal shakes his head again.

"You're clearly mad. And Jez is even more so, for leaving you in charge." He glares at me, then turns and stalks back to his car. I watch him climb into the Volvo, rev the engine like a toddler, then speed off.

Before I can even ask how the hell I get the sulky back to the farm.

am a strong, independent woman. I do not need man candy to help me get two dogs and a glorified tricycle back to the kennels. I leave the sulky where it is and detach the harnesses, using them as dog leads to walk the twins back down the road to the paddock, where I close the gate and turn them loose.

"Go on," I say. "Playtime."

Both dogs turn to me with a look of confusion, as if they haven't the faintest idea what they are meant to do. They sniff the grass for a moment, then lie down, like this is some sort of staging post on the next leg of the relay.

"Fine, suit yourselves. I'll be back in ten." I leave them in the paddock and trudge back down the lane to get the sulky. I drag it like a cart horse up the track and back onto the A road, cars whizzing past, trying my best to look nonchalant. Just as I am nearing the Cozy Canine turnoff I catch a glimpse of a familiar green sports car. It slows as it passes, then pulls in and stops. After a moment Handsome Hugo steps out and waves. *Ahoy there!*

"Are you all right? Do you need help?" he calls, motioning toward the sulky.

"No, I'm fine." With my free hand I wave back and Hugo gives me a bewildered smile. He comes a bit closer.

"I thought you might be in some sort of trouble." He indicates the sulky.

"No, just . . . out for a test drive," I say breezily, as if it is perfectly normal to be dragging a small vehicle behind me like a drudge early on a winter's morning.

"Oh. Right. How was it?" he asks, looking perplexed.

"Handles beautifully. Especially off road," I say.

"Excellent. Well, then. Guess I'll leave you to it." Hugo turns back to his car.

"Did you find somewhere to board your dog?" I ask. Hugo pauses and shakes his head ruefully.

"I'm afraid not. Everywhere round here was full up. He spent last night in the car. But the weather's getting colder, so . . ." He shrugs.

"Oh. I'm sorry."

"Yes. I haven't quite decided what I'll do. It's not shaping up to be much of a Christmas."

"Are you meant to be off on holiday?" I ask. He shakes his head.

"Nothing so glamorous, I'm afraid. I'm meant to be spending Christmas up the road with friends. But I'm afraid they're not dog people. In fact, they're fairly uncompromising on that point."

"Some friends!" I bark. Though I suspect they and I are kindred spirits.

"Well, they're not exactly friends," he adds. "They're sort of . . . in-laws."

My heart sinks. *Handsome Hugo is married. Such a waste.*

He gives an embarrassed shrug. "Or at least, *prospective* in-laws," he says. "So we're trying to be accommodating."

Prospective! Hugo is not yet lost! "We?" I ask.

"Malcolm and I." He motions to the car and I bend down to see the Great Dane seated upright in the passenger seat like a bodyguard, his head nearly touching the ceiling. "We're sort of . . . on trial, aren't we, boy? Anyway, thanks for asking." He starts to climb into the car.

"So you'll be staying down the road?" I ask.

Hugo hesitates. "Yes. It's only about five miles."

"So you could . . . look in on him?" *Often?* I think.

"Absolutely. Every day. Twice a day if necessary!"

"Well, perhaps we could manage it," I say tentatively.

Hugo looks hopeful. "Really? The other woman said you were completely full."

"Oh well, yes," I stammer. "The kennels *are* full. But . . . the house is free," I add rashly.

He looks at me, amazed. "You'd let Malcolm stay in the *house?*"

I hesitate. "Maybe?" I say. *As long as he doesn't hog the sofa.*

"He's incredibly well behaved. And I'd pay extra!" Hugo says quickly. He runs a hand through his hair. "Frankly, I'd pay *double.*" He looks at me desperately. *Double.*

"I'm sure we can come to an arrangement," I say with a smile.

am a strong, independent woman, and soon I will be shacked up with six canines. Hugo goes off somewhere to fetch various dog accoutrements, promising to return with Malcolm later in the day. He is practically bursting with gratitude, and I am feeling extremely magnanimous. Not to mention pleased at the prospect of double the fees, and twice-daily visits from Hugo to break the tedium. Even if he *is* engaged.

I return the twins to their cage and fetch Peggy, Slab, and Hulk from their respective beds, marshaling them out to the paddock like recalcitrant teens. Peggy and Hulk immediately squat to do their business, but Slab manages only a brief, trembling leg-rise against a tree, before he turns and looks at me. "Come on, Slab. You can do this," I say coaxingly. He watches me doubtfully with his less-cloudy eye. Perhaps if we walk a little, I think. We embark on a forced march around the perimeter of the paddock, Peggy eyeing me resentfully, Hulk picking her way daintily among the thistle and nettles, and Slab managing a sort of weak stagger, but with no result. Eventually I decide that Slab's treatment can probably wait until later in the day. Surely it is best to give nature every opportunity to work its magic?

All the dogs seem relieved when I return them to their respective beds. And I am just settling down with Agatha Christie when I hear a truck pull up outside. I leap to the door in anticipation of my flat-screen delivery, and see an attractive woman in her late thirties, with close-cropped salt-and-pepper hair, hauling what appears to be a tall, trussed-up fir tree out of the back of a truck.

She hoists it onto her shoulder like a scaffolder and approaches the house. I open the back door.

"Hello?" I ask. The woman gives me a cheery smile, then lifts the tree off her shoulder and thwacks the trunk down at my feet.

"Good morning! Is Jez around?"

"Sorry, I'm afraid she's away."

"No worries. I've brought her tree." She thrusts the top of the tree toward me like an oversized baton.

"Um. Jez is away for the holidays," I say tentatively. The woman frowns.

"Really? That's odd. She never said."

"It was kind of a last-minute thing," I explain.

"Oh. No matter. Here's her tree. You may as well have it. I cut it especially for her."

Seriously? "Um. I wasn't really . . ." I start to say but decide that it might seem churlish to refuse. "That's very kind," I say instead.

"I'm Stella. I own the pig farm down the road. Christmas trees are just a seasonal sideline," she says with a grin. I introduce myself and Stella helpfully offers to bring the tree inside and set it up for me. Once again I nearly decline but don't want to appear rude. Besides, the tree does smell delicious, and fresh-cut Christmas trees are one of the few items on my pro-Santa list. Stella directs me toward a kitchen cupboard, where I locate a small red tree stand high on a shelf. She fixes the trunk into the stand, then deposits the tree in the corner of the kitchen, slicing off the netting efficiently with a razor, and giving the tree another thwack and a hearty shake. "There," she says, beaming.

"It's . . . lovely," I say politely. In fact, the tree is curiously mis-shapen, with the upper half tragically sparse and the lower half bushy on one side, spindly on the other. The top four feet of the tree is completely bare and crooked to boot. Stella beams at it.

"Aren't homegrown trees charming?" she says. I nod, unable to formulate a coherent response. The tree looks pathetic, and I suspect we both know it, but one glance at Stella suggests otherwise. From her place on the sofa, Peggy sits up and regards the tree with what appears to be disdain.

"Thank you so much," I murmur.

"That should get you in the spirit!" Stella says.

I peer at her. *Is she being ironic?* Apparently not. "Yep." I nod.

Stella crosses to the door and turns to me. "If you need any help, I'm just down the road. Hollyhox Farm. You can't miss it."

I hesitate. She's a pig farmer: she is *obviously* experienced with animal husbandry. "Actually, there *is* something," I say quickly, and Stella turns to me enquiringly.

Stella doesn't seem to mind at all. In fact, she seems positively *pleased* to be of use. She deals with Slab's bottom rocket with admirable efficiency. Just one quick lift of the tail, a small shove, and the entire business is over and done with in a flash. I am suitably gushing in my gratitude, Slab looks patently relieved, and the three of us part company the best of friends. A few minutes later I wave her off cheerily from the doorway and she gives a small toot of her horn as she drives off. *Why are women so much more congenial than men?*

After a shower, a blow dry, and a trawl through Jez's wardrobe for something vaguely alluring to wear, I am ready for Hugo's arrival later that afternoon. I don't hear the car in the drive and when a light tap sounds at the kitchen door I look up to see an enormous canine face looming in the window. The dog's pale white head is the size of a large dinner plate and completely obscures most of the window. His brown eyes sweep across the kitchen balefully, and if I didn't know better, I would swear he was sizing up his new digs with something akin to regret. Off to one side I can just make out Hugo, who appears to be bent over, fiddling with an oversized wheelie bag at his side. I open the door and Hugo stands up.

"Hello! We've arrived," he greets me cheerily.

"I can see that." I turn to the dog, struggling to take in the sheer *scale* of him. Though I have already caught a glimpse of him folded into the seat of a sports car, standing Malcolm is a very different proposition. The top of his head comes almost to my shoulders, which puts his gaze roughly in line with my breasts. He is entirely pale white, like a massive canine version of a snowy owl, except his eyes are hazel and very slightly pink-rimmed. I look down at his legs, which seem to go on forever and end in meaty dog hocks, with paws the size of giant putting irons.

"And this is Malcolm," says Hugo proudly.

Who is clearly not a normal size!

"Of course it is," I say. Now I know exactly why Hugo's prospective in-laws were not keen. And I am in complete accord with them on this point.

"Um . . . should we come in?" asks Hugo.

The idea of sharing the same living quarters with Malcolm

seems suddenly outrageous. I am a fool for suggesting it in the first place. Nevertheless I open the door wide.

"Please do," I suggest, as if it was my idea.

Hugo leads Malcolm into the kitchen and, behind me, Peggy sits up with alarm from her spot on the sofa, ears alert, hackles raised along her back. Malcolm turns to Peggy and I swear he dips his head to her: the dog practically *genuflects*. Or curtsies. Or whatever. Peggy relaxes slightly, still eyeing him, but clearly less concerned. She slowly lowers her laden belly back down onto the sofa with a harrumph. Pecking order has been established, and unsurprisingly, Peggy remains top dog. I turn to Hugo.

"Would you like a drink?"

"I'm frightfully sorry, but I'm afraid I can't stay."

"Oh?" *What a pity.*

"It's just . . . I'm needed at some sort of neighbor's drinks party." He rolls his eyes. "Command performance, and all that." He holds out a large dark blue wheelie bag, the sort that would clearly not fit in an overhead compartment on a plane. "Here are his things." I look down at the bag.

"Your dog has his own luggage?" I ask. I cannot disguise the incredulity in my voice. Hugo gives an embarrassed laugh.

"Well, it's just odds and sods, really. His bed, a blanket, a food bowl, a couple of leads. And his favorite toy. Oh, and some treats. Just in case." His voice trails off.

Hugo is clearly a nutcase. A rich, handsome nutcase, but a nutcase all the same.

"In case of what?" I ask.

"He can be a little sensitive."

Alarm bells begin to toll. "Sensitive how?"

"Oh, not to worry, nothing sinister. All rescue dogs are sensitive."

"He's a rescue?" I ask. The bells are tolling louder.

What sort of person would rescue a dog like this?

"And Malcolm especially so, because of his disability," Hugo continues.

Disability? The bells are actually clanging now. I turn to appraise the dog, looking for clues I'm not seeing. No missing limbs or ears or tail.

Hugo carries on speaking, oblivious to my burgeoning sense of alarm. "I got him from Battersea. I practically had to sign my life away before they let me take him home."

"Did you say disabled?" Hugo pauses and looks at me, his handsome face all innocence.

"I'm sorry, didn't I mention? Malcolm is deaf."

chapter
11

A deaf Dane. It is almost Shakespearean. After Hugo takes his leave, we are left with Malcolm's hulking presence in our kitchen. It is difficult to know what to do with him. I deposit his enormous dog bed in the corner by the door and endeavor to coax him over to it by waving my arms like a lunatic, but perversely Malcolm positions himself squarely in the middle of the room. He doesn't so much lie down as lower himself into a sphinxlike pose, regarding us with wary eyes.

Peggy looks over at me as if to say: *Seriously?*

It is inhibiting, to say the least. But I instruct Peggy to get over it and endeavor to follow my own advice. Between the Dane and Stella's tree the kitchen has shrunk considerably. Before he left, Hugo turned to the tree and cocked his head a little sympathetically.

"Wouldn't it benefit from . . ." He hesitated.

"Burning?" I suggested.

"I was going to say adornment."

"We were going for the natural look."

He frowned. "I'm not sure it's working."

I decide to ring Sian to let her know that I won't be coming back to London until after the holiday. "She left *you* in charge of the kennels?" Sian asks. "That's rich. What do your duties entail?"

"Not a lot, as far as I can see. The dogs don't do much besides eat, sleep, crap, and lie around scratching."

"Oh God. Don't come home with fleas."

"They don't have fleas," I say. *Which is only a teeny-weeny bit untrue.* "Anyway, it's not like we're cohabiting." *Also untrue.*

"That's good to know."

I tell her about the deaf Dane and Handsome Hugo.

"Seriously? And he's rich?"

"Apparently."

"This could be the best thing that ever happened!"

"But he's engaged."

"Doesn't matter. Sixty percent of all engagements come to nothing."

"Really? Is that true?"

"Nah, I made it up. But if you include divorces down the line, I suspect that figure's not far off. So you'd be doing him a favor. Think of all the legal fees he'll save."

"I'm not sure he'd see it that way. Besides, it sounds like his fiancée is out of my league. She's some sort of royalty."

"So are Beatrice and Eugenie."

"Good point." Sian has long maintained that Beatrice and Eugenie will single-handedly bring down the monarchy, simply through their choice of hats.

"So what does Handsome Hugo do for a living?"

"He told me he's some sort of commodities trader."

"Which is what, exactly?"

"No idea. He mentioned something about aluminum futures."

"Is that like . . . prospecting for tinfoil?"

"Who knows? But there appears to be money in it."

"God, I knew I shouldn't have retrained as a counselor."

"But you *like* working in the caring professions."

"Do I? Tinfoil sounds much more lucrative."

"Not to mention malleable."

"True. Though when it comes down to it, I prefer cling film."

"How's my favorite godson, anyway?"

"He's recovering from gastric flu."

"Oh wow, sorry."

"Yep. He threw up four times last night. In the end I swapped his bedding for a plastic tablecloth and he didn't even notice. I might use it all the time from now on. Saves me doing laundry."

"I'm surprised you didn't ring me."

"I would have, but he threw up on my phone."

"Nice."

"We were out of rice, so I had to bury it in Rice Krispies. Worked a treat."

"Very innovative. Be sure to post that tip on Mumsnet."

"I already have."

"And please tell me you threw out the cereal."

Later that evening I am halfway through a bottle of Chilean chardonnay and have almost discovered the killer on the Orient Express, when Peggy rolls herself heavily off the sofa, walks over to the tree, and sniffs at the lower branches. She turns to me with a look that says she's clearly underwhelmed. I get up from the sofa with a sigh and search the cupboard where I found the tree stand, but it is devoid of anything that could even vaguely be described as an ornament, much less a strand of lights. What I do find are lots of dog supplies: disposal bags (helpfully colored poo-brown), a dozen spare leads, a bag of old tennis balls, a carton of bone-shaped rawhide chews, and a box of squeaky toys.

Needs must.

Fifteen minutes later Peggy, Malcolm, and I survey my handiwork. The leads have been strung together in a long garland, which I have wound several times around the branches and clipped almost to the top. I've stuffed tennis balls into the poo bags and tied the handles into a sort of bow to decorate the ends of the branches, and the rawhide chews and squeaky plastic toys have been dotted about the denser parts of the tree. Peggy sniffs with interest at one of the lower-hanging poo bags, and Malcolm turns to me with an enquiring look, as if to say: *Are we done here?*

For a moment the three of us regard the tree.

"It's missing something," I say finally. I return to the cupboard to root around, and emerge triumphantly a moment later clutching a neon orange Frisbee with a hole in the center, which I balance at the very top of the tree. Malcolm responds by prostrating himself directly at its base, as if the tree is now somehow worthy of worship, and even Peggy signals her approval with a long, satisfying scratch beneath its boughs.

Bah, humbug, I think with satisfaction.

I pass a pleasant enough evening with my canine companions, but in the morning when I come downstairs I find the Great Dane in exactly the same position as I left him: crouched low, facing the tree, ears rigid, and a decidedly worried look in his eye. I stare down at him.

"Malcolm, have you been here all night?" I ask.

He's deaf. Not to mention a dog. So it's a purely rhetorical question. Still, he seems to intuit that I'm addressing him and swings his oversized muzzle toward me like the barrel of a cannon, his eyes alighting on me for the briefest of instants, before swiveling back to gaze steadily at the tree. I glance over at Peggy, who is faking slumber on the sofa. She opens one eye, gives a dismissive snort, then closes it again, indicating that Malcolm is unworthy of her attention. I bend down and lightly run a hand down his back: he flinches; his spine as taut as a violin bow, but apart from that he takes no notice of me, his eyes are stapled to the tree. It's like he's cornered it and doesn't know what to do with it—as if the tree is somehow *prey.* I get up with a sigh and make coffee, trying to remember what it is they say about mad dogs and Englishmen. I'm beginning to realize that double the fees may not be enough to compensate for Malcolm's eccentricities.

Armed with sixteen ounces of freshly brewed dark roast, I cross to the office, where Jez houses her professional library in an enormous wooden dresser. It's the old-fashioned sort with shelves above and drawers below, the kind that people used to display crockery on in the old days, but this one holds an impressive collection of books on a wide variety of canine topics including breeding, training, evolution, dog psychology, and health.

The titles range from the obvious (*Perfect Puppy*) to the ridiculous (*Train Your Dog the SAS Way*) to the hilarious (*Know Your Bitch!*) to the frankly baffling (*Canine Cognitive Dysfunction*) and to the sublime (*Follow Your Dog into a World of Smell*). Who knew that dogs were even capable of cognition? They eat, sleep, shag, and fart—but do they really obsess about doing so, the way we do? None of this is getting me any closer toward understanding what is wrong with Malcolm and I briefly consider phoning Hugo, but decide that a little due diligence is in order first. So I select a title to peruse over breakfast: a slim volume, promisingly titled *Dog Sense*, whose cover features a cock-eared boxer with a sardonic look in his eye. Peggy raises her head and frowns at me as I sit down next to her with the book, like I'm some sort of pretender, but I fix her with my most authoritarian glare and she turns away.

I'm a strong, independent woman, I think huffily.

Why shouldn't I become a dog expert in the space of ten days?

The book is about canine personality profiling, a concept that immediately strikes me as oxymoronic (or at the very least moronic). According to the author, every dog has genetically determined behaviors that can be grouped into three drives: *prey*

drive, *pack* drive, and *defense* drive. The first is associated with hunting and eating: dogs that stalk, chase, bite, or dig are all exhibiting prey drive. I glance up at Malcolm. He may have cornered the Christmas tree, but something tells me his behavior isn't about food. His body is rigid with apprehension, as if the tree might combust at any moment. I skip forward to chapter two. Pack drive is all about loyalty, order, and cooperation—dogs that sniff, groom, mount, or play with one another all exhibit pack drive. I look up at Malcolm and Peggy. The idea of them grooming each other is laughable: they couldn't be less of a pack. So far, we're definitely barking up the wrong tree.

But chapter three is more promising. The defense drive is about survival and self-preservation, but confusingly it can result in either fight or flight behaviors, making the dog aggressive or fearful, depending on how they're inclined. Fighting dogs will growl and stand tall with their hackles raised. Flighty dogs will prostrate themselves, retreat, or even hide. *Bingo*, I think. Malcolm is in flight mode. He's an enormous canine coward.

I turn to Peggy, who somehow seems to defy all three categories. She's calm, cool, and self-contained, and fight-or-flight seems definitely beneath her. Peggy doesn't really strike me as a *dog* at all. Peggy is like Jeanetta, my überorganized but condescending upstairs neighbor in Nunhead, who sighs with dismay when I ask to borrow a teeny-weeny drop of milk for my morning tea, but gives it to me anyway because, at the end of the day she may be obsessively efficient, but she's not a jerk.

I decide that dog psychology is mostly common sense, and canines aren't much different from humans. In fact, as soon as I saw the list of traits associated with prey drive, an image of Lionel popped into my head. Lionel was the classic alpha male—confident, charismatic, competitive, and a little bit arrogant. In truth, it was these qualities that attracted me to him in the first place, because who among us isn't secretly drawn to the pack leader?

I first met Lionel at a barbecue in Hyde Park on a sunny night in June. It was one of those golden summer evenings in London—which are so rare they instantly take on an almost mythic quality—when the air is clean and sharp, the grass luridly green, the temperature fuzzily warm, and the city seems to almost shimmer with energy. It was a night made for exuberant living and I went along, like most others that evening, determined to have a whale of a time.

Even if one of my closest friends *had* just lost his job.

Lionel was working at one of the top legal firms in London and the barbecue was a leaving do for a colleague of his who had been a roommate of mine at university. Joss had recently been made redundant, sidelined in the vicious up-or-out world of London law, and although the event hadn't been billed as a leaving do per se, we all knew why we were there: to cheer him up because his contract hadn't been renewed. Someone from their office had gone to masses of trouble to compensate: there were tables laden with platters of salads and cold dishes shipped in from a trendy Chelsea deli, each with a handwritten label in perfect calligraphy. Everything seemed to be either charred or fancily dried: air-dried beef, sun-dried tomatoes, wind-dried salmon, and some sort of Asian daikon salad that had probably been blow-dried. The drink flowed, too, with massive jugs of lethally strong Pimm's that were replenished by smiling staff as soon as we emptied them. There must have been forty or so people in all, including a half dozen of my old university mates, and within a few hours we were all pretty tanked. Then someone started the games: tug-of-war, three-legged race, four-in-a-sack—the latter causing much mirth, more than a few contusions, and at least one person vomiting behind the bushes.

The final event of the night was the egg-and-spoon race, and for this we were all organized into heats. Lionel was put next to me, and as he stepped forward I noticed that he didn't so much walk as *swagger* into the starting position. He was tall and lean with a long, narrow nose, a prominent chin, and dirty blond hair cut short so that it stood up like a brush. His clothes were casual but chosen with care: Nike trainers, Diesel jeans, and a dark blue T-shirt that read TRUST ME in white letters across his chest. *Typical metrosexual garb*, I thought.

After he'd taken his place at the starting line he turned and looked at me dead on. Though I'd clocked him earlier as one of the better-looking guys there, we hadn't yet been introduced, and there was something unnervingly direct about the way he met my gaze: like he could tell *exactly* what I was thinking. Which at that precise moment was that if we ended up in bed that night, I wouldn't be sorry.

"May the force be with you," he said with mock solemnity.

"And with you," I replied evenly. He nodded, as if accepting my challenge, then turned toward the finish line, thrusting his egg out in front of him.

Needless, to say, the force wasn't with me. I lost, rather spectacularly. It had all been going swimmingly well, with me lurching forward at breakneck speed, the egg hovering in front of me like a tiny flying saucer, and Lionel matching my pace with seeming ease—when suddenly I stumbled, the momentum launching me like a rocket. I landed facedown in the grass and lay there, gasping with laughter while Lionel went on to win the heat amidst raucous cheers and shouts. When I stood up I discovered that the egg had smashed beneath me and was now fetchingly smeared across my chest. Lionel walked over to where I stood, still holding his perfectly balanced egg on the spoon. When he reached me, his eyes flicked down to my yolk-stained T-shirt, lingering for an instant on my bright orange breasts. "I usually like poached," he said. "But scrambled will do." Then he reached in the back pocket of his jeans and pulled out an actual cloth handkerchief (*Who carries cloth hankies these days?* I thought) and started to dab gingerly at my breasts, which caused us both to crinkle with laughter. He handed me the hankie. "Think this might be one of those *too-many-cooks* situations," he said with a grin, then turned away.

He went on to win the next two heats, until it was only he and Joss left to battle it out in the final. We all watched as they took their starting positions, and the fact that it was Lionel against Joss made me feel suddenly uneasy. I'd learned during the interim heats that Lionel and Joss had both been put forward for the same job, and it was Lionel who'd been given the promotion. I watched as Joss gave his egg a quick kiss for luck, then placed it firmly on his spoon, his face unnaturally pink from drink, heat, and exertion. He had a worryingly manic look in his eye, as if there was too much at stake, and I saw a shadow pass briefly across Lionel's face. They set off and both men strode confidently across the grass, though with his long legs Lionel cut a more impressive figure and seemed certain to win. They were neck and neck right up until the last twenty paces, when I saw Lionel start to pull ahead, and Joss fall back a little, his hand beginning to tremble slightly, as if he was losing focus. When Lionel was only a few paces from the finish line, he glanced back over his shoulder at Joss, and as he did he tripped on a small dip in the grass and went down, sprawling flat, while Joss practically leaped over him to cross the finish line, his egg miraculously balanced on the spoon. Joss roared with victory and flung his egg high into the air. Lionel stood up, smiling, and I saw that his egg had broken all down his T-shirt, just as mine had done. He clapped Joss heartily on the back, offering his congratulations, then turned, his eyes searching the crowd.

They landed on me. He smiled and walked over to where I stood. I handed him the handkerchief and nodded to his egg-smattered shirt.

"Bad luck," I said.

"Or not," he replied. He looked at me with his piercing gaze and I felt my knees buckle. Then he smiled. "I thought you might not want to eat alone," he said.

He did end up in my bed that night, and the next, and the one after that. And in less than six weeks, we'd moved in together. At the time it seemed like the most natural thing in the world, even though my mother expressed alarm over what she termed our "undue haste." Lionel's lease was up and we spent most of our evenings together anyway, I argued, so it made sense to pool our resources and save on rent. The fact that it took him several months to set up the standing order for his share of the bills only slightly worried me, but not enough to spoil our idyll. That first year passed in a miasma of lust. At home we were in bed more often than not, and most of that time Lionel was funny and attentive and spontaneous. He brought me freshly brewed coffee in the mornings, introduced me to his friends, and showed me his favorite London haunts. He was a keen climber and even tried to persuade me to join his gym so we could climb together, something I resisted instinctively, without really knowing why.

But one day about eighteen months into our relationship, when he'd already begun to grow distant, his best friend, Tony, made a casual remark that thrummed somewhere deep inside me. "Lionel's a serial hobbyist," he declared lightly one evening over beers. We were in a pub outside of the gym waiting for Lionel to finish. By this time Lionel's obsession with climbing had morphed into one with kickboxing, and he spent every waking hour outside of work training. "He has the attention span of a gnat," said Tony. I frowned. Did that extend to his relationships, I wondered.

I think I knew the answer even then. But it took two more years and one more hobby (rowing) before Lionel finally left me. Over that time, the alpha-male traits that had initially enthralled me had slowly begun to grate: by then his confidence struck me as overblown, his charisma insincere, his competitiveness annoying, and his arrogance boorish.

The truth is, I should have left Lionel long before he left me.

chapter
12

Hugo rings me later that morning to check on Malcolm, and I confess that things aren't going well. With a great deal of coaxing I'd managed to get the Great Dane out to the paddock after breakfast, but only because he'd reluctantly followed Peggy and the others. Once he'd done his toilet business, he'd stood next to the gate staring longingly in the direction Hugo had departed.

"He seems a little unsettled," I say.

"He doesn't adapt well to new environments," Hugo admits.

Now you tell me. "Perhaps you should visit?" I suggest hopefully.

And take him away?

"We're just off for a ride now," he says breezily. "And then there's a bit of a lunch thing later, but I promise to come by later this afternoon." The weather outside is blustery and freezing: why anyone would want to ride out in it is beyond me. They are forecasting a blizzard for later in the week. But no doubt Hugo and his fiancée will be kitted out in the most expensive riding gear money can buy. And Hugo is clearly a pack animal: he will do as he's bid.

Instead, it's Valko who arrives in the middle of the afternoon, stamping his feet and blowing on his hands. "Outside very cold," he says, shaking his head. He motions to the kennels. "Dogs will be freeze."

"The kennels are heated," I say breezily. *Surely they must be?*

He raises an eyebrow. "Not so much, I think."

"Enough for animals, I think."

Jez would never let the dogs freeze. I think.

Valko takes the twins for a long walk and afterward, over tea, he tells me the story of his Moldovan bride. It seems he met her on a website catering especially for men seeking Moldovan women for marriage. Sometimes I think I'm better suited to the Victorian Age, I tell him, as I'd no idea such websites even existed. Valko googles *Eastern European Bride* on his phone and shows me the results. There are dozens of sites. We click on one and I see with relief that it is not just men seeking women, but women seeking men. But when I click through to the detail, I realize that the men are all from the UK, the US, and Australia, while the women are only from Eastern Europe. Further research reveals that the women are all under forty and, without exception, stunningly attractive—while the men are uniformly dumpy, fat, balding, wrinkled, or a combination of all four. I look up at Valko and, sadly, with his gaunt features and leaden eyes, he fits the profile.

For twenty-five dollars a month he was given access to dozens of Moldovan women's details: he could search by age, ethnicity, education level, or simply by photo. The woman he chose to correspond with was called Laska. She was thirty-one, divorced, peroxide-blonde, and unlucky: she'd been raised in dire poverty by a father who was more often drunk than sober and a depressed mother who, when Laska was twelve, took to her bed and never got up again; an older sister had run off at sixteen with a Russian man twice her age; and her younger sister had married a local man who impregnated her with twins, then promptly disappeared. Laska herself had been married to a man she had believed loved her: he drove a truck across Europe delivering goods for IKEA and was absent three weeks out of four. One day he went out drinking with mates and left his mobile phone behind; it rang, and when she answered it the caller demanded to know why a strange woman was answering her husband's phone. It turns out he had not one, but two other wives, and was engaged to a fourth. Laska waited until he left town, then made an enormous bonfire of his possessions in front of their flat and texted a photo of it to him, together with the news that she was filing for divorce.

When Valko relates this sorry tale in halting English, I shake my head with wonder. How did we ever manage to survive before modern technology enabled us to meet, marry, cheat, and divorce with such aplomb, I wonder aloud. But Valko doesn't seem to understand. I ask him what happened between him and Laska. He takes a deep breath and lets it out abjectly. "For her, it was not love math," he says with a tortured shrug of his shoulder. I frown.

"Do you mean *match*?"

"I am only . . . passport." He spreads his hands. "To new life in Britain."

"She came here?"

"After one half year she fly to London. I meet her at Heathrow with flowers, chocolate. She bring me socks she make herself," he says, jousting with his index fingers in an effort to mime knitting. "And to begin, she is nice. She is . . . kind." He shrugs. "Well . . . a little kind. I bring her to my caravan and she make it . . . more like home. We are happy. For some little time. I think."

He frowns and my heart twists for him. "And then?" I ask.

"She begin to be . . . not happy. First, it is she do not like my food. Then she do not like my cloths." He pinches his threadbare jacket. "Then it is place we live. The people beside us. The rain." He rolls his eyes.

I refrain from saying that she has a point with this last one.

"Until she like . . . nobody. No one thing. But most of all . . . she not like me." Valko seems to shrink with this last admission, as if his clothes are suddenly two sizes too large, and I understand that this mail-order woman has somehow reduced him to a pint-sized man.

"I'm sorry, Valko," I say.

"In end, she stay in bedroom. And I stay on sofa. She will not talk to my face. Only use Skype. Even though there is only . . . thin wall between us."

"Oh, Valko," I say sympathetically.

"Then one day she leave. With cow man."

"'Cow man'?"

"The man who come with milk," he grumbles.

"She ran away with the milkman?" I ask, incredulous.

He nods, and I wince. Mail-order brides and milkmen: Valko is living inside a tragic cliché. "Maybe it wasn't meant to be," I offer half-heartedly. "Maybe the Internet isn't where you find true love."

Though it seems to have worked for Jez.

"Then where?" he asks. I shake my head.

Beats me.

After Valko leaves I get a call from the courier service delivering my flat-screen TV. It seems that the parcel was accidentally sent to a warehouse in Motherwell instead of Launceston. "Motherwell?" I ask. "Isn't that in Scotland?"

"It always has bin," says a man with a heavy Scottish accent. I can practically see him chuckling down the line.

"So when will it be rerouted?"

"I assume yoo're awaur there's a' blizzard up haur," he says. I am, of course, aware that the much-vaunted storm has already hit the northern parts of the country. But we live in the twenty-first century. We have the means to clear transport routes, surely?

"So what does that mean?" I ask tentatively.

"'At means yur telly will be delayed."

No kidding. "Any idea how long?"

"Ach. Yoo'll be lucky tae see it afair Christmas now."

Nooooo. "But . . . is there an actual scheduled date of delivery?"

"I think we're operatin' purely in th' realm of theory haur at this point," he says.

Brilliant. A philosopher-courier. Just my luck.

"What's your best guess?" I ask.

"Ye want me tae guess?" He sounds bemused, as if guessing is somehow beyond his remit.

"Yes."

"Well, if I was tae speculate," he says slowly. "I'd say it was oan indefinite delay."

Perfect. My date with Audrey has been *indefinitely* postponed.

Later I escort the dogs out to the paddock and watch as Slab makes several valiant but unsuccessful efforts to purge himself. But each time he crouches down, his entire body begins to tremble uncontrollably, and he looks over at me imploringly, as if wanting me to intervene. *Seriously?* I kneel down beside him and place a steadying hand on either side of his fragile hips to try to support his frame. "Come on, Slab," I plead. "Concentrate." Slab strains and strains and finally something starts to emerge at a glacially slow pace. *Hallelujah.*

Though at the current rate we could be here all night. Just then I hear the sound of a familiar diesel engine behind us. Both Slab and I glance over to see the dark blue Volvo pull up beside the paddock. The engine dies and, after a split second, Bovine Cal climbs out. "Is he OK?" he calls over. Slab freezes, halfway through his business, poo dangling like low-hanging fruit from his bum. It is not a pretty picture.

"Um . . . maybe?" I call over.

"What are you doing?" Cal asks, coming over to the gate. I hesitate. He will think I am bonkers.

"Just . . . lending a hand."

Cal opens the paddock and walks over to us. He is looming over me with disapproval. "Did you use the suppositories?"

That would be a negative. "He had one yesterday. Or maybe the day before," I add.

He gives me a withering look. "So you thought *what* exactly? That you'd do it *for* him?"

"I just thought he might need a little support. That's all."

Cal stares down at us for a moment, then much to my surprise, he throws back his head and laughs.

"Constipation is no laughing matter," I say in an admonishing tone.

He nods and turns away. "Hang on for a second," he calls over his shoulder, trudging back to the car.

"We're not going anywhere," I reply.

He fetches the backpack from the front seat before returning to us, then reaches inside and pulls out a box of surgical gloves, snapping one onto each hand with brisk efficiency. When he finishes he reaches toward Slab's bottom, then pauses, turning to me.

"This is the part where you might want to look away," he says.

Yep. Too right. Still holding on to Slab's hips I avert my eyes, while Cal proceeds with relieving the dog of his burden. It takes several moments until he gives the all clear. "Think that should do it," he mutters. He bags the excrement in a black sack, then removes the gloves and places them inside, tying the handles shut. We both stand and Slab wobbles off gratefully to sniff the grass.

"Thank you," I say.

Cal nods.

"Look," he says. "I have to pass by here a few times a day. I can check on Slab if you're worried." His tone is suddenly more conciliatory. I wonder if he is feeling bad about his outburst over the sulky. Or maybe he's just worried about Slab. I nod.

"Do you want to come in and wash your hands?" I ask. I call to the other dogs and we walk back to the house.

As we go inside, Cal gestures toward Malcolm. "Where did he come from?"

"The owner's staying nearby. He needed somewhere to park him for a few days over Christmas."

Cal raises an eyebrow. "You're keeping him in the house?"

"He's deaf," I say, lowering my voice slightly, as if Malcolm might hear. "And *very sensitive*," I add in a loud whisper. "So I've agreed to keep an eye on him."

Cal looks at me quizzically, then goes to the kitchen sink and turns on the hot water. I watch, mesmerized, as he pours a liberal quantity of washing-up liquid on his hands and kneads them together over and over, slathering suds halfway up his arms. His soapy forearms are nothing short of exquisite. Eventually he shakes his hands dry over the sink and turns to me expectantly. I stand there, openmouthed.

"Tea towel?" he asks. I grab a clean tea towel out of a drawer and hand it to him, trying not to stare as he rubs his hands and forearms dry. *Vigorously.* Finally, he hands the towel back to me. I have to stifle the urge not to sniff it. "Thanks," he says with a nod. There's an awkward moment of silence while his eyes drift around the room, alighting on the neon orange Frisbee atop the Christmas tree.

"Cool tree," he says. And I feel a little clink of surprise. I am not at all sure what to do with Nice New Cal.

"Thanks," I say. "Would you . . . like something? A cup of tea?" I ask.

He hesitates. "Sure."

We drink tea at the kitchen table and Cal quizzes me about my life and work in London. I give him a much-pared-down version of recent events, including the explosion, but omitting any mention of Lionel and the breakup. In turn I ask him about his practice, carefully steering clear of any questions about his personal life. If Cal is taken, I really don't want to know—I'm only here for a few days—no need to spoil the illusion. (Though I've already clocked the absence of a ring, which, of course, means very little these days.) He tells me that he started the practice two years ago with another vet, but now runs it on his own after his business partner moved out of the area. "Must make it difficult to take time off," I say.

He shrugs. "There are locum services I can use. And anyway, when you're starting up a new business you expect to put in a load of time. I don't really mind."

"So, what's so special about cows?" I ask.

"I love all animals," he says. "But there's something special about cows. My uncle had a herd of Friesians when I was growing up and I used to help look after them during the holidays. They're clever. And loyal. And each one has its own personality. A herd of cows is like a village. There are feuds and scolds and secret alliances. It took me years of working with them before I understood how complicated their society is. Sometimes I prefer it," he adds with a sardonic smile.

"Maybe because, at the end of the day, you can go home and leave it all behind?" I suggest.

He nods. "Probably."

"When I was a child I stumbled onto a huge ant colony in a bit of derelict land near our house," I tell him. "I used to stop and watch the ants on my way home from school: coming and going, harvesting food, building the nest, guarding against marauders. It was all so purposeful and orderly. And cooperative! They all just pitched in and did their job. Sometimes I just wanted to be a part of it—all that enterprise and community."

He gives me an odd look.

"You wanted to be an *ant?*"

I lift my chin.

"Don't underestimate them. They have very complex social structures and can communicate with each other. Just like cows," I add for emphasis.

"Fair enough. But I can think of better things to be," he adds. He pins me with his gaze then. "So have you still got a thing for bugs?" he asks, the corners of his mouth curling upward. The question feels oddly loaded.

"Actually, I've moved on to mollusks," I say.

He laughs out loud, which makes him look even more handsome. *But I am sure he is taken.* So I rise and go to put the kettle on for more tea.

"So when will your flat be fixed?"

"No idea. The agency rang this morning to say they still don't have an estimate for the repairs, much less the insurance report. Think it might be a while."

"Will you stay on here until it's done?"

I glance over my shoulder at him. His expression is completely neutral: I can read nothing in it one way or another.

"I definitely have to go back to work after the holiday. So I guess I may be sofa-surfing for a while."

He nods and looks around the room. Darkness has fallen since we came inside and I am wondering if it would be indecent to offer him a glass of wine this early, when Malcolm suddenly rises to his feet and goes to the door, ears alert. Just then we both hear a car door shut in the driveway. Cal turns to me with a puzzled look and nods toward Malcolm.

"I thought you said he was deaf?"

"He is." I shrug. In the next instant we hear a knock at the door and I see Hugo peering through the glass with his chiseled good looks: he really is a West Country Adonis. I glance over at Cal. What did I do to deserve two buff men on my doorstep in the course of a single afternoon? I go to the door, where I have to budge Malcolm to one side with my entire body in order to open it.

"Hello," Hugo calls in a cheery voice. He greets Malcolm affectionately, kneeling down so they are muzzle to muzzle. Malcolm is beside himself with excitement, lapping at Hugo and clamping his massive paws one by one onto Hugo's shoulders in a doggy embrace, while I watch in amazement. The Dane has not shown the slightest bit of enthusiasm for me and I am more than a little offended. Cal, meanwhile, has stood up and is already putting on his coat, making way for my next gentleman caller. *When it rains it pours!*

Hugo eventually stands and nods to Cal. "We've met, haven't we? You're the local vet."

Cal nods. "Last summer. At the show. I'm Cal."

"I knew it," says Hugo triumphantly. "You were absolutely heroic with those goats."

I turn to Cal with an enquiring look.

"There was a small fracas," he explains. "Nothing serious."

"He's being modest," says Hugo. "Who knew goats could be so terrifying?"

"Pedigree goats can be a little highly strung," Cal says.

"It was Armageddon!" says Hugo.

I turn to Cal and say, "Bold."

"Just doing my duty," he replies.

"Well, I gave you full marks," says Hugo. "So did Constance."

For an instant I see a shadow flicker across Cal's eyes.

"How *is* Constance?" he says, after a moment's hesitation.

"Very well. Throwing herself into nuptial planning as we speak."

"Ah yes. I heard. Congratulations," says Cal. His face is suddenly a mask of impassivity.

"Constance and her mother seem to be approaching the whole operation like a military campaign," continues Hugo. "And I appear to be quite incidental. Just another squaddie." He barks a laugh.

"Knowing Constance, it will be a flawless occasion," says Cal evenly.

I peer at him. *How, exactly, does he know Constance?*

"I've got to run," Cal says then. "Thanks for the tea." He nods to us and we watch as he departs.

Farewell, Nice New Cal, I think a little wistfully. *Who knows which Cal will turn up next?*

Once he's gone, Hugo indicates Malcolm with a nod. "He looks in top form," he says.

"Trust me, he's been pining terribly."

"Well, it's good for him," says Hugo brightly. "He's been entirely too dependent on me these last few months. I fear he's been . . . overindulged," he declares. Hugo has clearly no intention of taking Malcolm away. I sigh and offer him a cup of tea, then, at the last second, suggest we have wine instead. He looks at his watch and frowns. "But it's only half past four," he says, a little taken aback.

"Really? I had no idea," I say peering outside at the dark. "I thought it was much later. Dog-sitting is just so . . ." I break off, searching for the right word.

"Exhausting?" he asks earnestly.

Exactly. Though it's not the mutts that tire me out. It's the men. I nod, and Hugo's forehead crinkles with concern.

"You poor thing," he says.

An hour later we are two glasses each into a bottle of Chianti, and Hugo has related much of his life story. Or the story of his love life, at any rate. Turns out he has been almost married three times before (*Seriously? Three?*), but each betrothal was thwarted by forces beyond his control, he explains obliquely. "What sort of forces?" I ask. My mind runs to extraterrestrials, jihadists, or maybe even El Niño, but it turns out he's referring to jealous ex-boyfriends, overreaching bosses, and too-exacting parents.

"Really? But you seem like the perfect son-in-law! What sort of parents could possibly object?"

"Mine," he replies with a shrug.

"Ah."

"My mother has impossibly high standards," he explains with what appears to be genuine regret. I'm about to ask which one of his ex-girlfriends fell afoul of his demanding mother when he suddenly brightens. "But she *loves* Constance," he adds.

Of course she does. Constance is fiancée number four and she comes garlanded with a veritable shopping list of enviable traits, apparently: she is clever, beautiful, rich, and naturally blonde. I know this because he has already showed me her photo and I shamelessly asked. On top of that she's practically *royal*; her family is descended from German nobility.

"So I have every reason to be optimistic," he says with an awkward laugh. Then he turns to me. "The thing is . . . I'm not very good at bachelorhood," he confesses. He makes it sound like some sort of weekend sporting activity, like shooting or polo. "I wanted to marry the first girl I fell in love with."

Blimey. But why shouldn't he be the marrying type? Just because he's got Y chromosomes doesn't mean he's genetically programmed to roam. "Which one was that?"

"Bonnie," he says. "We were only seventeen. But we fell madly in love. The way you do when you're young, you know?" He gives an embarrassed smile.

Did I? I didn't. At seventeen I struggled to even fall *in like*. But it wasn't for lack of trying: I had dozens of crushes on boys from afar. But as soon as I got within striking distance, something went awry each time. Between the age of fourteen and eighteen, my conversations with boys were either impossibly awkward or impossibly dull. It was as if my incompatibility with the adolescent male of my own species was somehow predetermined; like one of us was feathered, the other furred.

"How lovely," I say, deeply envious. Because I will never, *ever* be a seventeen-year-old madly in love, and that is a shame.

He takes a deep breath, like he's trying to inhale the memory. "Bonnie made me laugh more than anyone else has before or since," he says wistfully. "She was utterly without guile or self-interest. She was gentle. And kind. And fun. And I thought that I would spend the rest of my life with her," he says simply.

Wow. "What happened?"

"*Maman.* She persuaded me that we were too young. That we needed to get an education, start a career. That we had our entire lives ahead of us, and we shouldn't squander opportunity." He gives a melancholy smile. "So we squandered love instead."

"What happened to Bonnie?"

"She was devastated when I broke things off. So was I, though I couldn't let on. Almost straight away she enlisted in the army. She was very musical, you see; we both were, but Bonnie even more so. She played the French horn and it was her dream to play in the music corps. She ended up in the Band of the Household Cavalry. They're based in Windsor, and play at all the state occasions," he adds proudly.

"Did she marry?"

He nods. "Eventually. Some years later. A sergeant. Plays the tuba, according to his Facebook profile," he says grudgingly.

"You stalked him on Facebook?"

He shrugs. "After so many years, we no longer had friends in common," he admits sheepishly. "So I resorted to subterfuge."

"So you're not in touch with her?"

He shakes his head. "The year after we broke up, I wrote to her several times," he says. "But she never replied. I broke her heart, you see. And she never forgave me." He looks at me with a pained smile. Then suddenly he slaps his hands onto his knees.

"Good Lord," he says, jumping up. "Look at the time! Constance will be vexed!"

Malcolm stares out of the kitchen window as Hugo drives away, and once the car has disappeared round the bend, he resumes his sphinx position in the center of the room. But something has shifted; he seems slightly more acclimatized to Peggy and me, and lays his head on the floor, watching me quietly as I prepare supper. As I scramble eggs, I can't stop thinking about Hugo and Bonnie. Who says that the love you experience at seventeen is any less genuine than what you experience at thirty-seven? As if the heart of an adolescent is somehow not fully formed. The more I think about it, the more I feel that something extraordinary has been snatched from them, and when I climb into bed that night, I am quietly overcome with sadness for Hugo and Bonnie, and their lost love.

chapter 13

My mother insists my hair is auburn, but I would call it brown. On a clean day, in direct sunlight, it might be called rust. That pretty much sums up the difference between us; my mother bends the world to suit her idea of it, while she would say that I'm stubbornly rooted in reality. She likes to remind me at every opportunity that she's a glass-half-full person—which, of course, makes me the half-empty one.

Marriage is the closest thing she has to a vocation. She cycles through husbands faster than most people do secondhand cars. Richie is her fifth—and, admittedly, he has lasted longer than the others. Certainly he's lasted longer than my father, who only managed six years before my mother moved him on, like an ill-suited lodger. One day, when I was five, he failed to materialize at dinner. I looked across the table and realized that there were only two places set: hers and mine. "Where's Dad?" I asked as my mother ladled stew into a bowl.

"Gone," she replied matter-of-factly. And, with that one word, she neatly peeled him from our life.

Of course she didn't banish him completely. The next morning she explained that my father would not be living with us any longer, but that he would continue to visit, and I could telephone him if I wished. Over the next decade or so, I rang him every Sunday evening and saw him at regular intervals—birthdays, holidays, Father's Day. He was an academic who moved jobs every few years at first and, unlike my mother, never remarried. I have the impression that marriage for my father was like one of those bad package holidays that go wrong from the start—with me as the slightly awkward souvenir he picked up along the way.

I once said this to him, only partly in jest, and he blinked rapidly with distress. "You're not some sort of adjunct to my life, Charlie. You're . . ." He paused then, searching for the correct word, because my father is nothing if not precise. "*Elemental*," he said finally.

"Like radon?" I asked. He gave me a look.

"More like oxygen. Without you, I'd be . . ."

"Breathless?"

He swatted me with the journal he was reading.

I do love my father, even if his analogies are obscure.

For her part, my mother treated my father like a benign medical condition we had to tolerate, and pretty soon I couldn't imagine them ever having been together. When I was twelve, my father landed an associate professorship in the Philosophy Department at Sheffield University, a place that seemed to suit him. He was given a small one-bedroom flat near the university. That summer I spent a weekend with him for the first time. Oddly, it was my mother's idea; she was in the first flush of romance with husband number three, and I think she wanted to off-load me for a few days. I remember waiting anxiously on the station platform, clutching my purple plastic overnight case, scanning the crowd. Eventually my father came rushing up, red-faced and apologetic. He beamed at me, but I could tell by the look in his eyes that he was terrified at the prospect of a weekend alone with me.

That night he made me spaghetti and meatballs and I slept on a narrow cot he'd borrowed from a colleague. The canvas sagged down the middle, its edges closing over me like a coffin. In the morning I woke early and wandered around his tiny flat gazing at his possessions: my father had an *electric blender!* And a *toilet brush!* As if his home was some sort of bachelorhood museum. He took me to a long ribbon of park beside a winding river and we ate soggy ham-and-cucumber sandwiches, which he had made himself and wrapped in cling film. I remember being touched by this, as if ham sandwiches were somehow beyond his remit.

His academic specialty was Kant, and when I asked him what exactly he taught, he frowned and launched into an earnest explanation of the *categorical imperative,* which he said was a universal set of rules to live by, based on reason, rather than on personal gain or individual motive. It was many years before I understood this, much less realized the irony of it, because my mother's moral code is entirely subjective. For my mother, context is everything, and pretty much anything is justifiable. She is forever telling me to trust my instincts: it would never occur to her to question her own.

My father, on the other hand, is paralyzed by the minutiae of everyday living. For him, even small domestic dilemmas can mushroom into immense quandaries. I once arrived to find him painting his fourteenth swatch on the bathroom wall. The room was tiny, so he'd used up nearly all of the available space, and the colors ranged from pale yellow to burnt umber through to leaf green and sky blue. It looked like a sad patchwork quilt.

"Dad," I said. "It's a loo."

"But think of how much time I spend here," he protested.

"Not something I care to dwell on."

"*Important* time."

"Important for . . . smooth bodily functions?" I asked.

He rolled his eyes. "For *thinking*, Charlie. It's where I come to think."

In the end he decided that pale green was most conducive to deep thought, and eventually confessed to me that it was the first swatch he'd tried. Ironically, he should have trusted his instincts. But maybe Kant would have appreciated that he'd worked his way through the spectrum in a rational manner.

On the plus side, my father is also the most empathetic person I know. When faced with a problem he sees every possible angle, which to my mind is like being permanently trapped inside a watchtower. But it makes him my go-to person for outright sympathy. So, when Lionel walked out on me, it was my father I rang first, even before Sian. And it was to him that I confessed that, while I was furious with Lionel for being unfaithful, I wasn't nearly as sad as I should have been—I felt a sense of loss, but it was as if I'd been stripped of something that I hadn't really needed in the first place—my appendix, say, rather than my heart or lungs. As much as anything, Lionel's departure left me feeling *destabilized*.

"I'm not sure I ever really loved him, Dad. And I'm not sure what that says about me as a person," I confessed. Who was I all those years we were together? And who does that make me now?

His response was predictably evenhanded. "No one has ever successfully defined love, Charlie. Ask a scientist and they'll tell you it's chemical, that it's all down to testosterone and pheromones in the first instance, dopamine and serotonin later on. Ask a theologian and they'll tell you that love is a perfect union of mind, body, and spirit. Ask a psychiatrist and they'll harken back to Aristotle and the notion of love being ultimately rooted in self-love. Maybe love is all these things. And maybe you're just being too hard on yourself, maybe the real truth is that Lionel wasn't worthy of your love."

That was the closest thing to outright criticism that I'd ever heard from my father. I wondered how long he'd felt that way about Lionel, and whether he would have told me if we'd stayed together. "Were you in love with Mum?" I asked instead. He paused for a moment, and I could almost hear the gears of his mind turning.

"Your mother was . . . compelling. She burned very brightly. I admired her intensity, and her strength of will. She swept me up in her constellation, and for a long time I was content to be there. I learned a great deal from her. And she gave me you, of course. For which I'm eternally grateful."

As I listened to him speak, I heard only the space between the words: there was so much he didn't say, either because he didn't want to or because he didn't know how. But I really needed to know, so I pressed him.

"Was it painful when you separated?" I asked.

"Yes, it was," he said truthfully. His words pinched me somewhere deep inside.

"So you *did* love her."

"I suppose I did," he admitted.

I haven't spoken to him since the accident, so I decide to ring him now. My father is on sabbatical this year in Kaliningrad, a remote Russian city on the Baltic Sea, which also happens to be the birthplace of Kant, who spent virtually his entire lifetime within a ten-mile radius of the place. Last month, when I rang to let him know that Lionel had left me, he'd tried to persuade me to join him there for the holidays, promising meatballs, marzipan, and oxblood cocktails, for which the city is apparently famed. I'd graciously passed.

I dial him on Skype and he picks up after only a few rings. When I relay the events of the past few days, he is gratifyingly horrified.

"Good grief, Charlie, why didn't you let me know earlier?"

"I did try to ring you, Dad. But let's face it, there wasn't much you could have done from the Baltic Sea."

"Still. Your mother should have called," he says in a rare moment of irritability aimed in her direction. It's true. She should have. *Why am I not surprised she didn't?*

"Honestly, I'm fine."

"How's your cousin?"

"Couldn't be better." Which is true. I presume.

"Give her my best. Of all your mother's relations, she was always my favorite. When she was a child, she used to hold her hand out and ask me to read her fortune. I think she thought philosophy meant palmistry."

"It's palmistry of the mind, Dad."

My father hesitates for a moment. "I think you'll find that's neuroscience, Charlie."

Whatever.

"How are the dogs?" he asks.

"Oh, you know, they're dogs. Four legs and a tail. Lots of crotch-sniffing."

"Dogs aren't really your thing, are they."

"Not top of my list, no."

"Remember what Kant said."

"I don't, but I'm sure you'll tell me."

"He said that you can judge the heart of a man by his treatment of animals."

Yeesh. "I'll be sure to remember that, Dad."

I tell him I will ring him again on Christmas Day, and after I hang up I wonder what sort of life he is leading, all alone in the Baltic, with only his books, Kant, and oxblood cocktails for amusement. But my father is nothing if not self-contained. Indeed, he's the very antithesis of my mother. For her, relationships are like mirrors. Without them she would not exist.

How they ended up together is the eighth wonder of the world.

The next morning I receive a phone call from Gerry at the post office. It seems that my package has been delivered after all, and I practically yip with delight when I hear the news. I rush through the morning chores, hurry the canines through their various ablutions, then jump in the Škoda and drive into the village. But when I arrive, Gerry hands me a parcel not much bigger than a shoebox. I stare down at it with dismay.

"Something wrong?" she asks.

"It's not twenty-two inches," I say forlornly. She frowns at the parcel.

"True," she agrees. "But good things come in small packages," she says optimistically. I tear open the box to discover that my mother, with her almost uncanny instinct for what will annoy me most, has sent a Christmas-themed parcel. Inside I find a pair of fluffy pink reindeer socks, a green woolly hat with an enormous red bobble on top, and a ridiculous pair of bright red flannel pajamas adorned with cartoon penguins; apart from the size, the latter are the sort you would give to an eight-year-old—one completely devoid of taste. My mother has never displayed one iota of fashion sense, I think with resignation. Why should she break the habit of a lifetime now? I hold each item up for Gerry to appraise, and when I get to the pajama bottoms she tilts her head sideways. "Could be cozy?" she offers diplomatically.

I sigh. From the far side of the world, my mother has managed to both irritate and infantilize me. There is also a cheery card with a laughing Santa on the cover and a message on the inside: *A little something for under the tree! Enjoy your Christmas with Jez!* I have not yet disclosed to her that Jez has abandoned me to spend Christmas with an Arctic scientist, and I do not intend to.

Before I go, Gerry nods at the hat. "Best put that on. It's freezing outside." I pull the hat on and turn to her for approval.

"How do I look?"

"Very festive."

"That's what I was afraid of," I say. "Let me know if any *large* parcels turn up."

"I'll be sure to use a tape measure on the next one," she says.

Just then I hear the tinkle of the door chime and turn to see Cal step into the shop, wearing jeans and a cobalt-blue puffer jacket that suspiciously matches his eyes. Is he trying to color coordinate?

He stops short when he sees me. "Oh, hello," he says, clearly a little surprised. I smile cautiously, not sure who I'll be dealing with today. *Nice New Cal or Cranky Cal?*

"Is that what they're wearing in London?" He nods at my hat, and I see the corners of his mouth twitch upward slightly. *Hello, Mocking Cal.*

My face flames. It is too late to whip off the hat now without looking self-conscious, so I lift my chin a little defiantly. "As a matter of fact, bobble hats are all the rage this winter," I say. This is true, although my mother's choice is ludicrously wide of the mark. He regards the hat, tilting his head in almost exactly the same way Gerry did a moment ago.

"Really?" He shakes his head with regret. "We're always two steps behind here in the country," he remarks to Gerry.

"But isn't it nice to be brought forward," she replies pointedly. He indicates the hat with a nod.

"Best put one of those on your Christmas list," he tells her.

"I'd like a green bobble," she replies.

"I'll see what I can do." I look from one to the other and they are smirking conspiratorially. They burst out laughing and I am forced to chortle along.

Ho ho ho! Feel free to engage in mirth at my expense!

"Is that my parcel?" says Cal, indicating a large box on the floor.

"It just arrived." Gerry bends down to retrieve it and places it on the counter.

"Actually, it's for you," he says to her a little coyly. Gerry's eyes light up with delight.

"Really?" For an instant I see a look pass between them. She tears open the box and reaches inside. "Oh, Cal, you shouldn't have," she says, lifting out an enormous white poinsettia in a glazed terra-cotta pot. The plant itself must span at least four feet and is covered in a profusion of white blooms. Poinsettias are one of my mother's favorites, though the red ones have always struck me as rather garish and aggressive, with their spindly stems and spiky, blood-colored leaves. I've always thought they were really just a potted shrub masquerading as a flower, but this one is undeniably gorgeous.

"Where did you find it?" Gerry exclaims.

"A specialist nursery outside Taunton." Cal looks a little embarrassed but is obviously pleased at her reaction. I'm not sure, but I think he might actually be blushing.

"It's lovely, Cal. Thank you." Gerry beams at him, then leans over and kisses him on the cheek. Now he flushes beet red, his eyes darting nervously over her shoulder in my direction. *Hang on. What is going on here?* There's an awkward moment, during which I suddenly feel like a colossal third wheel. Now I'm the one who is embarrassed as I bid them a hasty good-bye and stumble out of the shop, whipping the hat off as soon as I get in the car. As I barrel down the road in the Škoda, I am wondering what exactly I've just witnessed. Could this possibly be a *Harold and Maude* situation?

Oh my God.

After *Breakfast at Tiffany's, Harold and Maude* is one of my top fave films ever. For two years at university, I had a boyfriend called Felix who was doing Media Studies and ran the Film Society; he was the person who first introduced me to Hal Ashby's early seventies black comedy about intergenerational love. When I saw that it was playing last summer at a pop-up cinema in Brixton, I had to drag Sian kicking and screaming with me to see it. She spent the first half hour loudly stage-whispering: "But it's pedophilia!"

It isn't really, because in the film Harold is twenty years old (though, as Sian pointed out, he looks about twelve) and Maude is a sprightly seventy-nine, so it's perfectly legal. It's just unorthodox, I told her. In the film Harold and Maude meet at a funeral and become friends. Harold is young, disillusioned with life, and obsessed with suicide; while Maude is spontaneous, unconventional, and fun-loving. It's true that she's four times his age, but somehow, when they fall in love it makes sense. She shows him the meaning of life, and he realizes that life is worth living. It is tender and romantic and life-affirming, and by the end of the film Sian was completely won over. I had to lead her onto the tube like a blind person, because she was weeping buckets over the ending.

But . . . *Gerry and Cal?* Gerry must be twice his age. Though she is also warm, funny, kind, and perceptive—not to mention remarkably spirited for someone so old—and still attractive in a

Dame Judi Dench kind of way. So why shouldn't he be drawn to her? The thought depresses me, though I'm not sure why. It's not as if I had any serious designs on Bovine Cal; he has been little more than a mild diversion this past week. But after my conversations with both Valko and Hugo, I'm beginning to feel like everyone around me is engaged in something vital and important, and that I've somehow missed the party.

Or maybe it's just the prospect of waiting until my seventies to meet someone I really like.

When I get home, I definitely need a mood swing. I realize that, apart from brief walks with the dogs out to the paddock, I've done almost no physical activity since before the accident—and I know from experience that if I don't exercise soon, I'll go mad. Endorphins are right up there with caffeine and alcohol in my holy trinity of chemicals: all three are fairly essential to my sanity.

In fairness, I have to credit Lionel with this. Before I met him, I hadn't taken proper exercise in years. But Lionel was fanatical about fitness and shortly after we got together, he started bugging me about going to the gym. The gym, for Lionel, was like a second *womb*; a complete ecosystem where he felt happy, comfortable, and sated. I swear he would have slept there if they'd let him—and he couldn't understand why I didn't feel the same.

For my part, I'd always been ambivalent about exercise in general, and *indoor* exercise in particular. The latter felt like a strange form of deprivation, a place where you were denied fresh air, natural light, and *reasonable* human behavior. Being surrounded by dozens of grunting, straining, sweating adults, all pushing themselves beyond the limits of endurance, made me uneasy. It also made me feel like an impostor. But I had to do *something,* so after a few months with Lionel, I grudgingly agreed to shop around.

At school I'd played field hockey, so I decided to join a South London women's league. But I soon discovered that my teammates took their sport *very seriously indeed;* if I turned up shattered after work, or worse, hungover from the previous night's excesses, glances of condemnation would be flung among them like angry pucks. Forget team spirit and jolly camaraderie: these women were out to *win,* and our occasional losses were usually followed by earnest debate and frenzied soul-searching. Even after winning matches, we rarely went out for drinks; my teammates would all cry off to get an early night, presumably so they could be fresh and ready to play hockey again the next day.

After one spectacularly bad performance on my part, I was demoted to a lower league, which I took as my exit cue from the sport altogether. When I threw my stick in the back of a cupboard, I was almost overcome with gratitude and relief. Then a friend from work talked me into rollerblading. He was in a club that met twice weekly by the Serpentine and it was urban, cool, and just the right side of edgy. But a little *too* edgy, I soon discovered. It became clear that *blading* wasn't my destiny, either: I grew up before dyspraxia was even a thing, but it didn't take a genius to work out I had balance deficiencies. And in spite of plastering my entire body with padded guards, after a few weeks my arms and legs looked like overripe bananas. In the end I decided that if God had intended me to *roll,* he would have given me wheels in lieu of feet.

So in the end I settled on running. I guess it was the path of least resistance. There were no expensive barriers to entry, little risk of injury, virtually no competition, no awkward personalities to contend with, no stuffy changing rooms, and no marching to someone else's timetable. It was just me, my feet, and the horizon. And while I found it painful to begin with, over time I grew to crave it, both physically and mentally. I loved the solitude, the autonomy, and the sense of freedom it gave me. So running became one of my things.

Right now I would like nothing more than to sling on some trainers and hit the road, but I don't have any gear—and anyway, I'm pretty sure it's too soon after the concussion. So there is only one other thing I can think of that will produce the desired effect—and even though I know that both Jez and Bovine Cal would disapprove, I decide to have another go with the twins and the chariot.

It's a clear day and although the mercury reads almost freezing, the wind is not as biting as yesterday. I pull on one of Jez's heavy-duty coveralls and march all six dogs out to the paddock, then go back to retrieve the sulky and harness. When I return I truss up the malamutes and attach them to the frame. By the time I finish, Peggy, Malcolm, Hulk, and Slab are all lounging in a sunny corner of the paddock, watching us with interest, like little Roman emperors. I climb into the sulky, take up the reins, then carefully release the brake. The twins twist round and fix me with a stare. "What's the problem?" I ask Remus. "Go on!" I snap the reins a little. "Come on, boys! Mush!" Remus paws the ground and whimpers, and Romulus gives a kind of massive shiver, as if his entire body disapproves. Just then I see Valko wobble up the road on his ancient, rusty bicycle. He cycles into the yard, jumps off, and leans the bike up against the fence.

"What do you do?" he calls over to me, looking puzzled.

"Taking the dogs for a run."

Valko shakes his head. "Not here." He motions to the paddock.

"Why not?"

"They no like grass."

Oh. Who knew sled dogs could be so fussy? Grass, snow, tarmac . . . surely it's all the same?

I climb out of the sulky and open the gate to the paddock, then lead the malamutes out onto the yard, where Valko is waiting. He looks at me doubtfully as I take my seat again.

"You know how to this?" he asks, gesturing to the sulky.

"Sure."

"I think is not safe," he says, shaking his head.

"And I think it'll be fine. We'll go on the track," I say, motioning toward the dirt track down the road. I strap myself in, plant my feet on the pedals, and release the brake. In an instant the twins explode like rockets, shoulders straining, paws outstretched, and the sulky practically takes flight. But instead of turning left out of the farmyard, the dogs immediately veer right, and in the next instant we are bombing down the A road in the opposite direction from where I intended. I hear Valko shouting behind me and I look back to see him jump on his bike and pedal furiously after us in a vain attempt to catch up. The dogs are working hard, running flat out in perfect syncopation, and the sulky sails along smoothly behind them. I lean back and let the wind buffet me, my heart pounding with a mixture of fear and delight; it is easily the most exhilarating thing I have ever done, and I find myself grinning madly.

I should have been a gladiator!

After a few minutes the dogs' pace starts to slow, and as we round a bend in the road I see Stella's pig farm looming ahead on the right, a neat cluster of white buildings next to a tidy cottage and a trim painted sign that reads HOLLYHOX FARM. As we reach her driveway, I tug sharply on the right-hand rein and the twins veer into her yard, coming abruptly to a halt in front of Stella's barn, the sulky lurching to a stop. We sit there for a moment, all three of us panting, then I throw my head back and give a little whoop of pleasure. The dogs' chests are heaving and their tongues are lolling from the effort, but I can tell from the spark in their eyes that they enjoyed the ride as much as I did, and Romulus gives a little yip of his own. I reach down and set the brake, dropping the reins.

Stella comes out of the barn just then, wearing enormous dark green plastic coveralls and wiping her hands on a rag. She glances down at her watch and then beams at us. "Right on time."

I give her a puzzled look. "For what?" I say, climbing out of the sulky.

"Jez always brings the dogs here for coffee on Thursdays."

"Really?" I turn to look at Romulus and Remus. *How on earth do they know it is Thursday?* I can barely keep track of the time, much less the days of the week. Just then Valko comes cycling up the driveway, puffing with effort. He reaches us and climbs off his bike. "This is Valko," I explain. "He was worried about my driving."

"I fear for safe," says Valko, shaking his head and pointing to the road.

"How sweet," says Stella. "I'll put the kettle on."

We follow her inside to the kitchen and it is like stepping into a grotto: the walls and ceiling have been festooned with fresh-cut evergreen boughs and strands of tiny white lights. Sprigs of bright red holly and bunches of mistletoe have been tied to the boughs with green ribbon, and the scent of pine wafts around us deliciously. Valko looks around, wide-eyed. "Like dream," he murmurs. I know exactly what he means, because the effect really is rather magical. Stella blushes.

"I get a little carried away at Christmastime," she says. We sit at the table and she serves us homemade scones with rhubarb jam, and I marvel at the strangeness of circumstance: only ten days ago I sat hunched over a computer screen in a shabby office near Elephant & Castle punching in code, and today I am drinking coffee with a pig farmer and a Bulgarian migrant in a fairy-tale kitchen. It turns out that although Stella has seen Valko cycling along the lanes, she did not know who he was until now. And Valko reveals that much of his childhood was spent helping out on his uncle's pig farm in Bulgaria.

"For me, pigs is first love. Before even . . . woman," he says exuberantly.

"Really?" I ask. Stella and I burst out laughing and Valko looks from one of us to the other, before his face flushes beet red.

"No! No! Not this!" he cries with alarm.

Stella and I hoot even harder.

We stay for only a short visit, as I'm conscious that we've left the dogs back at the kennels in the paddock. I give the twins some water before we leave, then I carefully position them and the sulky at the opening of Stella's driveway, facing toward home, before climbing in and taking up the reins. Valko takes up his post on his bike at the rear. "I go behind," he says. "Just in cases." I release the brake and Stella waves us off. The dogs know exactly where they are headed and need little encouragement from me, lurching off eagerly. They pull at a more sedate pace this time, but we still reach home in a matter of minutes. When we turn into the yard I'm surprised to see a smart, gray Mercedes sedan parked outside the barn and a well-dressed older woman peering into one of the kennel windows. I see with relief that the canine crew haven't budged an inch in the paddock. Why would they, when movement is such an effort?

The woman turns toward us as we pull up. She's in her early sixties, quite attractive, and immaculately groomed: her silver-blonde hair pulled back in a neat chignon, her eyebrows sketched in perfect dark arches, and her features suspiciously taut. She's wearing a long wool coat in charcoal gray with what appears to be a real fur plume around the collar—in fact, it looks remarkably like Remus's tail—and her boots are tall, black, and stylish, with killer heels. She waits for me as I climb out of the sulky, though I get the distinct sense that she is unused to waiting.

"Hello. May I help you?" I ask, approaching her.

"My name is Camilla Delors. I rang earlier this week. More than once, in fact." My mind flies to Jez and the woman who disguised her voice on the phone.

"I'm afraid the owner is abroad at the moment."

"I'm looking to kennel my setter over the holiday. The owner told me you were full." Her tone is cordial but vaguely accusatory.

"We are," I say, flashing my most courteous smile. *The customer is king!*

Just then Valko approaches with the four dogs on leads, whom he has retrieved from the paddock. He nods to us, then returns Slab and Hulk to their respective kennels and goes into the house with Peggy and Malcolm.

"You have eight kennels here," Camilla Delors says, nodding toward the kennels. "But I see only six dogs."

"That's because two are at the vet," I lie.

Camilla Delors frowns. She is wearing black leather gloves that match her boots and she holds one hand out in front of her for a moment, examining it.

"I only need five days' care," she says then. "He could board with one of the others, as long as they're both crated."

"I'm sorry, but we really can't manage any more dogs just now. Not with the owner away. I'm sure you understand." My tone is firm but placatory. *Jez would be proud.*

"Five hundred pounds," says the woman. She is still examining her glove, studiously avoiding my gaze, as if I'm not really worth looking at.

"I'm sorry?"

"That's what I'm prepared to pay," she says. "It's more than generous."

I stare at her for a moment. She is obviously used to getting her way. Everything about Camilla Delors smacks of entitlement: her hair, her clothes, her car, her attitude. Does she really think I can be bought that easily?

Obviously, the answer is yes.

"Fine," I say. I have just more than tripled my holiday earnings; if I'd known, I would have ordered a bigger TV. "What sort of dog did you say it was?" I ask.

"An Irish setter. He's a triple champion and very valuable. You do have a security system here, don't you?"

As far as I know Jez doesn't even lock the kennels at night. But for five hundred pounds, I think I can manage. "Yes, of course," I say.

"Fine. You'll have to take him now. I've got a charter flight from Exeter in less than two hours."

"Less than two hours"? What was she planning to do if I refused? Leave him with the baggage handlers? I watch as she crosses to the Mercedes and opens the back door. Inside, a tall, chestnut-brown dog sits bolt upright on the black leather seat, as if it is used to being chauffeured. "Come!" she barks. The dog carefully descends to the ground, then stands obediently beside her. He is tall and lean, with exquisite deportment, and his coat is truly prize-worthy: long, silky, feathery fur that literally gleams in the afternoon sun. *What shampoo does he use?*

Camilla Delors then opens the boot and retrieves a small bag of dog food, which she places on the ground next to me, then pulls out a lead and attaches it to his collar, handing the other end to me. "He should have only this food, one cup twice daily. There's a measure in the bag. And plenty of fresh water," she adds.

"What's his name?" I ask.

"Justice James Alexander of Welbeck," she says in one breathless sentence.

I peer at her. *Is she being facetious? Which of those does he answer to?*

Camilla Delors merely raises an eyebrow, as if to say: *Do you have a problem with that?*

"Fine," I say, deciding that I'll call him Judd. "Does he require any special care?" I ask. And now it's me who's being facetious, though Camilla Delors does not appear to notice.

"He needs exercise, of course. Preferably on his own. And his coat should be brushed completely through twice daily. Otherwise it will mat."

I hesitate. Until now, grooming has been a bit of a deal breaker. But then I decide that Valko can brush him. And as for being exercised alone, she's got a hope; Judd can lie in the corner of the paddock with the others.

"The main thing is to ensure that he's here when I return," she says pointedly.

"Of course," I reply. She retrieves an envelope from her handbag and hands it to me.

"Half your fee up front. Half when I return. My contact details are inside. I'll collect him at two o'clock on Boxing Day," she says with clipped efficiency, turning away. She does not say good-bye, either to me or to her prizewinning pooch, but climbs into her Mercedes and closes the door with a decisive *thunk*. A moment later the engine purrs to life and she speeds off, leaving Judd and me to stare after her. I open the envelope and count five crisp fifty-pound notes alongside a plain white business card with her name and mobile number.

Valko emerges from the house just then and walks over to us.

"This is who?" he asks, motioning to Judd. I grin at him.

"Your new best friend."

install Judd in the Royal Suite. It seems only fitting for a triple champion. When I show him to his quarters he walks over to the pale blue canopied bed and sniffs at it, then lies down on the floor with a world-weary sigh. I don't envy him. The life of a canine champion must be an endless parade of strange kennels, two-star motels, badly lit exhibition halls, desolate car parks, and peculiar humans with bad breath prying your mouth open to examine your teeth. All this, while maintaining an even temperament and impeccable deportment.

Once back at the house I flick to the page on Irish setters in the *Dog Encyclopedia*, thinking I might as well earn Judd's fee. The entry describes the breed as highly sensitive working dogs who thrive on companionship and activity. It cautions that they should not be left alone for long periods of time, as isolation can lead to boredom, depression, or worse. *What sort of worse?* I wonder.

Serial biting? Canine suicide? Camilla Delors must have known that Judd would be left alone in the kennel, so it's not really my responsibility if his mental health plummets over the course of the next five days.

Maybe tomorrow I'll ask Valko to give him a shampoo and set. That should perk him up.

Aftfter dinner Jez rings me to see how things are going, her voice crackling down the line from the frozen hinterland.

"All good here," I say cheerily when she asks. *No need to mention Malcolm. Or Judd. Or the extra fees.* "How's the North Pole?"

"Chilly!"

"And the Arctic anthropologist?"

"Extremely hot!"

I smile. "Sounds like the perfect combination."

"Eloise is amazing. She's got this fantastic research project with the reindeer herders up north. She's taking me to meet them tomorrow and we're going to camp for two nights in a real igloo!"

"Sounds exciting," I say. *And insanely cold.*

"I just wanted to make sure you guys were OK. How's Peggy doing?"

I glance over at Peggy, who for the past half hour has been steadily licking her own teats. "Peggy is fine. She's engaging in a little personal hygiene as we speak."

"And Slab?"

"Slab is . . . still alive," I say brightly.

"Great. Give Peggy a cuddle from me."

"Sure." *Unlikely. Peggy and I haven't even held hands yet.*

"I hope the twins are behaving," says Jez guiltily.

"The twins are great." *And the sulky is awesome!*

"I'll be out of contact for the next few days while we're camping," Jez says.

"We'll be fine," I reassure her. *All seven of us.*

"You're a lifesaver, Chaz." *It's true. I really am.*

Jez rings off and I glance over at Peggy, whose girth seems to increase by the hour. Over the past day she has become even more sluggish than usual and has developed a sort of glazed look in her eyes. This afternoon Valko frowned at her and said: "Dog will pop soon. Like balloon." I reminded him that the puppies aren't due until January—at least another fortnight away—by which time Jez will be back from her Arctic adventure. And I will be safely back in Nunhead.

The next morning I wake to a leaden sky and the sound of wind thrashing the trees outside my window. The temperature has plummeted even further during the night, bringing the promised blizzard one step closer, just in time for Christmas. It's the twenty-first of December and I remember, with a sinking heart, that the Christmas pageant is being held this evening on the village green. In a rash moment I have promised Stella that I'll attend, and have even offered Valko a lift in so he doesn't have to cycle in the bitter cold. More fool me.

I rise and dress in extra layers. I now have the full run of Jez's wardrobe and have abandoned any notion of a pilgrimage to buy clothes. Though her taste is completely different from mine, it's sort of refreshing to see myself in someone else's attire, like looking through a filtered lens at a not-quite stranger, one who surprises me each morning with possibility. Today I pull on dark blue corduroy jeans and a magenta cowl-neck sweater. Warm and functional, but something I would never in a million years wear in London, where my favorite outfit is a black pencil skirt and a cropped gray *Agnès B* tunic that I bought for a song at a sample sale in King's Cross. Staring in the mirror, I wonder whether clothes really do maketh the woman. And if so, then who have I become?

Valko turns up just after breakfast, his nose pink from the cold. He bustles into the kitchen and shakes his head, jerking his thumb toward the outside. "Something not right in kennels. Too cold."

"Really? But they were fine yesterday evening," I say dismissively.

"Not fine now," he says emphatically, shaking his head.

I sigh and bundle on a heavy coat and boots and we walk out to the kennels, where I discover that the temperature inside is subarctic. When I exhale I can see my breath. I find Slab and Hulk shivering in their respective beds and see, with dismay, that their metal water bowls are frozen solid.

Whoops.

I rush to the Royal Suite, where I find Judd curled in a tight spiral on the canopy bed. He doesn't stir when we enter and for a moment I think that he has *literally* frozen. My insides lurch sickeningly at the thought of telling Camilla Delors that her dog is an ice-pup. But after a moment he raises his head to give us a beseeching look, his nose quivering with cold, and I am flooded with relief.

"The heating must be broken," I tell Valko. "I've got a phone number for the boiler guy back at the house. I'll give him a ring, but we'd better take them inside."

Valko scoops up the two small dogs in his arms and I lead Judd back to the kitchen. He is so cold he can hardly walk, tiptoeing along on frozen paws beside me. I instruct Valko to deposit Slab and Hulk on Malcolm's massive dog bed in the corner and I position Judd next to them, budging them up together for warmth. The dogs are so cold they do not even resist.

Peggy sits up with alarm and sniffs the air when we enter, while Malcolm turns and blinks proprietarily at his bed. But after a moment they both return to their former positions, apparently unfazed. I ring the boiler man's mobile and it goes straight through to his message service. Owing to the cold snap, he's not available to take my call at the moment, and his voice mailbox is full.

Of course it is.

Valko takes the twins for out for a walk while I stoke up the Rayburn in an effort to thaw the three dogs. Hulk is still shivering so I root around in the linen cupboard and find three old towels, tucking them in tightly around each dog until they look like canine sausage rolls. *Maybe I should give them each a little dish of brandy?* Just then I hear a knock on the kitchen door and look up to see Hugo peering in through the window. At once Malcolm is on his feet at the door, his giant muzzle pressed to the glass, tail lashing like a bull whip.

"Hello, boy," Hugo says cheerily when I open the door. He bends over to pat Malcolm, who showers him with sloppy licks.

"Sorry I didn't make it round yesterday," Hugo apologizes, as if Malcolm can somehow keep track of the days. He straightens and turns to me. "How's he been?"

"He secretly adores us. He just doesn't like to show it."

"Sorry about yesterday. Constance dragged me halfway across Dartmoor to a point-to-point," he says. "We didn't get back until late." Hugo turns and frowns at the three mummified dogs lying in a row. "Good Lord. What's wrong with *them*?" He asks.

"The heating in the kennels broke. I had to bring them inside to thaw them out."

He looks around. The room feels rather crowded, and smells of old dog. "Poor you. Isn't there somewhere more . . . convenient you can stow them?"

"Like where? The bedrooms?"

"I suppose not. Well, it's certainly very cozy in here," he says unconvincingly. "Do they all get along?"

"Who knows? I think they're too cold to fight. But I expect the Duchess will keep them in line," I nod toward Peggy on the sofa, who at the moment is sprawled across a pile of cushions in a decidedly throne-like posture, looking out across the room imperiously. Hugo regards her for a moment.

"She does look like a fierce maiden auntie."

"Except that she's pregnant."

"Ah. Not quite maiden then."

"No. But Peggy is every inch her own bitch."

I make us both a coffee and when we're seated at the kitchen table, I ask him how things are going with his prospective in-laws. Hugo frowns.

"Difficult to say. I *think* they approve of me. But they aren't very demonstrative. Constance is the same. When we first started going out she seemed perfectly indifferent for the first several weeks. I actually thought she disliked me."

"What happened?"

"One weekend, when I didn't ring her, she turned up at my flat and demanded to know why." He takes a sip of his coffee and shrugs. "And we've been together ever since."

"But . . . when did you decide to marry?"

"Well, I think we knew fairly quickly that marriage was in the cards. Constance is very decisive. She isn't one to mess about."

"But how did *you* know?"

Hugo frowns, considering this.

"It's difficult to pinpoint, to be honest." After a moment, his face brightens. "One day we popped into Harrod's and Constance suggested we put our names down on the wedding registry."

Seriously? I look at him askance.

"It was more romantic than it sounds," he adds hastily.

"But . . . you never exactly *decided* to be with Constance?"

He frowns at me. "I'm not sure I understand the question."

"Was there ever a moment when you looked at Constance and thought: *yes.*"

Hugo raises an eyebrow and considers this for a moment. "There must have been," he says. "Or we wouldn't be together. But, honestly, I don't remember it." He gives an awkward smile. "Does that sound strange?"

I sigh.

"Actually, it sounds quite common," I say.

Hugo gives me a sardonic smile. "I can promise you that Constance is anything but *common.*"

ring the boiler guy about a thousand times over the next several hours and each time it goes through to his answering service. Peggy continues to clean herself like she has suddenly developed canine OCD, and late in the afternoon Malcolm shifts position so that he is facing her instead of the Christmas tree, which both of us find unnerving. In the early evening, when I try to coax them all out to the paddock for a wee, all five dogs look at me as if I am trying to make them walk the plank.

I'm almost relieved when it's time to drive into the village for the Christmas pageant. Valko and I park on the outskirts of the center, where the streets are already chockablock with cars. A ring of trees circles the village green, and each one has been strung with dozens of tiny white lights. I am forced to admit it does look jolly. Crowds mill around the green: children bundled in colored parkas tumble about, grannies kitted out in homemade scarves greet one another warmly, and babies languishing in pushchairs chew the ends of their mittens. As we walk toward the green, Valko asks me to explain the purpose of the event. I shake my head. I have only the haziest idea what will take place: I was only half-listening when Stella told me about it. Something to do with farm animals and a race.

"God only knows," I say.

Valko frowns. "So this is *religious* festival?"

"Not quite."

I look around. A large fenced-off circle has been erected in the middle of the green, and the village folk are all clustered around the outside, waiting for the festivities to begin. Inside the fence, we can see about a dozen people dressed in identical bright green tunics, each tethered by a long rope to an animal, also wearing a green tunic. Both humans and animals wear green peaked hats: there is even a ferret with a tiny green cap attached to its head with a piece of elastic.

"Oh, dear Lord," I mutter. "*Elves.*" One of my Christmas top tens. Valko looks at me as if I've whispered some sort of prayer. I point at the contestants.

"I think they're meant to be elves," I say. Valko looks bewildered.

"I do not understand. Why do animals wear clothes?" he asks.

"Why indeed?"

"This is normal English custom?" asks Valko.

"This isn't normal English anything." I crane my neck to get a better view. The animals appear to be in all shapes and sizes: there is a pig, a sheep, a cow, a cockerel, a duck, a dog, a cat, a Shetland pony, a llama, a rabbit, a ferret, and what appears to be a large antelope. Except it isn't an antelope. I realize after a few seconds that it's a reindeer and it is tethered to Bovine Cal, who looks suitably ridiculous dressed as an elf, but no more ridiculous than the reindeer beside him, whose hat has been carefully notched so as to allow its antlers to poke through.

"I do not understand," says Valko.

"I'm not sure we're meant to."

After a minute, someone blows a whistle and the human elves shuffle slowly toward the starting line, each pulling on their tethered animal, some of which are more compliant than others. The cow plants its feet and bellows loudly, refusing to budge, while the ferret makes a mad dash around all the other animals, jumping momentarily onto the Shetland pony's back and causing it to buck. The llama cranes its head right back and bares its teeth in a sort of sneer, while the cockerel paces back and forth nervously. Both the cat and the rabbit have to be more or less dragged into position.

"I think this is not real race," says Valko doubtfully.

"Um . . . no."

"So the purpose is?"

"A mystery to us both."

An older man with a goatee and a red vest appears to be officiating. He has a whistle around his neck and is waving a clipboard. We watch as he marshals all the contestants toward the starting point, after which he announces the rules to the audience in a loud voice. Each contestant must make a complete circuit of the course, accompanied by their beast. Any carrying of beasts is strictly prohibited, as is any form of punishment. Food may be used as an inducement, but any interference from the audience is not allowed.

"And may the fastest elf win!" he shouts, blowing the whistle loudly. The crowd erupts into cheers and out on the green chaos ensues, with animals scattering in every direction. The dog pulls away from his owner and dashes across the green into the crowd, barking madly; the cat bolts from its handler's grasp and skitters up a nearby tree; the Shetland trots off in the wrong direction, then stops dead; the ferret runs back and forth among all the other animals in a frenzied jig; while the cow, the sheep, the llama, and the rabbit remain obstinately still, munching on grass. The crowd continues to cheer like football hooligans—even though *there is no actual race*. It is the most demented event I have ever witnessed, and I instantly take a shine to it.

Meanwhile Cal is quietly coaxing the reindeer, step by step, around the ring, one hand on the animal's halter and the other palming bits of something to eat, all the time whispering into its ear intently. The pony's owner has retrieved it from the far side of the ring and is persuading it to walk in the right direction. Soon the Shetland is closing the distance on the reindeer's lead, with the pig about ten paces behind, though the latter keeps pausing to snuffle about in the grass. But just as the pony draws near, the reindeer glances back and honks loudly, making a deep, guttural, grating noise that bounces across the green. The Shetland shies, spins round, and trots off quickly in the opposite direction, leaving Bovine Cal and the reindeer a clear path to the finish. Twenty paces behind them is the pig, which steps daintily along in second place, and a surprisingly compliant tethered duck manages to waddle into third.

When he reaches the finish line, Cal throws his arms up in jubilation and the crowd roars with approval. The entire event has lasted maybe three minutes. A burly, red-faced man wearing a black-and-green checked coat steps forward offering Cal a shot of whisky, which he quickly tosses back. I spy Gerry just beside the finish line, grinning broadly, and she, too, leans forward—and gives Cal a kiss. No one around the couple seems fazed, so it would appear that their romance is no secret, I conclude. It was a chaste kiss, but they would hardly have a congratulatory snog in public, would they?

I turn away with something akin to envy, just as Handsome Hugo emerges on the far side of the crowd, an attractive long-haired blonde clinging to his arm. The woman is leaning into him conspiratorially, chuckling about something. She is slightly taller than me, and everything about her is flawless. Hair, makeup, clothes, demeanor . . . The entire package is perfectly choreographed. She wears an expensively tailored ivory wool coat and a Russian-style white fur hat with a hot-pink mohair scarf, which matches her lipstick, wrapped around her neck. I see, with dismay, that her prominent cheekbones are flushed prettily from the cold.

Even from a distance, I do not like her.

When Hugo spies me, his expression brightens; he quickly makes his way through the crowd to where I'm standing, with Constance in tow. She fixes me with a cool smile as he introduces us, and I have the distinct impression that, in her constellation, dog minder is roughly on a par with parking attendant.

"Did you get hold of the plumber?" Hugo asks. I shake my head.

"Afraid not."

"Oh dear. What will you do tonight?" Hugo asks.

"Canine slumber party!" I say, grinning. Constance looks at me with disdain.

"Well, I can't thank you enough. *We* can't thank you enough," Hugo says, squeezing her arm. "Isn't that right, darling? We're so grateful."

"Eternally," she says with glacial politeness.

"Do you come to this event every year?" I ask her. She scrutinizes me for a moment, as if trying to decide if I'm being facetious.

"My family started the pageant," she informs me. "We still sponsor it. And Winston is ours, of course."

"Winston?" I ask.

"The winner."

"Oh! You mean the reindeer?" Now it's my turn to be perplexed.

"Daddy rescued him from a traveling zoo years ago. He was in a terrible state. He lives on our deer park now." She says this as if owning a deer park is no more remarkable than owning a caravan.

"Apparently he wins the race every year," chips in Hugo. "So you know who to bet on next year!"

"I'm surprised you don't lead him round yourself," I say to Constance in a vaguely baiting tone.

"Oh, we leave that to Cal. Cal and Winston have a special bond. He helped rehabilitate him. Isn't that so, Cal?" She looks past me, and I turn to see Cal materialize out of the crowd beside me, still wearing his elf suit. Which up close looks surprisingly fetching on him, I have to admit. Who knew elves could be sexy?

"Isn't *what* so?" he asks.

"You and Winston; you were made for each other."

Cal looks at her, and the space between them suddenly crackles with enmity. *Whoa. What have I missed?*

"Winston is much too good for me," says Cal, holding her gaze.

Hugo frowns and Constance slips her arm proprietarily into his. "Time to head back, darling. Mummy and Daddy will be waiting."

"Yes, of course," he says obediently. "Good night." He nods to us both, and Constance smiles pertly as she pulls him away.

Cal turns to me. "I see you've met the local landed gentry."

"I'm speechless in the face of such charm and breeding."

Cal laughs and once again I can't help but notice that Jolly Cal is even more attractive than Brooding Cal. *Strike that thought! Because he is taken.*

"Old friend of yours?" I ask. He shrugs.

"I've known Constance all my life. Her father's done a lot for the village over the years," he says evasively.

"Apparently this is all down to them." I motion to the surrounding event.

"Constance's father started the pageant, and she organizes it now. Though you won't see her clearing up at the end," he adds wryly.

"I see." *Actually, I don't quite see; what's the real story here?*

"But that's being churlish. In the interest of full disclosure . . . Constance and I have a bit of history," he admits. *Bingo.*

"I see."

"Ancient history," he adds.

"The follies of youth?" I ask.

"Something like that." Cal looks decidedly uncomfortable. I decide to change the subject; I've heard quite enough about Constance for one night.

"So why is it called a *pageant*?" I ask.

"Well, you can hardly call it a race."

"True. But why elves?"

He colors. "I'm afraid that's Gerry's doing. She's got a thing for elves." He looks down with embarrassment at his costume. Up close I can see that it is rather beautifully made of soft green felt, with immaculately turned edges and hand-stitching round the seams.

"The elf look suits you," I say. "You should wear it more often."

"Well, Gerry would like that," he says. Now it's me who flushes. *Let's not go there.*

"Apparently you and Winston are unbeatable."

"Well, it's not much of a contest. Winston's addicted to these." Cal reaches in his pocket and pulls out a handful of tiny mushrooms. "Don't tell anyone," he adds.

"Why? Are they hallucinogenic?"

He lifts a brow. "They're shiitakes."

"I'm only asking."

"Anyway, Winston's getting on in years now. I don't know how many more pageants he's got left in him."

"She said he was in a terrible state when you rescued him." He shrugs.

"Animals are very loyal; they have long memories."

"Unlike people."

"Unlike people." He gives an awkward cough. "So, how are the dogs?"

"Cold. The boiler in the kennels broke."

He raises an eyebrow with alarm.

"Don't worry. I brought them inside."

"You've got them in the house?" he asks.

I nod.

"Together?" He frowns.

"Yep," I say. "Actually, they all seem to get along fine. We're one big, happy canine family."

Cal seems surprised. Or impressed. Or maybe both. Just then Gerry appears at his side. She slips her arm through Cal's in a way that definitely seems proprietorial. "You made it," she says warmly to me. "Wasn't it splendid?"

"'Splendid' is the word," I say.

"Time for the pub." She turns to me. "I hope you're joining us?" she asks. I hesitate. The thought of crashing their twosome is unbearable, and all of a sudden Cal also looks deeply uncomfortable.

"Oh no, that's very kind," I stammer.

"I'm sure she has better things to do," Cal says quickly.

"Nonsense," says Gerry. "You must come. Cal, tell her she has to come."

He hesitates a beat, looking straight at me.

"You should come," he says.

So we all repair to the Sheep's Head, which sits at the far end of the village green. I've not yet visited the village's only pub. It's the traditional sort, all gabled brick and ivy-clad, with leaded pane windows and wooden picnic tables set out in front. When we push open the heavy oak door, a warm wall of air buffets us. I see that half the village has already arrived: a throng of people stands between us and the long wooden bar, and I spy several elf costumes as we thread our way through the crowd.

Some country pubs are frosty to outsiders, but the vibe here seems jovial enough. Cal draws congratulatory backslaps from a number of people we pass, which he handles more graciously than I would have imagined; and no one looks at me as if I'm some sort of alien interloper. Cal seems genuinely pleased to be here as he leads us to a small table in the corner, not far from a blazing wood fire. The mantel has been trimmed with holly and bright red balls that gleam like jewels in the firelight. Beside us sits a bushy tree trimmed with wooden ornaments. It would all be thrillingly romantic—if I were not date-crashing.

Cal goes to the bar to fetch drinks and Gerry smiles at me. I'm wondering whether I can casually quiz her about their relationship (*Who made the first move? How exactly does intergenerational sex work?*) when she hits me with a question.

"Do you live alone in London?"

I nod. "I have a flat south of the river." No point in saying where; even Londoners have never heard of Nunhead.

"I've never lived on my own," she muses, throwing a darting glance in Cal's direction. She leans forward. "I imagine it might be quite nice," she confides.

"There are definite advantages," I say, not quite sure what to make of her declaration. Is there trouble in paradise?

"No arguments over what to watch on telly. The freedom to have popcorn for supper or leave dirty dishes in the sink. And you could dispense completely with personal hygiene, if you felt like it."

"Or clothing, for that matter," I say.

"How glorious." She laughs.

"Actually, I used to live with my boyfriend, but he moved out a few weeks ago."

"Oh. I'm sorry," she says. "I hope I haven't spoken out of turn."

I shake my head. "No. Things had run their course."

She considers this. "Modern love does seem very . . . fluid these days," she remarks. "Don't get me wrong, I don't think that's necessarily a bad thing. In my day, relationships were like treacle. You could get stuck fast if you weren't careful."

I think of how quickly my life with Lionel unraveled: four years undone in a matter of moments, ostensibly because of a photograph. Was that a good thing or bad?

"That's why I admire Jez for taking her time," Gerry continues. "She and Eloise have courted the old-fashioned way, long and slow. And there's something in that."

I peer at her. Is she being ironic? Apparently not.

Cal arrives then, clutching three glasses. "I hope mulled wine is OK." He places them on the table, the scent of cinnamon and cardamom wafting up.

"Lovely. You're an angel," says Gerry, reaching for one and handing me another. I have to concede it smells delicious, and I remember guiltily that mulled wine was another thing on my Christmas list of *don'ts*.

"Cheers," she offers, raising her glass. Suddenly her attention is distracted by a large, burly older man who has just come through the door. "Is that Dibber?" she asks. The man wears a battered tweed blazer and a checked wool cap. His hair and beard are snow-white, but his eyes are alert as they sweep the room. They alight on Gerry and he doffs his cap in her direction theatrically. She laughs.

"The old rogue. Excuse me for a moment while I just say hello."

She gets up and moves through the crowd. I see Cal frown slightly as his eyes follow her. Is he jealous? We watch as Gerry reaches Dibber and greets him warmly.

"Old flame," says Cal, a little grudgingly. "From a previous life."

"Odd name," I say, eyeing him.

"He owns a bulb farm down the road."

"Well, that explains it."

Cal detects the sarcasm in my tone and raises an eyebrow. "Flowers?" he says.

"I got that much."

"Guess you're not a gardener."

"Tricky. In a third-floor flat. But I do own a very resilient cactus."

"A *dibber* is a tool you use to plant bulbs."

"Ah."

"People use them in the city, too."

"I'll take your word for it." He tilts his head and regards me.

"So, what *do* you do for fun? In the great metropolis."

I hesitate, my brain flying through several possible answers. What *do* I do for fun? Any number of things, which will all sound totally lame if I say them aloud. "I run," I say finally.

"Run what?"

"Surely you mean *where*?"

"OK. Where?"

"Along the river mostly. Hyde Park. The Serpentine. Wherever the mood takes me."

"On your own?" He aims his too-blue gaze right at me, and I feel my cheeks flame in response. Is he probing me for my relationship status? If so, it feels a little disloyal. I glance over at Gerry and she is laughing up at Dibber, so I turn back—and something catches inside my chest.

"I always run alone," I say. "It relaxes me." I do not say what else I am thinking: that there are times, living in a city of eight million souls, when I have an almost physical craving for solitude. And calm.

He nods, staring at me with an intensity that seems inappropriate, given the circumstances. Defiantly, I take a much too large gulp of wine, and endeavor to grapple the conversation back onto safe terrain.

"What about you? Do you engage in . . . country pursuits?"

He smiles, raising a skeptical eyebrow. "'Country pursuits'?" he asks.

Aren't country pursuits a thing? I think.

I'm sure they are. But he has a way of turning everything I say inside out. I lift my chin. "You know, like . . ."

"Shooting?" he offers.

I nod. Exactly. I *knew* there were country pursuits.

"I'm a vet," he says. "I heal animals for a living. So I would hardly go around shooting them during my spare time."

"Right." I flush. So maybe *not* country pursuits.

"But I'm a keen badminton player," he says then.

Badminton! This I did not expect.

"Of all the racquet sports, that's the last one I would have put you down for," I say truthfully. He looks mildly affronted.

"Badminton is surprisingly athletic," he says.

"For an elf."

He laughs.

"Do you play with the other elves?" I ask, only half-joking.

He shakes his head. "I'm in the Southwest Men's League. We play in Taunton, mostly. Sometimes in Exeter."

There's an awkward pause, while I briefly imagine athletic men wearing elf suits flinging themselves around a badminton court. I take another swallow of wine and see that I have already downed most of the glass.

"I thought I hated mulled wine," I admit. "But this is delicious."

He looks at me, incredulous. "How can anyone hate mulled wine?"

I freeze, struggling to formulate a coherent response. "I think it's more about what it stands for," I say. "You know, all that relentless merrymaking and good cheer."

"You don't believe in *good cheer?*"

Oh God. He makes me sound like Satan. Which is an anagram of Santa when you think of it. "Not . . . when it's forced."

He looks around us. "Is this forced?" he asks.

I flush anew. "No. Of course not. This is very . . . congenial."

"OK, so let me get this right. Congenial is OK. But *merrymaking* is not." He's doing it again: twisting my words, bearing down on me with all that blueness. It is like a conversational assault, but with a flirtatious edge. The corners of his mouth are turned up in a sardonic smile, and there is definitely a spark of something seductive in his gaze, not to mention in his tone.

Or maybe I am already drunk.

"I can make merry," I stammer. "When the situation . . . warrants."

Now it sounds ludicrous. And a little obscene.

"That's good to know," he says, still staring right at me, as if he knows all that blueness will render me incapable of a response. Which it does.

Finally, he looks away. Which leaves me both relieved and disappointed.

His gaze travels around the room. "Fair point," he says, after a moment. "About the forced good cheer. Expect there's a bit of that going on around us right now." His tone has taken on a slightly rancorous edge.

Welcome back, Bovine Cal.

"Those are harsh words, coming from an elf," I say.

He looks back at me a little accusingly. "Don't tell me you have a problem with elves, too?"

Uh-oh.

Gerry slides into her seat at the table just then and Cal looks over at her expectantly. Not a moment too soon, I decide.

"So? How's Dibber?" he asks.

"Oh, much the same. He's talking about selling up."

Cal raises an eyebrow. "The farm?"

"He's had a good offer, apparently."

Cal frowns. I see him check himself from asking more. His eyes alight on my empty glass. "Do you need a refill?" he asks. But something in his tone has shifted and I can tell that he is no longer really present. I shake my head.

"No, thanks. I should be going."

"So soon?" says Gerry.

"The dogs will be waiting."

Cal nods, just once. Which is my cue to go.

chapter

15

When I arrive home the dogs are beside themselves with relief, as if I have been away for months, rather than hours.
And a teeny-weeny bit of me is genuinely gratified by all that tail-
wagging and crotch-sniffing, even if it is partially motivated by
cupboard love. I parcel out their dinner, tossing in a few extra bits
and bobs—some leftover pepperoni pizza, a few old hunks of
cheese and salami—it's almost Christmas, after all—then I mar-
shal them out to the paddock in the dark. It's a clear, freezing night
and the grass is crisp beneath my boots. A slim quarter moon
perches just above the horizon and the sky is blanketed with stars.
I throw back my head and gawk. How have I managed to live so
long without stars?

The dogs, too, are happy to be outside, content to wander
about in the darkness, sniffing the earth, raising quivering nostrils
to the breeze, pawing the dirt, and snapping randomly at lanky

bits of frozen grass. Even Peggy and Malcolm seem energized by the cold, while Judd attaches himself to Hulk, trailing her everywhere, his delicate chestnut nose pinned to her fluffy white bum. A battered white van trawls slowly by—drawing attention to itself—and I resent the intrusion, glaring fiercely in its direction until the taillights disappear round the bend. I feel suddenly protective of both the dogs and the farm—but most of all, of the peace and quiet and the unending sense of calm. We linger outside a long time, until I can no longer feel my fingers or toes, and the numbness is strangely exhilarating.

Later, I sleep like the dead—until I am woken in the small hours by a chorus of barking. It sounds like a canine rave and I throw on my dressing gown and stumble down to the kitchen, flicking on the overhead light. The dogs are clustered around the back door, baying, hackles raised, and Malcolm's massive muzzle is plastered to the window. I rush to look outside and see the same battered white van speeding off down the lane. The dogs round on me, bristling with energy, eager to divulge what they've seen, with Malcolm towering over the others. "OK," I say, trying to pacify them. "Whoever it was, they've gone." I double-check the locks, give them all fresh water, and order them to lie down. But once back in bed, the image of the white van keeps driving slowly through my mind.

Jez rings again early the next morning and I decide not to tell her about the white van. It would only worry her and there is little she can do from afar. Hopefully, whoever it was will have been deterred—few burglars would choose to go head-to-head against five dogs, one of them the size of a small pony. I will definitely mention it to Valko, however. He may have seen the car on the road these last few days.

"So how was the igloo?" I ask Jez.

"Freezing. I thought my face would fall off. The scenery was amazing, though. I took loads of pictures. Turns out ice isn't very photogenic, though."

"Can't wait to see *those*," I say. "Meet any polar bears?"

"No, but we saw lots of reindeer."

"Hey, we have reindeer here in Devon." I say. "I saw one wearing an elf suit last night."

"Oh, the pageant! How was it?"

"Daft," I reply, "but in a splendid sort of way."

"I thought it might amuse you," she says. I consider asking her how long Cal and Gerry have been an item but decide against it.

"And Eloise?" I ask. "How's it going?"

Jez pauses for a second.

"Well, I think it's safe to say we're over the first flush. Just trying to get to know each other now. You know, habits, foibles, irritants."

"Does she know you're phobic about moldy cheese?"

"Not yet. I'm waiting for the right moment."

"And have you shown her your toes?"

"What's wrong with my toes?"

"Just show her."

"Thanks."

"No worries. What's family for?"

"I'll be sure to return the favor when Mr. Right comes along."

"Who will no doubt turn out to be Mr. Wrong."

"Don't be such a pessimist."

"Besides," I say. "Who needs men when you have mutts?"

Jez laughs. "Too true," she agrees.

After we hang up, I decide that I am only half in jest. Pickle and Pepper notwithstanding, I have to admit that dogs make perfectly pleasant housemates. They are loyal, companionable, reasonably well behaved, and reassuringly predictable. Unlike men, they respond well to prompting, rather than resenting you for it. And they are streets ahead when it comes to personal grooming and eating everything put in front of them without complaint. Admittedly they are rubbish at housework, but then, so is every man I've ever known. And Malcolm aside, dogs are better listeners than men, *by far*. So apart from the obvious (sex, which is clearly a nonstarter) dogs outperform men in virtually every realm of daily life. Why has it taken me so long to discover this?

But today I am worried about Peggy, who is suddenly so fat she can barely waddle over to her water bowl without assistance, her belly swaying like an overloaded lorry. She drinks long and hard, as if it is her last drink *ever*, as if water is the key to salvation and the afterlife, then collapses heavily on her side with a grunt. In the last twenty-four hours she has abandoned the sofa (which I can see has taken on Everest-like proportions), so I made up a bed for her out of old blankets and cushions in the corner opposite from the others (she likes her privacy.) But she remains remarkably tolerant of Malcolm, who follows her everywhere, like a worried, ineffectual, oversized bodyguard.

I reach over and gently place a hand on her stomach: it is taut and lumpy, with sharply jutting bits that I imagine are tiny paws and muzzles and haunches and, eerily, every now and then something shifts beneath her skin. She locks her eyes on mine with an expression of quiet desperation, one that suggests she would prefer to give the whole thing a miss, if at all possible. I place a hand on her head in a gesture of female solidarity. She has every right to be terrified, frankly. I know I would be. Birthing one baby is hard enough, but several in one go? No one should have to endure that.

I scour the bookshelves to see if there is any sort of advice about how to make her more comfortable, to no avail. Suddenly, rashly, I decide to ring Cal.

He picks up on the sixth ring, and if it is possible to sound irritated in only two syllables, he succeeds. I explain that I am ringing about Peggy and say that she really does look worryingly large.

"She's not due for almost a fortnight," he says.

"What happens if she's early?"

Cal sighs. "Canine gestation isn't like human's. You can generally set your watch by it."

"But she seems so . . . lethargic."

"That's because she's lazy at the best of times."

"But what if something's wrong?"

"Such as?"

"I don't know . . . maybe she has preeclampsia!"

"I doubt it."

"How can you be sure?"

"Does she have tremors?"

"No."

"Can she walk?"

"Yes."

"Then she doesn't have preeclampsia."

"Oh."

"Look, I don't mean to be rude but . . . I'm actually in the middle of something."

"Sorry."

What sort of something? I wonder as I hang up. Suddenly my mind flies to the possibilities: Perhaps he and Gerry are sharing a lazy postcoital afternoon? *In which case he never should have answered his phone! Though perhaps it's mandatory in the caring professions?* This isn't a line of thought I care to dwell on, really. Luckily, Valko is due to come by any minute to exercise the twins. Who knew that I would so look forward to visits from a depressed Bulgarian migrant worker?

But Valko is uncharacteristically upbeat when he arrives a few minutes later. I see that he is freshly shaved and wears a shirt that is marginally less frayed than his others. "You're looking tidy today, Valko," I say. He blinks a little self-consciously.

"*Tidy.* Is good, yes?"

I nod. "Have you got plans later?"

"Oh. No. Just . . . I go to see Stella. For . . . small time." He shrugs in an effort at nonchalance.

"Of course."

"To help with pigs. Or . . . some things."

"Absolutely. Some things. Why not?"

We take the twins for a walk and I tell him about the white van. Valko stops and frowns. "This not good, I think."

"It was probably just someone trying their luck."

"But . . . you are alone. In house."

"I'm not alone. I have seven dogs to protect me."

He shakes his head. "You need gun, I think. Gun is good for protect."

"Valko, I'm not going to use a gun!"

"No need to use. Just . . . have gun is good."

"Where would I even get a gun, anyway?"

"To get gun is not difficult," he says. "I maybe know someone."

"What exactly did you do back in Bulgaria?" I ask suspiciously.

"Some things."

"Some things with guns?"

He shrugs. "Some things with guns. Some things with no guns." He says this casually, like he is ordering pizza: *one with cheese and one without.*

"I think I'll stick with dogs," I say, eyeing him.

He grunts. "Guns is better."

Late that evening I'm sacked out on the sofa, reading the newspaper, when I hear a noise outside. Malcolm and I both sit up and he suddenly swings his head from the maternity corner toward the door, his large brown eyes blinking with startled anticipation. Has the white van returned? But in the next instant Hugo's face appears blurrily through the window, peering in. Through the glass I can see that he is wearing a mustard-colored scarf wrapped around his neck so many times that it looks as if he's being strangled by a woolly anaconda. When I open the door, he gives a little wave. "Hello," he says.

"Hi. Um . . . What are you doing here so late?" I ask.

He sways slightly, one hand shooting out to grip the door frame.

"Hugo, are you drunk?"

He squints at me. "Fractionally."

"You didn't drive, did you? Where's your car?"

"Actually, I rode," he says with a hint of pride.

"Rode *what?*" I say with alarm, scanning the yard for a horse.

"That. I found it in the barn." He points toward an old bike leaning against the kennels. Then he frowns. "But it took longer than I thought. I must have taken a wrong turn somewhere." He turns and stares at the road. "And I had no idea it was so cold out," he mutters.

"You'd better come in."

I lead him inside and put the kettle on. Hugo walks over to where Malcolm is guarding Peggy and bends down to fondle him for a moment. "Hello, old boy," he says. "Just needed a little canine sustenance, didn't I?" He straightens and walks over to the sofa, collapsing onto it while I set about making coffee.

"What happened?" I ask. "Where's Constance?"

"Constance is playing bridge with her family. Nothing has happened. Nothing *ever* happens at Constance's house, I've discovered. It is all a seamless occurrence of the expected."

"So why aren't you with them?"

"I'm on furlough." He grins. "Self-appointed."

"Meaning she doesn't know you're here?"

He sucks in air. "I suspect not," he says.

"Maybe you should ring her."

He shakes his head. *"Definitely* not."

"She might be worried."

"The thing is . . . Constance doesn't really *do* worry. She does anger."

"Hugo, what are you doing here?"

He looks perplexed and a little bit wounded.

"I mean, why have you come?"

He frowns. "To see *you*, of course. And Malcolm." His eyes roam around the kitchen. "I *like* coming here. It's warm. And comfortable. And . . . cozy." He looks at me. "Life is easy here. *You're* easy."

I shake my head. "Not a compliment."

"In contrast with Constance. Who is decidedly *not* easy. Who is decidedly . . . complicated."

"People are complicated, Hugo."

"But Constance requires so much . . . *fealty*. It can be exhausting. You've no idea. I'm not sure I can summon all the energy required to meet her standards."

"But, Hugo, you're engaged."

He frowns. "Yes. I know. That is a—a troubling detail."

"Do you love her, Hugo?"

He hesitates, his eyes glazing slightly. "That is a trick question," he says slowly.

"Call me old-fashioned, but people who marry should be in love."

He exhales. "I *esteem* her," he says.

"That's not exactly truly, madly, deeply, is it?"

"I *deeply* esteem her."

"Look, have you considered the possibility that this engagement might be a mistake?"

He sinks back into the sofa despairingly. "How difficult can it be to get married and live happily ever after?"

"Quite difficult, actually."

"Other people seem to manage."

"I think you'll find that a lot of people fail."

"Well, I appear to be a *serial* failure."

"No, you're not."

He turns to me. "Would *you* marry me?"

"No."

"I rest my case." He slaps his hand on the sofa.

I hand him a mug of coffee. "Here. Drink this."

Hugo takes a sip. He looks down at the mug. "And you make *fantastic* coffee. You really do have to marry me."

I sit down next to him on the sofa. "Does Constance love you?"

"I've no idea."

"Has she told you?"

"I asked her once. She said, *Of course.*"

"Huh."

He takes another drink of coffee and sighs. "I'm sorry. I've no right to impose myself on you like this."

"It's OK. You're paying double." I grin at him.

"Ah yes. I nearly forgot."

"If it's any consolation, my love life is worse than yours. My ex-boyfriend cheated on me with his personal trainer."

Hugo makes a face. "How thoroughly unsporting."

"Anyway, I've decided dogs make perfectly good life partners."

"Really?" He looks at me askance.

"No. But they'll have to do until something better comes along. Something without a tail, preferably." He shakes his head.

"I don't understand," he says. "You're attractive. And clever. And funny. And kind. Any man would be lucky to have you." He looks at me intently and I realize all at once that it could be so easy. Because he, too, is kind. And clever. And handsome. And rich! "Perhaps we're being idiots," he says.

"I'm not sure I follow," I say cautiously.

But I know perfectly well what he means.

In the next instant Hugo leans forward and kisses me, and even as sirens start to blare in one half of my brain, the other half has leaped right up on that wagon, happy to go along for the ride. We kiss for a moment and, as we do, the computer in my brain is rapidly analyzing the metrics of the encounter (about a five on a scale of one to ten, which is disappointing, though his aftershave smells absolutely divine, so maybe a six) but the sirens grow more insistent and suddenly I realize that they're competing with a noise from *outside* my brain. It takes an instant before I recognize the sound of someone banging on the back door, and another instant before I realize that Hugo and I are not alone—that someone is standing just outside, staring directly in at us through the glass.

Someone with absurdly blue eyes.

Awkward.

I practically fling myself across the room to open the door. Outside, Bovine Cal stands there, stony-faced.

"I thought I'd better check on Peggy," he informs me coldly.

Oh. Crap. "Thanks," I say. I open the door wide and he steps into the room.

"I've been tied up in clinic with an emergency," he says tersely. "Or I would have come earlier." He turns toward Hugo, who jumps to his feet and steps forward to greet him. Cal gives the briefest of nods and sidesteps him, crossing to where Peggy lies in the corner, panting. He squats down and splays both hands across her abdomen, while Malcolm, Hugo, and I look on. Cal palpates Peggy for a moment, then pulls a stethoscope out of his coat pocket and listens to her heart for a minute. Eventually he rises, turning to us.

"She's fine," he says. "Keep her quiet and give her plenty of water."

"OK."

For an instant, there's an uncomfortable moment of silence.

"I'll leave you to it," he says then, flinging the words like stones. And he does.

After he has gone, I give Hugo a ride home in the Škoda. Neither of us says a word about the kiss, which hovers around us like a bad smell. When Hugo gets out of the car he gives me a sheepish little wave—a wave that says he's feeling like an arse. But I am no better; I had no business kissing Hugo, and no business flirting with Cal in the pub. The thing about infidelity is that it preys on the weak, I decide on the way home. Lionel was one of the weak. I am not.

I am a strong, independent woman.

Or at least I used to be.

chapter

16

wake the next morning feeling sheepish. Last night was not my
finest hour. Though a part of me can't help wondering why Cal
was so angry? Perhaps he was offended on Constance's behalf. Or
perhaps he simply thinks I have no business meddling with other
people's engagements. If so, then he is right. Today will have to be
a day for making amends. It is the eve of Christmas Eve and, for
once in my life, I will throw myself into the holiday spirit. I will
ring Gerry to say thank you for the other evening (and to make up
for flirting with Cal); I will apologize to Hugo for unwittingly
leading him astray; I will be kind and supportive to Valko—and I
will keep Peggy well watered.

I will even groom Judd.

Obeying my own call to action, I go to Jez's wardrobe and ferret around for something festive to wear. Apparently everyone on
the planet (apart from me) owns a Christmas jumper, so it is simply a case of finding where she hides it. I rummage through all her

drawers and all her hanging clothes to no avail. Perhaps she has taken it with her? I am on the verge of settling for a Kelly green cardigan when I spy a large plastic box on the floor at the back of her wardrobe. I drag it out and voilà! It is basically a dressing-up box for grown-ups. Inside I find silky purple Arabian nights' trousers with sparkly gold trim, thigh-high pale pink vinyl boots, a leopard-print catsuit *(Meow!)*, an enormous shaggy, dirty-white onesie *(Not sure what look she's going for with this one? Yeti?)*, a floor-length, hooded dark brown robe *(Jedi? Franciscan monk?)*, and a minuscule, flouncy black minidress with ruffles and gold tassel *(Ooh la la! French maid? Or maybe sexy pirate?)*. As I rummage through the stack I feel as if I'm seeing an entirely different side of Jez. Life in the country is clearly more adventurous than I'd realized. I am just about to settle on the catsuit *(The dogs will love it!)* when I pluck a folded red knitted sweater from the bottom of the box.

I hold it up and laugh out loud.

Dear Lord, I cannot possibly wear this!

It is indeed a Christmas jumper. But instead of a reindeer or Santa emblazoned across the chest, there are two perfectly round plum puddings, each placed strategically over one breast, complete with dripping icing and cherry nipples. The effect is both seasonally jaunty and surprisingly lewd. I pull the jumper on and turn to face the mirror. My plum puddings stare back at me, cherry nipples winking. It is almost certainly an optical illusion, but my breasts appear to have gone up a cup size or two. I turn to the side, admiring my more buxom profile. The sweater does feel festive. And it is surprisingly soft and warm. Besides, who apart from the dogs will see me?

ater that morning, Sian rings. "How's the mutt house?" She asks.

I sigh. My plum puddings and I are squeezed on the sofa between Hulk, Slab, and Judd, who as soon as Peggy vacated, decided that dog beds were passé. When I came down this morning, Hulk and Judd were cozied up together at one end of the sofa, sniffing each other's hindquarters, while Slab stood quivering beside it, waiting to be lifted on.

"Actually, I think the house might be starting to smell."

"So are you now, probably. Is the boiler still out?"

"Yep. The boiler guy appears to have fled to warmer climates."

"How's the Dishy Danish?" Sian has dubbed Hugo the Dishy Danish, even though I have pointed out to her on more than one occasion that he is a) not Danish, and b) well, there is no b actually, because he *is* quite dishy. I relate the previous night's events.

"So what's the problem? It sounds like his girlfriend's a miserable cow."

"Fiancée. The problem is that it's wrong. And infidelity is always a bad launchpad for a relationship."

"OK, so persuade him to break up with her first."

I frown. Constance isn't the only reason, I think. As nice as Hugo is, his kiss was only barely a six. I suspect Bovine Cal would score much higher. But I definitely can't go there. "Actually, I think Hugo's still in love with his childhood sweetheart," I say.

"Really?"

I tell Sian about Hugo and Bonnie and the Band of the Household Cavalry.

"No way!" she says. "Owen and I adore that band! We just went to see them play Christmas carols on the Mall."

"I thought you hated the monarchy."

"I do. But I still like the trappings. Anyway, what's not to love about horses and horns? And the uniforms are fabulous! They wear shiny black, thigh-high boots, and gold jackets. Owen has been begging me for a trumpet for Christmas."

"Good luck with that."

"It's way cheaper than a pony."

"True." Sian is nothing if not pragmatic.

"So . . . are there really no decent prospects for romance in the West Country?" she asks. "What happened to the brooding vet?"

Something inside me curls with shame. "He's taken, apparently. Plus, he thinks I'm reckless."

"Ah." An awkward silence follows.

"Sian, this is the point where you're supposed to reassure me that I'm not."

"Right," she says. "You're not. Most of the time."

"Thanks for the vote of confidence."

"What happened to the *Star Trek* guy?" she asks.

"What *Star Trek* guy?"

"You know, the one who helps you with the dogs. The Vulcan."

"Valko?"

"Yeah, what's wrong with him?"

"Nothing really. He's perfectly nice. If a bit . . . odd."

"So? Odd can be good."

"He's not really my type."

"In what way."

"Um . . . physically."

"Don't be so shallow! You two could be *Beauty and the Beast*."

"I don't think so."

"Why not?"

"Because he lives in a caravan. Not a castle. And I can't sing."

"That film has a very important message. *Don't overlook what's in front of you.*"

"The dogs are in front of me. Or, at least, beside me."

"I'm serious. *Beauty and the Beast* is our top-fave film ever. Owen and I must have watched it like nine million times. Except now Owen thinks there's a little man with a French accent living inside our alarm clock."

"Anyway, I'm pretty sure Valko's already got something going with the local pig farmer."

"Wow," she muses. "You can't even compete with a pig farmer?"

"I wasn't trying to."

"Sounds like you've only got one option left."

"What's that?"

"The dogs."

I look over at Judd and Hulk, who are gazing lovingly into each other's eyes. Even *they* are already taken. But there's always Slab.

"Yep," I say.

"You could do worse," says Sian.

After I hang up, I remain glued to the sofa, overwhelmed by the crapness of my life. I realize now that *dog days* do not only occur in late summer. The fact is, life can paralyze you at any time. All the resolution I felt upon waking seems to have ebbed away, like someone reached in and pulled the plug on my spirit.

Slab leans up against me, snoring, and I fondle his ears absent-mindedly. Apart from his smell, he really is rather sweet. He has a gently imploring way about him, as if to say: *please don't give up on me.* I look down at him. Perhaps his life, too, has not gone quite according to plan. Perhaps he would not have chosen to be institutionalized in his final years. Perhaps he misses his former owners, or perhaps he would have preferred a livelier household. One with children, say. Or cats. Or maybe he would have loved to spend his days by the sea, to be a beach dog, chasing rocks, biting at seaweed, jumping in and out of waves. But he didn't get to choose. Slab has had to make the best of things. He has persevered. And so must I.

Outside the sky is leaden, and the temperature has plummeted even lower. I drag myself off the sofa and pull on three quilted jackets, one atop the other, as well as two scarves, a woolly hat, and two odd mittens, because I cannot find a matching pair. When I'm finished I look like a West Country version of the Michelin Man in random shades of hunter green mixed with country plaids. My plum puddings will definitely be toasty.

I commandeer all five dogs and frog-march them out to the paddock in a rough formation, where they sniff halfheartedly at the frost before squatting gingerly in the face of the biting wind. Malcolm stands facing east, his pale pink nostrils quivering, as if he can smell Hugo from afar, and I think again about what Hugo said last night. Maybe he and I are *both* serial failures. Having watched my mother navigate a long string of disastrous marriages, and my father use the jump seat after only one, it occurs to me that

serial failure might even be an inherited trait: perhaps I am genetically *programmed* to fail at relationships.

When we get back inside, the phone is ringing. "Good morning," says Gerry cheerily when I answer.

"I was just going to call you," I say, which might even be true.
"To thank you for the drink the other evening."

"No thanks needed. We were delighted to have you along."

We, I think. Gerry is part of a *we.* And I am part of an *I.* That
is my genetic destiny. I'd better face up to it.

"I was just ringing to say that a very large parcel has arrived,"
she says. "In fact, it's more like a shipping container."

"Really?" All at once I brighten. I'd virtually given up on the
TV delivery before the holiday, but maybe Father Christmas
really *does* exist. "That's fantastic," I say. "I'll be right over."

Simple pleasures, I think, as I jump into the Škoda. I may be
terminally single, but I can still be a cultural slag.

Maybe the dogs and I will watch *Beauty and the Beast.*

When I pull up to the post office, the first thing I see is Cal's
old blue Volvo parked outside. *Damn.* I assumed he'd be at
the surgery. I really do not want to come face-to-face with him so
soon after last night's unfortunate episode. But I really *do* want the
TV, so I park the Škoda and go inside. When I enter, Gerry is
behind the counter sorting out the post, and a massive wooden
crate sits in front of the counter off to one side. Fortunately, Cal is
nowhere to be seen, and I feel a little flare of relief. With any luck
I can be in and out in a trice. Gerry looks up and smiles.

"There you are," she says, nodding to the crate propped against the wall. "Good thing you warned me it was coming. I might have refused delivery." She laughs.

"Wow." I turn to the crate. It is far, far bigger than I expected, rising almost to my chest and taking up half the wall in width. Surely it can't be twenty-two inches? I peer at a label on the side and buried among the fine print I see that, in fact, it is sixty-two inches! How did I manage to order a sixty-two-inch television without realizing? And what on earth did it cost? On top of that, the crate has been trussed up like a small-arms shipment, with a wooden frame and miles of tightly wrapped cellophane, which will no doubt require a small army of ninjas to open. I'm not sure it will even fit in the Škoda. "OK, well, I'll just see if I can . . ." I try lifting one end and realize that there is absolutely no way I will be able to move it on my own. And it is much too heavy for Gerry to help.

"Why don't I call Cal?" she offers. "He's in the back."

"Oh no," I say quickly. "I'm sure I can manage."

But she has already walked to the back of the shop and is bellowing his name loudly while I cringe. After a moment, Cal appears. Once again he is color coordinated: this time it's a royal blue crewneck sweater that makes his eyes look like they are lit from inside. I swear the man practically *glows* blue: like a tall, handsome Smurf. When he sees me he stops short and his gaze suddenly darkens like a mood ring.

"Oh," he says. He does not smile.

"She can't possibly move that carton on her own," says Gerry, completely oblivious to Cal's reaction. "Be a darling and help her take it out, won't you?"

Cal looks from me to the crate, drawing a breath through his nostrils. His jaw is clenched tight. I can just make out a tiny pulse throbbing on one side. He nods once, and without a word crosses around to the front of the counter, positioning himself on the other side of the box. Together we lift it and stagger toward the door, which Gerry quickly opens for us.

"What the hell is in here, anyway?" he mutters as we descend the steps.

"Um . . . just something for the house," I say, grunting with effort. Technically, this is not a lie. Every home should have one.

"Like a new boiler?"

Ah. Well *that* would have been a good idea. But if the dogs and I sit close enough to the screen, it might just keep us warm. I do not answer him because, really, it is none of his business. We set the carton down beside the Škoda and I open the back door. He looks at me as if I'm mad.

Because it is blindingly obvious that the crate will not fit in the Škoda.

"Um . . . It won't fit," I say.

"No kidding." There is no mistaking the hostility in his tone. He is obviously furious about last night, although he has no right to be. I glare at him and take a step forward.

"What is your problem?" I hiss quietly, aware that Gerry is just inside.

"*My* problem? I'm not the one who—" He stops himself.

"Look, I don't judge you for your *ch-choices*," I stammer.

"Oh! Is that what you were doing last night?" he interjects. "*Choosing?*"

I stare at him uncertainly. What exactly is he getting at?

"Maybe that's because my choices aren't so stupid," he continues, practically spitting the words at me. "And what do you know
about my choices, anyway? You know nothing about me."

Gerry has come to the door and is watching us through the
glass. I glance over and see her frown. She opens the door and calls
out. "Cal! You'll have to take it over for her in the Volvo!"

He turns to me expectantly but says nothing.

No. Absolutely not.

I will not grovel to this man.

Cal crosses his arms over his chest and waits.

I breathe in. He is sure to offer. If I can just hold on.

But he doesn't. I wait another long moment.

Truly, he is rudeness incarnate.

Gerry leans out again from the doorway. "Cal?" she calls, a
little puzzled.

Cal fixes me resolutely with his stormy blue gaze.

I exhale. Really, it is more like a snort.

"Would. You. Mind." I say. Though I do not form it as a
question.

He jerks his head toward the Volvo, then bends down to lift the
box. When we finish loading it into the back of the car, he slams
the door.

"I'll have to drop it off later," he says curtly. "I'm due at the
surgery now."

"Fine," I snap. I start to turn away but hesitate. He *is* doing me
a favor, after all. "Thanks," I add. But I needn't have bothered.

Because he climbs into the car and drives off without a word.

I return to the shop, where Gerry has gone back to sorting the
post. "Thanks very much for your help," I say.

She turns and smiles. "A pleasure," she says.

I laugh uneasily. "I'm afraid *he* didn't seem very pleased."

"Who? Cal?" She waves a hand. "Don't mind him. Mornings aren't his best."

I *really* do not want to hear what Cal is like in the mornings.

"He's always been that way," she continues. "Ever since he was a little boy. He used to eat his breakfast cereal under the table, so he wouldn't have to speak to us." She laughs. I stare at her.

Oh my God.

Not only am I stupid. But I'm a world-class idiot.

Gerry is Cal's *mum*.

Harold and Maude! What was I thinking? As I barrel down the road I run through the reasons that led me astray. First, there was the fact that they have different surnames. Second, there was the gift of the poinsettia, not to mention Cal's embarrassment when he gave it. Then the deliberately chaste kiss of thanks. Deliberately chaste *because she is his mother.*

Crap. What must he think of me?

All at once I understand what he meant by *choosing*. Cal thinks that I have chosen Hugo over him. Hugo, who is already engaged to Constance. And who is barely a six. I really am genetically programmed to fail.

chapter
17

By the time I get home I'm feeling low. Maybe not stick-your-head-in-the-oven low, but definitely eat-your-way-through-an-entire-pint-of-Ben-and-Jerry's-Karamel-Sutra low. Which I do. But afterward, I only feel worse. So I do what I should have done in the first place: I call my father on Skype.

When he answers, he looks at me dubiously. "Charlie, what's that you're wearing?" he asks. I instantly fold my arms over my chest. I'd completely forgotten about my plum puddings.

"Just something I found in Jez's wardrobe," I say, coloring. But then I peer at him, because he, too, is dressed in seasonally strange garb. My father is not exactly fashion-forward. His preferred look is a plain white business shirt, and on a day when he's feeling especially daring, he might don a pale blue version. But today he appears to be dressed in a bright red tunic with silver embroidery around the collar. He looks like a skinny Russian version of Kris Kringle. "I might as well ask you the same," I say.

He sighs and dabs at the shirt with his fingertips. "It's some sort of traditional Russian garb. My colleagues gave it to me last night. We had a small departmental celebration, so I thought it would be diplomatic to wear it today." He pulls at the collar uncomfortably. "It's meant to be linen. But I have a feeling it's something less . . . benign."

"I'm not sure it's you."

"I'm not sure it's anyone," he says. "Are you OK?" His forehead creases with concern. "I wasn't expecting to hear from you until Christmas Day."

I sigh. "OK is a relative construct."

"You're not still suffering headaches, are you?"

"No. My head is fine. But I think my heart might be concussed."

"Oh, Charlie." His voice is so full of sympathy it makes me want to cry.

Instead, I tell him about Hugo and Cal, and my theory that I am genetically programmed to fail.

"I'm not sure genetics enters into it," he says gently. "I think when it comes to relationships, nurture wins over nature. But you haven't exactly had the best models in your mother and me. And for that I can only apologize."

"I blame Mum more than you," I say grudgingly.

"She seems very happily settled now," he points out.

"Fifth time lucky," I reply, my voice laced with sarcasm.

"It took her a long time to decide what she wanted in a partner," he says equably.

"It took her a long time to find a partner who could tolerate her."

"Don't be so harsh, Charlie."

"What about you, Dad? When will you find someone you can settle down with?" My voice is laced with desperation, as if my happiness is somehow pinned to his.

He shrugs. "It's not something I dwell on. Believe it or not, I'm very content on my own. Besides, I have you."

"I know." Funnily enough, I do believe him. I also know that I do not want to be like him. Which feels disloyal, somehow.

"Kant said that in order to be happy, we must first make ourselves *worthy* of happiness," he says. "He wanted us to live honorable lives. To live each day as if our every action counted for something."

I frown. "So you think I haven't earned my happiness?"

"I'm not saying that. I'm saying that you must strive to be the best person you can be. And happiness will follow."

Great. Last night when I kissed Hugo, I was definitely *not* being the best person I could be.

"He also said that we must never use each other as a means to an end."

Noted. Guilty as charged. Almost certainly. My father frowns.

"I sometimes think I violated that rule when I met your mother," he says thoughtfully.

"Really? Why?"

"Because I got you."

The idea that my father used my mother as a means to an end stays with me long after we end the call. I'd always assumed it was the other way round. But it is true that parenthood seems to have tethered him to the world in some vitally important way. Although he didn't raise me, I know from speaking to his colleagues and friends that being my father is an enormous part of his identity. The fact of my existence has enriched and deepened him, has given him a reason for being. Ironically, it has enabled him to remain alone. The same is true of Sian and Owen. This thought lifts me a little. We all need love, but maybe love itself is infinitely mutable, able to spread itself thinly and wrap itself around all manner of beings.

I look down at Slab, who has nestled his body up against mine on the sofa and is snoring contentedly. Behind us, Malcolm keeps vigil over Peggy, his head on his paws, his eyes alert. Over in the corner, Hulk and Judd have retreated to one of the dog beds, where they are curled around each other in a tight canine whorl. I sigh and give Slab a little pat. Perhaps when it comes to love I should heed Sian's advice. *Don't overlook what's in front of you.*

That afternoon I bundle on extra layers and take the twins for a long walk. The wind slaps my cheeks as we head out across the fields behind the farm. We find a footpath eventually that leads into a large wood. Once inside the forest, the twins race about happily, winding in and out of trees, scrambling up and down ravines, joyously ambushing squirrels like canine freedom fighters. By the end of the walk I cannot feel my face, but the dogs are muddy and content: tongues lolling, chests heaving, eyes bright with gratitude.

It is dusk when we arrive back at Jez's yard. I feed the twins and return them to the kennel, but when I come around the side of the house toward the front door I see the same white van that was there the other night pulled over by the side of the road. Inside the car I can just make out a dark-haired man with an enormous mustache peering at the kennels through binoculars. He does not see me at first, but when he does, he drops the binoculars, starts the engine, and pulls out onto the lane. I pull out my phone and quickly take a photo of the car as it drives off, congratulating myself on my presence of mind. Perhaps I should ring the police. But what would I say? Thus far, the man is guilty of nothing more than being a Peeping Tom. Anyway, his interest seems to be in the dogs, not me.

Which seems to be an ongoing theme these days.

I go inside and feed the rest of the dogs, then decide to cook a proper meal for myself, rather than pilfer my supply of frozen pizzas and meat pies. I search out some seasonally appropriate music from Jez's CD collection, and root around in her freezer, finding a small packet of mince that I thaw in the microwave. I chop up onions, garlic, peppers, and chilis, and fry them with the mince for several minutes, adding in a tin of tomatoes and some herbs. But when I eventually turn around from the cooker, all five dogs have lined up behind me like a row of little sous-chefs. Even Peggy has dragged herself out of the maternity corner at the prospect of home-cooked food. They sit in an orderly line, muscles tensed, their bodies ready to spring lest I drop the smallest scrap.

I stand in front of them like a conductor, clutching a small morsel of meat that I raise like a baton. All five sets of eyes swivel upward. "Malcolm," I say in my most commanding tone. I throw the mince straight to him, and his gigantic muzzle opens and snaps shut with a squelch. *Impressive,* I think. *We could take this on the road.* I turn to Slab and say his name, then throw another morsel. Slab doesn't quite manage to catch it midair, but he moves more quickly than I've ever seen him once it reaches the ground, practically snorting it. Judd does much better, managing the catch with minimal movement and maximal grace, as befits a triple champion. And tiny Hulk makes a bold effort, rearing up on her hind legs to catch the meat in her dainty jaws. I carry on until I get to Peggy: I don't want her to risk injury, so I simply hold a piece of meat out for her to eat off my palm, which she does rather demurely. But just as I do I hear an impatient rap at the door and when I look up I see a pair of too-familiar eyes staring at me accusingly.

In the dark they appear to be a steely gray, like the sea before a storm. When I open the door, he nods toward the dogs, who, to their credit, are still seated in an orderly line in front of the cooker. "What are you doing?" he says.

"Cooking dinner."

"What are *they* doing?"

I pause. "They're helping."

I realize that he is staring straight at my face, as if every fiber of his being is trying *not* to look at my plum puddings. *Why, oh why am I wearing this?* He jerks his thumb toward the Volvo. "Your box is outside." I follow him out to the car and together we lift the crate, carrying it inside. "Where do you want it?" he grunts. I cast my eyes quickly around the room. Where indeed? In front of the sofa would be ideal, but there isn't space, so in the end I settle for against the far wall. We set it down on the floor and he straightens, giving me a funny look.

"What are you listening to?"

I lift my chin a little defiantly. I have chosen one of my all-time favorite Disney soundtracks, but it is extremely difficult to maintain your dignity when "Do You Want to Build a Snowman?" is playing in the background. I walk over to the stereo and switch the music off, then turn back to Cal.

"Do you . . . want a drink or something?" I ask.

He shakes his head. "I should get going. Mum's waiting on me for supper."

I wince at the word *Mum*.

Cal doesn't leave though, he just stands there staring at me. He takes a deep breath. "Look," he says a little awkwardly, running a hand through his hair. "About this morning. I'm sorry about all the hostility. I had no right. What you do is your affair. It's no business of mine—"

"I thought you and Gerry were together," I blurt out, cutting him off.

He looks at me, his face suddenly blurry with confusion.

"That's what I meant by *choices*," I add sheepishly.

"You thought *what*?"

"You know—I thought you were having some sort of—of intergenerational romance." His eyes widen.

"You thought I was having an incestuous relationship with my seventy-five-year-old mother?" His voice is raised now, quite high-pitched; higher, in fact, than I've ever heard it.

"No! No, of course not! Not *that*. I had no idea she was your mother. How was I to know? No one ever introduced us properly. And besides, you have different surnames," I add a little feebly.

"Because Mum kept her maiden name," he says pointedly. He is staring at me like I'm a lunatic. "You obviously have an extremely vivid imagination," he says after a moment.

"Sometimes too vivid," I say.

I can't be sure, but the corners of his mouth twitch slightly upward. "I can't wait to tell her," he says, with barely concealed delight.

"No! You mustn't!"

"Why not? She'll think it's hilarious."

"No, really. Please. I'd be mortified."

"All the more reason," he says in a challenging tone. As if mortification is what I deserve.

Now he is no longer smiling.

"Look, last night was an accident," I say awkwardly. "It never should have happened. And no one should have witnessed it. Least of all . . . you." For a moment we are both silent. I realize that I am holding my breath.

"But I did," he says.

"I'm sorry."

He nods, just once. We stare at each other. He takes a deep breath, and as he does his eyes seem to thaw. Perhaps I haven't ruined things after all. And perhaps I am not genetically doomed to fail. He takes a step toward me, and maybe it's my overly vivid imagination, but it's almost as if he is going to—

Suddenly there's a knock at the door.

We both turn to see Hugo standing just outside, the giant gold anaconda scarf wrapped tightly around his neck.

Nooooo.

"I should go," Cal says quickly, his eyes clouding over again.

"Cal—" I stop short. I have already apologized.

"You should get the door," he says.

chapter
18

Hugo and I watch from the doorstep as Cal drives away. "Is he always so grumpy?" Hugo asks.

"You have impeccable timing," I say, pushing the door open.

Hugo steps into the kitchen and his eyes dip to my plum puddings with something akin to alarm. "I hadn't pegged you as the Christmas jumper sort," he remarks.

"It's just a *sweater*, for God's sake," I mumble.

"And an appalling one at that," he says.

I sigh and fold my arms, obscuring the cherries.

Hugo clears his throat with purpose. "Anyway, I wanted you to be the first to know," he declares. "I've broken things off with Constance." He throws his arms open wide, as if to say: *ta da!*

Oh God. I eye him warily, preparing to fend him off, if needs be. But then he thrusts his hands in his trouser pockets, turning to contemplate the Christmas tree.

"You were right, you know," he muses. "It wasn't *me* she was in love with. It was the *idea* of me. Or, at least, the idea of being in love with me. I was more like . . . an accessory to the crime."

"I'm sorry, Hugo."

He shrugs.

"How did she take it?"

"Rather well, actually. She really is an awfully good sport. I think she must have realized from my behavior these last few days that something wasn't right. And Constance is nothing if not practical. In fact, she's asked me to stay on for the holiday."

I look at him askance. "Really? Why?"

"She said it was no use spoiling Christmas. Her entire clan is turning up. And the table plan has already been done."

I raise a skeptical eyebrow. *Wouldn't want to mess with that.*

"There's just one small complication," he continues.

"Which is?"

"Her Christmas present."

"Oh. What did you get her?"

He winces. "That's the issue," he says. "They're being delivered tomorrow. And I agreed to a firm sale," he adds sheepishly. "So I really can't cancel."

"Delivered from where? And what do you mean by 'they'?" I ask.

"The owner is driving down from the west of Scotland." My mind instantly flies to the possibilities: a crate of whisky, matching kilts, a giant haggis.

"I thought it was the perfect gift," he says, shaking his head. "Because of Winston and the deer park. And, frankly, they were bloody difficult to locate in the first place! Plus, I had to get a permit." He sighs.

"Hugo, what are you talking about. *What* needs a permit?"

He turns to me. "Alpacas."

"You bought her an alpaca?" I ask, incredulous.

He shakes his head. "I bought her *two* alpacas. Because you can't just have one. They're herd animals. They'd perish on their own."

"Oh, Hugo," I say with dismay.

"Mmm. It's all rather sticky."

"What are you going to do?"

"The thing is . . . under the circumstances, I really can't go through with it. The gift, I mean. It doesn't seem appropriate."

"No. I can see that," I agree.

"So, I was hoping . . . Maybe you could take them for now? Until I can sort out an alternative?"

"What do you mean?" I ask warily.

He looks around. "Well, you have all this *space*. Not that they need much," he adds hastily. "They're quite efficient that way. They don't need to roam. But they do need to graze."

"Hugo, I can't have alpacas here. Are you mad? We're a *dog* kennel."

"Why not? They could live in the paddock. It's the perfect size. I already checked with the breeder," he adds quickly.

"The dogs use the paddock!"

"Alpacas are very sociable. They get on brilliantly with other types of livestock," he says. "And they're very hardy. They can live outside all year round. They positively thrive on the outdoors, in fact."

"Hugo, you do realize that I don't own Cozy Canine Cottages? My cousin, Jez, does. I'm only looking after things here for a few weeks."

His face falls then. "Ah. Quite. I'd rather forgotten that."

"You'll have to find somewhere else."

He looks at me plaintively.

"But I spent all morning ringing round," he says. "There *is* nowhere else."

I am a strong, independent woman, and soon I will be shacked up with seven dogs, a colossal flat-screen TV, and two alpacas.

Now all I need is a partridge in a pear tree.

Later that evening, I unfurl the telly. It is nearly as wide as I am tall, but when I check the receipt it appears that, somewhat miraculously, I have only been charged for the smaller one. *Happy Christmas to me!* I have a brief moment of moral angst *(What would Kant do? Do I care?)* before setting about installing it with glee. After several minutes of peering at the instructions, then casting them aside, I manage to hook the thing up and turn it on. I switch off all the lights and bathe the room in a soft, electronic glow, while the digital receiver scours the surrounding countryside for signals.

Within a matter of seconds the Snowman appears on the screen, soaring high above the earth, a small, pajama-clad boy clinging to his arm. A split second later the speakers roar into life, and a quivering falsetto, accompanied by a rolling baritone piano, sweeps across the kitchen. The sound is so loud it reverberates right through me. I stand, mesmerized, in front of the giant screen, and all at once I, too, am walking in the air, floating in the moonlit sky. The Snowman, the ginger-haired boy, and I circle over icy mountains and pine forests while the northern lights bloom on the horizon and snow blankets the land. It is not exactly the sort of viewing I'd imagined when I ordered it, but even I have to admit that, blown up nearly to life-size, *The Snowman* is pretty magical.

Suddenly I look round and see that all five dogs have sat up and turned their muzzles toward the screen, their eyes wide with curiosity. Malcolm seems particularly affected, his body rigid, his giant head cocked slightly at an angle, his enormous nostrils quivering with apprehension; even Peggy has stopped panting to focus intently on the scene. My phone pings suddenly with a text from Sian.

What you up to?

Watching Snowman on telly. Mutts v keen. Who knew?

Us, too! Owen keeps asking why snowmen need hats. Presume not for warmth?

Think it must be style choice.

In that case they need fashion help. Would start with carrot nose.

What veg would you suggest?

There is a brief pause while Sian considers this.

Beetroot.

Snowmen with bulbous red noses? Like giant, flying alcoholics?

OK, maybe jalapeño pepper.

Seriously?

Always fancied guys with hooked noses.

Think you might be in the minority there.

Owen also asking why they have no willy.

Think maybe they're asexual.

There's another brief pause on Sian's end.

Will let you explain. Maybe wait a few years.

Thanks.

Ran into L at gym. He asked after you.

Bastard.

Apparently, he and trainer are history.

Couldn't care less.

Really?

Really.

As I type this I realize it's not true. A part of me is secretly delighted that Lionel's new relationship has gone awry so quickly. Perhaps he will come to recognize that novelty and constancy are like yin and yang: one cannot exist without the other, and you need both to make a relationship work.

Sian's response pings on my screen.

Good. 'Cause I told him you already hooked up with tall, classy Danish guy.

I look over at Malcolm. He *is* quite classy. And he is definitely tall. As well as being male. So that's pretty much spot on. But I think he and Peggy are already an item.

Suddenly all five dogs swivel their heads toward the door. I hear a faint noise outside, behind the rousing orchestral score on screen, and realize that the twins are baying in their run behind the house. The sound is rare enough to make the hairs stand on the back of my neck. The twins have never barked like this before, so I grab a jacket and race out into the night, slamming the door behind me.

By the time I reach their enclosure Romulus and Remus have gone almost ominously quiet. They stand like statues at the gate, ears alert, hackles raised. But the lock on the pen is intact and they seem unharmed. I stop short and look around to see what first aroused them, but can discern nothing in the darkness. "What is it, guys?" I ask.

Remus whimpers slightly, then lies down with a grunt, as if to say, *You're too late.* I open the cage and step inside, squatting down to give them both a stroke. It was probably a badger, I decide. But then I hear an engine roar into life in the distance, followed by the sound of a car screeching away. By the time I extract myself from the cage and circle round to the front of the house, I see only tail-lights disappearing down the road. Someone was here, I think, and whoever it was disturbed the twins. As I turn to go inside, I look across the yard and see that the kennel doors all stand wide open, like darkly gaping teeth. Whoever it was, they're definitely not interested in me.

They're after the dogs.

chapter
19

I sleep uneasily, which is to say not much at all, and the next morning when I ring Jez there's no answer. I leave a vague message, asking her to call. But when I check my e-mail, I find a hasty message from her, explaining that Eloise has booked a surprise dogsled excursion for two nights over Christmas, somewhere even more remote, and she is likely to be out of mobile range until they return on Boxing Day.

A part of me is relieved—I don't want to dampen her festivities. Besides, I have very little concrete information to offer, beyond the fact that someone has been snooping round the kennels. I decide the dogs will be safe with me as long as they remain in the house; clearly the twins can look after themselves outside in the run.

Anyway, what sort of person commits a crime on Christmas Eve? Surely even criminals observe the holidays?

Later, when I escort the dogs out to the paddock, another problem surfaces: Peggy behaves like a lunatic, roaming from spot to spot, pawing frantically at the near-frozen earth, as if she is burying invisible bones. Malcolm trails obediently behind her, his giant, putty-white brow furrowed with alarm. Judd, Hulk, and Slab cut her a wide berth, as if they know she is having a bad day, while Romulus and Remus stand stiffly at the gate, guarding the road like muscular canine sentries. When we finish, I consider bringing the twins in the house with us for protection, but decide against it. Seven dogs in one kitchen definitely feels like too many cooks.

Once back inside Peggy declines breakfast, sniffing at her bowl listlessly, then waddling away. Malcolm and I eye her suspiciously, while Judd waits a moment, then sidles over and casually wolfs down her portion. For the next hour, Peggy refuses to settle, drifting about the kitchen restlessly, panting and glassy-eyed. Eventually I coax her over to the maternity corner and she burrows her nose repeatedly in the blankets I have laid down, deliberately (and perversely, it seems to me) messing them up. I think about ringing Cal, but he was so dismissive the last time, I decide to ring Valko instead. When he answers, I hear grunting in the background.

"Valko? Are you OK?"

"Yes. Am fine."

"What's that noise?"

"Is pigs."

Ah. I can almost feel Valko blushing through the phone. "I am help Stella," he adds awkwardly. *Sure you are. With what, exactly?*

"I'm worried about Peggy," I tell him. "You couldn't come over, could you?"

Ten minutes later I watch with relief as Stella's truck pulls into the drive. As they climb out, I see that she's carrying a large, dark green plastic toolbox. Once inside she deposits the box on the kitchen table with a flourish.

"Farrowing kit," she announces.

"Which is . . . ?" I ask.

"Technically, for birthing piglets. But whelping puppies is much the same. They all have four legs and a tail," she says with a shrug. She opens the lid and inside I see a bewildering array of equipment: rubber hoses, suction bulbs, scalpels, clippers, syringes. She rummages around for a moment and pulls out a long digital thermometer, holding it up. "First things first. If she's about to whelp, her temperature will let us know." She walks over to where Peggy lies panting in the corner and strokes her abdomen for a moment, before moving to her bottom and quickly lifting her tail, shoving the thermometer up her bum. I laugh a little nervously, hastily looking away so as to give Peggy some dignity.

"Hadn't quite realized it would be rectal," I joke. Stella gives me a look that suggests I am dim beyond measure.

"You can't exactly ask a bitch to stick out her tongue," she says. *Fair point. Though I know some bitches who would.*

"If her temperature drops below thirty-seven degrees, you can expect labor to start within forty-eight hours."

"Perfect," I mutter. *Merry Christmas!*

The three of us wait anxiously for the thermometer to beep. Peggy's eyes dart around worriedly, as if to say: *Is this going to take long? Because it's already kind of crowded down there.*

When it finally does, Stella carefully withdraws it and squints down at the window. "Thirty-six point four."

"Oh God," I say, a volcano of panic rising up inside me. Stella stands, wiping the thermometer with a tissue *(thank goodness)* and returning it to the kit before placing a reassuring hand on my arm.

"Relax. Dogs have been giving birth for millennia."

"Not in my kitchen."

"Peggy's an old pro."

"Shouldn't we ring Cal?" I say quickly to Valko, who shrugs in response.

"If I were you I'd lay in some snacks and a few box sets and put your feet up," says Stella. "The litter might not appear for another few days. And you might never need the vet."

"Really?" I feel a twist of disappointment. *Surely we'll need the vet? Or maybe it's just me who will need the vet . . .*

"With any luck they'll pop out like poop," says Stella with a broad smile.

Nice image. Thanks for that one.

"Cal said the litter was large," I say. "How large would that be, exactly?"

Stella looks at Peggy and shrugs. "Eight? Ten?"

Ten little canines? Surely there can't be that many little bodies inside her?

"They won't all come at once. She'll have contractions in between each one, so the whole thing could take several hours. And don't worry about the afterbirth," she adds, nodding toward Peggy. "Mum will take care of all that. Just keep her clean and comfortable."

Doggy afterbirth? Please tell me that is not a thing.

I watch in desperation as Stella and Valko pull on their coats and move toward the door.

Generally speaking, I am not good with blood, guts, or unsavory matter; pain makes me extremely anxious, even when it is not my own. As they climb into the truck I must suppress the desire to fling myself out the door after them. Once they have gone, I experience a minor panic attack; black spots dance before my eyes. I lower myself into the recovery position, take deep breaths, and tell myself forcefully to get a grip. Eventually, my vision returns. I move over to Peggy and kneel down in front of her. She is panting steadily, her eyes bulging, as if she can't quite believe she's landed herself in such a tight spot. I place a hand gingerly on her abdomen, which feels like an overstuffed Christmas stocking, and she looks up at me balefully.

"Whoever he was," I say. "I hope he was worth it."

I ring Sian, who rallies appropriately. "Right," she says with brisk efficiency. "First things first. You need to pack a birth bag."

"We're not going anywhere, Sian."

"Fine. But you still need to stock up on supplies."

I explain about the farrowing kit.

"No, I mean like snacks, extra cushions, rawhide, tennis balls."

"She's hardly going to want to play fetch during labor."

"The tennis balls are for massaging her spine. Works a treat. Trust me."

"Um. Right." *Sian has clearly been at the Coco Pops too long.*

"So you think she'll be hungry?" I ask.

"Ravenous. And thirsty. She'll need lots of water. Straws are good."

"Except she has no *lips*."

"Fine. But make sure she stays hydrated."

"OK. What is the rawhide for?"

"To bite down on. Helps you stay on top of the pain."

"You chewed on rawhide during labor?"

"It was either that or the midwife's arm."

"Oh God. I'm not sure I can do this," I say, suddenly feeling nauseous.

"You don't have to. She does."

Good point.

"But what if they get stuck?"

"Gravity. Works wonders. Just keep her on her feet."

Eventually Peggy falls into a deep sleep, her massive belly looming in front of her like a zeppelin. Malcolm lies facing her, unblinking, his giant brow crinkled with concern. I channel surf for a while, unable to settle on anything for more than a few minutes at a time, and at half past eleven Hugo turns up, as arranged. He has promised to be here when his consignment arrives. He enters the kitchen clutching a large carton of eggnog and a bunch of lilies, which he thrusts in my direction a little awkwardly. "What are these for?" I say cautiously.

"To express my immense gratitude."

"I don't want your gratitude, Hugo. Immense or otherwise."

"Nonetheless, you have it," he insists.

I sigh and put the lilies in water, the eggnog in the fridge. "When are they coming?"

"Who?" he asks insouciantly.

"You know who. Your furry, four-footed friends."

"Soon, I think," he says, glancing at his watch.

"Coffee?"

"No, thanks." He fumbles for his keys and begins to sidle toward the door.

"Hugo, where are you going?" I ask with alarm.

"Just popping out on a quick errand. I'm afraid I've been tasked with fetching Constance's grandmother from the station."

"Why can't Constance do it?"

"She and her mother are busy trimming the tree. They've gone all Teutonic on me. You know, stringing cranberries, dried orange slices, wax candles. The lot."

"Hugo, you are *not* leaving me here on my own to take delivery of the alpacas."

"You'll be fine. Just turn them loose in the paddock. I'll be back later to check on them. I promise."

I sigh. "Are they paid for?"

"Not entirely. I've paid a deposit. But the balance is cash on delivery." He removes a bulging white envelope from inside his coat pocket and hands it to me.

I look at it askance.

"How much is in here?" I ask.

He hesitates. "I'd rather not say," he says coyly.

"Hugo?"

"Enough to fund a small skirmish in Central America."

"Good grief. They'd better be well behaved," I say.

"I've been assured they're the finest alpacas money can buy."

As Hugo drives away, I finger the inch-thick packet of cash and wonder how far it would get me. Costa Rica is meant to be lovely at this time of year. I've always longed to see the cloud forest. I glance at my watch. If I left now, I could be at Heathrow in less than three hours.

Then I look over at Peggy, who has risen from her slumber and is now panting like an Olympic athlete. She needs me. And maybe I need her. For the first time I feel the stirrings of genuine fondness well up inside me and I am suddenly bathed in goodwill. Perhaps I *am* a failed human, after all, and perhaps it is time to redeem myself. I move over to where she lies and crouch down beside her, stroking her fondly, and as I do her enormous belly suddenly rises up and convulses like a massive boa constrictor, and in the next instant she gives a giant heave, and a small dark sac pokes through from her bottom.

Apart from the point of exit, it is just as Stella said.

A little poop of puppy.

chapter 20

scream. And then I panic. Properly.

I have not readied the birthing bag.

I have not kept her hydrated.

I have not massaged her spine with a tennis ball.

I have not fed her snacks to keep her strength up.

I have done, quite literally, *nothing.*

But in spite of my ineptitude, Peggy has heroically produced a poop of puppy—all by herself. I stare at her in awe. She is a goddess, a woman warrior, a canine Valkyrie, and I am reduced to shell-shocked admiration. At a loss for how to help, I lean forward and place a limp hand of reassurance on her head.

"Come on, Peggy. You can do this," I mutter.

I wait, my breath frozen in my chest, as her massive belly seizes up again with another contraction, and in the next instant the remainder of the gelatinous sac slithers out from the space between her legs. Without hesitation, Peggy curls around on herself and noses the sac, then nibbles it gently, breaking the membrane and releasing its tiny wet inhabitant. A spotty alien tumbles out— plump, covered in not-quite fur, eyes screwed shut, limbs like little nibs. Apart from the color, it looks like a tiny Moomin. It lies there unmoving, like a discarded soft toy, and an icy stillness settles on the room. Both Malcolm and I lean forward, horrified. For several seconds, nothing happens. Peggy merely stares at the Moomin, then turns away, and Malcolm whimpers anxiously. I am not a religious person; indeed, I cannot remember the last time I set foot in church, but right now I say a little prayer for the tiny inert form in front of me, promising God that I will never, ever cross the road again to avoid a devout young man clutching religious pamphlets on Oxford Street.

Just let the damn puppy survive.

Exhausted, Peggy lies back down again, as if she has forgotten that she has just shed another life-form. She lies there for a moment in a sort of daze, panting and blinking, and just when I think we might have to intervene, she startles up and turns back to the lumpen shape behind her. At once she begins to worry it diligently and repeatedly with her tongue, as if she can somehow lick it into being. *And lo!* Somewhat miraculously, it works! After thirty seconds or so of assiduous licking, at about the point where both Malcolm and I are practically witless with apprehension, the tiny puppy suddenly coughs and splutters into life, lifting its little quivering head. It shivers, then sneezes, and I laugh out loud with joy. Even Malcolm judders with surprise, then looks decidedly relieved.

I reach a tentative hand out to finger the baby-soft, warm pelt.

At once the puppy senses me, moves its tiny nose toward my hand, nuzzling blindly and instinctively, seeking sustenance, or maybe just connection. Suddenly Peggy's rear end gives another massive heave and a fistful of membrane and fluid spews out, together with a tangled line of cord. *Oh dear Lord.* Malcolm and I recoil involuntarily, as if we are watching a scene from a horror film. All at once the room fills with a slightly rank smell that is both sweet and sickly, and my stomach heaves uneasily.

And then, with nary a thought, with not even the *slightest* ounce of hesitation, Peggy the beagle dispatches with the afterbirth in the most efficient way possible. Just as Stella said she would.

And I nearly lose my breakfast. Just as Peggy wolfs down hers. As Malcolm and I watch her swallow the last bit of cord, an internal gong of relief sounds somewhere deep inside me. Because I know with utter certainty that I will never, *ever*, have to do the same. In that moment I decide that I've never appreciated being Homo sapiens more. I may well be a dog person.

But thank God I'm not a dog.

After ward, we are exhausted. Malcolm and Peggy and I lie on the floor, wrapped in a postnatal stupor that is bizarrely reminiscent of after-sex fatigue. The only one who is lively is the puppy, who has somehow managed to blindly feel its way to Peggy's tummy and is valiantly struggling to suckle, making tiny squeaks and adorable grunts as it bashes its nose against one teat after another. Peggy occasionally sniffs at it, but mostly leaves it to do as it pleases. I admire her mindless approach to parenting.

The afternoon passes in a long miasma of labor. We rest, we wake, Peggy squeezes out another puppy, we worry it into life, then we collapse; after which, we repeat the entire process again. Over the course of several hours I lose all sense of time. The only thing I keep track of is the puppies, who burst forth from Peggy's bottom at regular intervals in a seemingly endless stream. I do my best to keep her hydrated and feed her treats between births, which she wolfs down eagerly. But when I try to run a tennis ball down her spine, she almost snaps at me. *Fair dues.*

By half past four, there are seven little black-and-white Moomins lined up along her belly, jostling blindly for milk. Peggy's teats have become engorged over the course of the afternoon and are now practically bursting with milk. She lies back and lets the puppies do as they will. She no longer pants and seems much calmer, as if her work is finished, and I peer down at her belly. It has definitely lost most of its bulk.

Are we done here?

I have not eaten all day, nor have I taken the other dogs out. Miraculously, Judd, Hulk, and Slab have lain quietly on their beds by the door all afternoon, their eyes averted, as if they know that birth is a very private affair. Malcolm is asleep, exhausted from his vigil. I rise and put the kettle on, and as I do I hear a knock at the door. I turn and see an old man with a snow-white beard and bright red cheeks peering in at me through the glass. He wears a scarlet cloche-style wool hat. For a split second I cannot help myself: *Santa Claus!* Then I gather my wits and open the door, taking in the battered wool blazer, faded olive corduroys, and knee-high Wellington boots. On top of that he has the largest hands I have ever seen, with fingers like enormous chafed sausages.

"Can I help you?" I ask.

"Guid evenin'," he says in a broad Scottish accent.

"Um. Hello," I say tentatively.

"We had a wee holdup, or we would've been here oors ago."

I stare at him blankly. *We?* The Scottish Santa senses my confusion. He beams at me, then jerks his giant thumb over his shoulder, where I can just make out an old, dark green Land Rover parked out by the paddock, with a small, white horse trailer attached.

"Ye ordered two alpacas?" he says.

Where, oh where is Hugo? In the course of the afternoon I have completely forgotten about him, not to mention his four-footed friends. I follow Scottish Santa out to the horse trailer and he unlatches the back and flings open the door. Inside, two enormous nut-brown creatures peer down at me, their small, round heads perched atop elegant, elongated necks. Their eyes are dark and large, framed by ridiculously long lashes, and their coats are shaggy and luxurious. They shift around uneasily when they see me, bumping off each other like giant marbles, their hooves scrabbling noisily on the metal base of the trailer.

"Easy does it, lads," cautions the bearded man, reaching inside for some harnesses coiled on the floor.

Lads? Couldn't Hugo at least have bought females?

"They're going to need a wee drink and some supper. I've brought some hay to start ye off." He waves at the paddock.

I nod mutely as he pulls out a long metal ramp, then clips the harnesses onto each of the animals. They are surprisingly light on their feet, skipping daintily down the ramp and into the paddock, where he turns them out. They both trot a few feet, then wheel around to stare at us, blinking. One of them works its mouth anxiously in a sort of circular rotation. I watch as Scottish Santa unloads a large bale of hay and deposits it in a corner of the paddock, then looks around. "Have ye sorted out some water?" he asks.

"Um . . . not yet."

"They'll be wanting plenty of it. Make sure it's clean and fresh."

"OK," I say, nodding. *Where the hell is Hugo?* If anyone is going to cart gallons of clean water out to the paddock, it should be him. I watch as Scottish Santa packs up the ramp and closes the back of the trailer. He turns back to me.

"So," he says expectantly, clapping his massive hands together with a merry twinkle in his eye.

"Yes?" I ask.

"I'll be wanting the balance of payment now. Cash on delivery?"

"Oh! Right. Yes, of course." I pull the fat envelope out of my pocket and hand it across, thinking ruefully that I will probably never see the cloud forest. Scottish Santa opens the envelope and quickly thumbs through the bills, then nods and stuffs them in his jacket pocket.

"Been a pleasure. Look after them. They're good lads. Won't give you any trouble." He starts to turn away.

"Are they OK with dogs?" I ask quickly.

"Aye. They're OK with most things." I watch as he climbs into the Land Rover. "Except badgers," he adds thoughtfully. "They've a passionate dislike of badgers."

"Are you driving straight back to Scotland now?" I ask.

He smiles and nods.

"Promised the missus I'd be home in time fer Christmas."

Scottish Santa touches his hat and then drives off with a cheery wave. Once he is gone, I turn back to the alpacas. I walk up to the gate and stretch out a hand. They eye me warily for a moment, then one of them takes a few steps forward. Eventually he comes close enough for me to touch, and I let him sniff my open palm for a moment, then fondle each spear-shaped ear, before stroking the fur on his neck. It is dense and silky and I bury my hand in it. The alpaca looks at me, his dark eyes bright and inquisitive. I realize that I forgot to ask their names. But names, at least, I am good at.

I will call them Nick and Noel.

When I return to the house I go at once to check on Peggy, who is panting again and glassy-eyed. The puppies are asleep in a tangled heap by her side, but something in her demeanor alarms me. I stoop down and splay my hands across her abdomen. There is a hard lump on one side and I know instinctively that something is wrong. I quickly ring Cal's mobile, willing him to answer, but eventually it goes through to his voicemail. It is Christmas Eve; no doubt he is out carousing with friends or family. I leave a garbled message telling him that something is wrong with Peggy, then return to her and splay my hands across her belly.

As I do, I feel another massive contraction. I wait a few moments to see what happens, but there is no sign of anything. "Come on, Peggy," I mutter. Peggy pants and pants and I hear

Sian's voice in my ear. *Keep her hydrated.* I grab her water bowl and practically shove her nose in it, but she twists away and refuses to drink. Another contraction sweeps across her abdomen and Peggy whimpers, but once again, nothing emerges. *Gravity.* I reach out and grab Peggy's collar. "Up you get," I say loudly. "Come on, Peggy." I coax her onto her feet, holding on to her sides, and force her to walk a few steps, which she does, haltingly. And just then I see the telltale sac burst through from between her legs. "That's it," I say encouragingly. I reach behind to catch the pup, and after one more contraction it slides warm and wet onto my hand. Peggy buckles then, lying back down on her side, and I lay the sac gently in front of her to nibble. She looks at it, dazed, and for a moment I'm afraid she won't even try, but then she tears at the membrane with her teeth and a scrawny pup tumbles forth. It is smaller than the others and deathly still. Peggy noses it for a moment, but does not try to lick it, then she lies back down and shuts her eyes.

"No!" I say desperately. "Come on! You can't just leave it." But Peggy does nothing, and the tiny pup just lies there motionless, little more than a sack of bones and some skin. I grab a clean dishcloth and carefully pick up the puppy, cleaning the mucous from its face and nose, then rubbing it gently with the fabric. For a long minute nothing happens. I peer at its tiny muzzle.

Perhaps I should try mouth to mouth? How exactly would I do that?

I blow warm air onto it instead, and suddenly, without warning, the puppy splutters into life. I cradle it gently for a moment, making sure it is breathing, then hold it in front of Peggy's nose for her to see. She gives it a few halfhearted licks, then collapses again, and I push the puppy right up to one of her engorged teats. After a moment it opens its tiny mouth and begins to suckle.

God in heaven, please can we be finished now?

Just then I see headlights in the drive and hear a car pull up outside. *Hugo! The rotter! High time, too!* I rise from the floor and cross over to the door, only to come face-to-face with a pair of ludicrously blue eyes.

chapter
21

open the door. "You're too late," I say. Cal's face instantly blanches.

"Peggy?" he asks anxiously.

I nod.

"What's happened?!"

I step to one side and Cal dashes across the room to where Peggy lies snoring in blissed-out postnatal exhaustion, a mound of pups wriggling around her belly like a pile of plump mealworms.

Cal stops short and turns to me.

"Wow. You did it," he says in a stunned voice. Clearly, he did not think I was equal to the task. I shrug. *Technically, Peggy did it.* But I am happy for him to think otherwise.

"Are the pups OK?" he asks, dropping down on his hands and knees. One by one he picks up the puppies, examining them carefully, wiggling their stubby limbs, lifting their little tails, and peering inside their mouths. Finally, when he gets to the smallest, he frowns. "This one might not make it," he says doubtfully, shaking his head. I drop down beside him and gently remove the pup from his grasp.

"*Bah, humbug,*" I say stubbornly. "Of course he will." I rub my finger over the little pup's belly and it sneezes. When I look up, Cal is watching me.

"Job well done," he says quietly.

"So much for your diagnostic skills," I reply with a smile.

"Not the first time I've been wrong," he admits. Suddenly I have the impression that we are now on a new topic. I flush slightly.

"Guess it was a good thing I was here."

"I guess it was." He stares at me and I feel my insides do a giant stadium wave. I swear, this man has the power to incapacitate me with nothing more than a glance. I put the puppy gently down and rise to my feet a little awkwardly. Cal, too, stands.

"So . . . what now?" I say, motioning toward the pups.

"Keep them warm. Keep the area clean. Give Peggy plenty of food and water. She'll do the rest."

"OK," I say, nodding. Cal suddenly shoots me an odd look.

"Why are there two alpacas out in the paddock?" he asks.

Ah. Yes. Why indeed? My mind races through the possible answers. Clearly a revised version of the truth is needed.

"I'm just boarding them temporarily," I say quickly. "On behalf of a friend," I add. Cal frowns.

"Does Jez know?" he asks. *None of your business!*

"Absolutely," I say. *Teeny-weeny little lie.*

"Have you got water out there? Alpacas need a lot of water."

Enough with the damn water already! Not to mention the patronizing tone.

"We've got it covered," I say.

"We?"

"My friend and I."

Just then I hear a car door slam outside, followed by the crunch of footsteps. We both turn to see Hugo peering in at the window, wearing his giant gold anaconda scarf. Cal turns back to me.

"Is that your friend?" he asks quietly.

I hesitate.

"It might be." My voice is barely more than a whisper. Cal looks at me for a long moment, then takes a deep breath, and lets it out slowly.

"Aren't you going to let him in?"

I sigh, then go to open the door. Hugo grins broadly and points toward the paddock. "They're here! Why didn't you call me?" he exclaims, stepping into the kitchen.

"They've only just arrived."

"Aren't they splendid?" he asks, beaming. He looks past me to Cal. "Excellent! We could use some expert advice." Cal is standing with his arms folded across his chest, his sleeves rolled up three-quarters of the way. I can just make out his forearms. Even Angry Cal has glorious forearms, I think regretfully, which after tonight I will probably never get to fondle.

"What do you know about alpacas?" Hugo asks Cal in a jaunty tone.

"They make great sweaters," says Cal stonily.

"Ha!" Hugo turns to me. "Well, you're a little ahead of us. Right now we just want to keep them alive."

"You need to sort out some water in the paddock," says Cal.

Hugo nods solemnly. "Right. I'll get straight on it."

"And they'll need hay. The grass out there won't be sufficient to keep them in winter. Beyond that they should be fine," Cal says, and I detect a note of weariness in his voice. He turns to me and nods toward Peggy. "Keep an eye on her," he says.

"OK." I stare at him.

Don't leave. Inevitably, Cal moves toward the door. Once there, he pauses.

"Happy Christmas," he says, his eyes sliding up to mine.

"You, too," I reply.

Then he goes, leaving me with fifteen dogs, two alpacas, a giant flat-screen TV, one clueless-but-well-meaning suitor, and a much-diminished heart.

Hugo spends the next half hour lugging fresh water out to the paddock. He finds a giant barrel and fills it nearly full by carrying bucket after bucket out to it. When he is finished, he comes back into the kitchen and sinks down onto the sofa. "Thirsty chaps!" he exclaims. I am stretched out beside the puppies, running the tip of my finger down the runt's back. Every few minutes he gives a little shiver. I am thinking that this puppy holds my entire future. Clearly, I was not designed to bond with other humans. I am fit only for animal consumption.

"So," says Hugo. "Are you going to give them names?"

I frown. I have managed to screw up most aspects of my life thus far. Whatever I choose, it will need to be easy to remember:

there are eight puppies, after all. Perhaps something that hearkens back to the occasion of their birth. And then it hits me because, in fact, it is perfectly obvious. The little one I will call Rudy.

And the other seven, just as soon as I can tell them apart, will be Dasher, Dancer, Prancer, Vixen, Comet, Cupid, and Blitzen.

Once Hugo leaves, I take the dogs out to the paddock. As we approach the gate, I spy Nick and Noel grazing about twenty meters away. When they hear us coming, they stop and raise their heads in unison, as if an invisible puppeteer has pulled a string. Malcolm is the first to see them and stops dead, his enormous nostrils quivering with alarm. I give him a reassuring pat on the head, then go to open the gate. Slab and Peggy only manage to walk a few feet inside before doing their business, then they lie down on the grass. Hulk takes one look at the alpacas and picks her way to the far side of the paddock in order to complete her toilette in privacy, but Judd is instantly curious. He approaches them casually, sniffing the grass in a repeatedly circular pattern until he is only a few feet away. Noel (or is it Nick?) watches him carefully, and when Judd is within striking distance the alpaca slowly leans forward, stretching his long neck down toward him. Judd remains very still, and for the briefest instant, their noses touch in an impromptu greeting. Then both animals return to sniffing the grass.

Simple! Humans take note.

Afterward, I hit the eggnog. Who knew a frothy mixture of sugar, rum, cream, and egg yolk could be so delicious? And because it has eggs, it must be nutritious, so I pour myself an extra-large second glass and pop a pepperoni pizza in the oven. Then I text a photo of Peggy and the pups to Sian. At once she replies:

OMG you did it!!!

Cannot take ALL credit . . .

Not bad for a novice!

Might set myself up as canine midwife.

Wouldn't give up the day job.

How's Owen? All ready for Father Christmas?

Delirious with excitement. Had to resort to drugs at bedtime.

Nice one. Mumsnet would be proud.

Am enjoying the smorgasbord he has laid out for FC.

Such as?

Carrot sticks, apple slices, pink marshmallows, and a large glass of whisky.

Nice combo. I'm guessing the latter was your idea?

I merely suggested that FC might be sick of milk by the time he got to ours.

Btw, in addition to 15 canines, am now proud minder of 2 alpacas.

Huh. Struggling to picture an alpaca.

Like a very tall sheep with an extra-long neck.

Are they as stupid as sheep?

Will have to let you know.

Later, when I have polished off the pizza and the entire carton of eggnog, I fall asleep on the sofa with Slab across my feet. My dreams are fueled by sweet rum and recent events: I dream of Nick and Noel flying through the sky, pulling the massive wooden TV crate in sleigh-like fashion. Scottish Santa sits inside the crate waving cheerily with his great, burly hands and shouting, *"Ho ho ho."*

When I wake in the morning, I have a stiff neck and a nasty hangover. My feet sting with pins and needles, as Slab is still sprawled across them. I look around: Peggy is snoring and the pups are curled against her side in a jumbled heap of tummies, tails, and tiny muzzles. Thankfully, the other dogs are quiet and I am so grateful I could weep. *God bless everyone!* I gingerly shift Slab off my legs so I can sneak upstairs and run a bath. I fill it to the brim with extra hot water and pour in loads of bath salts. As I sink down into the tub my neck muscles begin to uncoil and my rum-soaked head starts to unclog. I sigh with pleasure.

Happy Christmas to me!

And then I hear a loud knock at the kitchen door. Seriously? Who the hell comes calling early on Christmas morning? I decide to ignore it, but the second knock sounds even more insistent; really, it is more like someone banging. I sigh and scramble out of the tub, snatching a hot-pink towel off the radiator and hurling myself down the stairs, dripping wet and trussed up like a sausage roll. No doubt it is Hugo, come to water the alpacas, or maybe Valko. But as I round the corner into the kitchen I stop short. Cal is crouched over peering in through the window with his outrageously blue eyes. When he sees me in the skimpy towel he pops up like a jack-in-the-box, his cheeks instantly two bright spots of color. I consider turning tail but decide that it is too late. Instead, I gather what little dignity I have remaining and open the door. Cal looks me straight in the eye, trying not to glance at my moist cleavage. His face is practically on fire.

"Um. Happy Christmas," he says awkwardly.

What on earth is he doing here?

"Happy Christmas," I reply cautiously. He takes a deep breath.

"Sorry. I . . . caught you at a bad moment." He gestures toward the towel.

No kidding.

"No problem." My voice is calm and cucumber cool.

"I was just passing. One of Stella's sows got cut on the fence, so I thought I'd better look in on Peggy." He is clearly mortified. I fling the door open wide.

"Be my guest."

He swallows and nods, struggling to avert his eyes. The towel I have chosen is not overlarge; I reckon it covers approximately 40 percent of my body, and we are both clearly aware of the bits it does and does not conceal. Cal slides past me and crosses directly to Peggy in a way that says he means all business. He squats down, palpates her abdomen, checks her heart rate, then quickly picks up each of the puppies and examines them, before hastily standing up again.

"All good," he says with brusque efficiency.

"Fine," I say. "Thank you," I add. He nods and moves toward the door, eyes glued to the floor. At the last second he pauses and clears his throat, still looking at his shoes.

"Um. There's something else. Gerry would like to invite you to lunch," he says in a stilted voice. "Unless you have other plans."

"Gerry," I repeat.

"Yes," he says. I wait for him to say something else, perhaps something about him, but his mouth is clamped in a tight line.

"Today?" I ask. *Just want to be sure.*

"Yes."

"So . . . you mean . . . Christmas lunch?" *Because I really do need to be sure.*

"Yes," he says emphatically. "That's the idea," he adds. He is clearly more than a little exasperated. I hesitate for a moment, forcing him to wait.

"I assume you'll be there?"

He rolls his eyes. "Of course."

"But what about them?" I nod toward Peggy and the pups.

"Um, they're not invited."

"Will they be OK?"

"For a few hours? I should think so."

"Fine," I say. "Tell her I'd be pleased to accept." He stares at me.

"Fine," he says stiffly. Did I give the correct answer? I cannot tell if he is relieved or angry. "See you about one," he says, and practically dives out the door. I watch the Volvo disappear around the bend and, as I do, the first flakes of snow begin to drift from the sky. The long-promised blizzard has finally arrived, just in time for Christmas.

Hark the herald angels sing! Glory to the newborn me!
Never in my wildest dreams did I envisage the scene that has just unfolded. I climb the stairs slowly, replaying it in my head. Did Gerry force him to invite me? Or was he secretly keen? The man is like a human version of a Rubik's Cube: deceptive, frustrating, confounding. Basically, impossible. I sink back down into the bath, my heart banging like a bass drum in my chest, secretly hoping for the best. Perhaps my luck is finally changing for the better. *(The question is, what did I do to deserve it?)* But then, a far more important question lodges in my brain.

What in God's name will I wear?

After breakfast, and a quick sprint round the paddock with the dogs, I raid Jez's wardrobe. I plunge deep into the back, pulling out items I've never clapped eyes on before, and strewing them all over the bed. Among other things, I find a pair of silky magenta trousers circa 2010 (all pleated front and gathered legs), a slinky off-the-shoulder dress in black-and-white stripes (perhaps a little too va-va-voom for a day honoring the birth of Christ) and a pair of dark blue corduroy culottes that must date from Jez's uni days. In the end I settle on black tights, a simple A-line charcoal wool skirt (cut well above the knee but not indecent, bless you, Jez) and an emerald green crop top that feels vaguely seasonal but does not scream *Good Tidings!*

When I get back downstairs my phone lights up with a text. I see, with a sickening gut-lurch, that it's from Lionel. The message contains only two words:

Happy Christmas.

I stare down at the screen and feel myself yanked back in time. Suddenly I am back in Nunhead, confronting Lionel across the kitchen table; he is red-faced, earnest, and not quite contrite, and I am reeling with pain, shock, and indignation. It is not a happy memory, and certainly not one I care to revisit on Christmas morning. What is he doing, texting me out of the blue? Perhaps he is just being considerate, concerned that the holidays might be weighing heavily upon me? But knowing Lionel, this seems unlikely. What seems far more likely is that his new relationship has gone awry and he has begun to reconsider.

As if all that has transpired between us can be erased with a few keystrokes.

I contemplate this for a few moments. If I could undo all that went wrong between Lionel and me, with the mere press of a button, would I choose to do so? My mind flicks back through the memories: Lionel and I on a ski holiday that first winter, we spent more time horizontal than on the slopes; Lionel and I both sick with flu over the holidays, when we missed our family celebrations and ended up toasting each other with mugs of Lemsip on Christmas morning; Lionel organizing a surprise anniversary picnic in Battersea Park, when after sinking two bottles of champagne, he insisted we re-create the egg-and-spoon race, with predictable consequences.

These happy memories flicker like decades-old home movies: they are faded, crackling, fuzzy. And not surprisingly, they end abruptly, swallowed by a host of more recent, painful ones— casually disapproving remarks, caustic retorts, abrupt arguments that bloomed out of nowhere, lonely evenings spent texting to no avail, and grudging sex. These later memories loom all too large and, unlike the earlier ones, they are crystal clear, like watching big-screen telly, with surround sound.

It does not take long to reach a verdict, and the answer is definitely no.

So that leaves only the question of how to respond to his text. I could oh so easily ignore it, especially given the timing—most people would be midway through their Christmas-morning festivities. How irritating that I am not; almost as if he knew I was on my own. I could send a heavily barbed reply, replete with expletives—a very tempting prospect indeed. Or I could pretend it is nothing more than an ordinary holiday greeting and return it in kind. This is by far the most civilized response, so in an effort to seize the moral high ground, I opt for number three.

You too, I type.

After a moment he pings back a reply.

I miss you.

I stare down at the gray bubble of letters, and as I do another gray bubble appears beneath it.

xx

And in the space of an instant, I swan dive off the moral high ground. *No, sir!* He does not get to *xx* me after all this time! What about the broken kettle? What about the rowing machine? These things cannot be undone with a few character strokes. I type a furious reply.

You LEFT me! Remember? You said our relationship had run its course.

In a matter of moments another gray bubble appears.

Not the first time I've been wrong!

I stare down at it. It's the exclamation point that wrangles most.

I quickly type:

Has it occurred to you that this is yet another instance when you are wrong?

His answer comes with lightening swiftness:

No.

That's the thing about Lionel: always so sure of himself. Even now.

So I do the only sensible thing I can think of. I turn off my phone.

And cuddle a puppy.

By lunchtime there is almost an inch of snow on the ground. It is the wet, cloying variety, with great big flakes that flutter down like damp butterflies. I don Wellingtons (country chic!) and an array of outer garments, then trudge outside to clear off the Škoda. But when I climb inside and turn the key, the engine coughs weakly, then refuses to turn over.

Nooooo.

I rest my head on the steering wheel in despair for a moment, then gather my wits and consider my options. There is no chance of a cab in this part of the world on Christmas Day. I could walk, but it will take me at least forty-five minutes, by which time I will be more than fashionably late, and my newly blow-dried hair will be ruined. I could ring Cal and ask him to collect me, but somehow that feels a little too damsel-in-distress.

So there really is only one option remaining.

I grin madly as I trudge behind the house to the run. Cal will go mental if I arrive in the sulky, but it will be worth it to see the look on his face. I grab the harnesses out of the shed and call to the twins, who as usual are more than eager to oblige. After they've relieved themselves, I hook them up and climb inside the sulky—

the only trick will be getting them to go in the right direction. The good news is that, between the weather and the holiday, there will be virtually no traffic on the roads, so we should have a clear run into the village. I release the brake and let the dogs go, pulling hard on the reins to steer them left out of the drive rather than right, and the sulky careers out onto the lane. In fact, it handles beautifully on the snow, better than I could have hoped for, and arguably much better than the Škoda would have done. Hurrah!

As we barrel down the road, the snow pelts my face and eyes, but the surrounding countryside is undeniably picturesque blanketed in white. In a grudging nod to my mum, as I flew out the door I grabbed the bobble hat she sent me and I have to admit that I'm grateful for it. The twins pull as if their lives depend on it, relishing the opportunity to run: clearly snow must be hardwired into their DNA. We reach the outskirts of Cross Bottomley quickly. As I navigate the sulky through the quiet lanes in my festive bobble hat *(Ho ho ho!)* I feel a vague sense of euphoria, which may or may not be the spirit of Christmas. By the time we reach Gerry's, the twins and I are breathless from the ride. I pull on the brakes and the twins come to a halt, panting hard.

As we do, Cal appears from behind the house carrying a shovel. He freezes when he sees us, then shakes his head, glaring.

"I can explain," I call out.

"You are certifiable!"

"The Škoda was dead!"

"So you risked your life instead of calling me?"

"We were fine. The roads were empty." I grin at him. He looks at me and his expression eases. Perhaps I even detect a glint of grudging admiration in his eyes. I climb out of the sulky, and when I am finally standing in front of him, staring straight into the crevice of his gaze, I nearly tumble into it. How is it that I lose my bearing so quickly in his presence? A snowflake lands on his nose and I reach up with my mitten and dab at it lightly. Cal raises his face to the sky and laughs.

Just then Gerry opens the front door. "Happy Christmas!" she calls out. Her eyes sweep to the sulky. "How marvelous! And very eco!"

I shoot a smug glance at Cal and he raises a dubious eyebrow.

Once inside I see with relief that I am not the only guest. Dibber is standing by the fire chatting to a middle-aged man wearing a clerical collar, and an elderly woman, wearing a pale pink wool suit worthy of the queen, rises at once from an armchair to greet us. Gerry shepherds me into the room and introduces me around, before placing a glass of something fizzy in my hands. The cleric is the local vicar, fresh from Christmas service, and the older woman is a well-to-do cousin who lives in a nearby village. Almost instantly Gerry marshals us into the dining room, where the table looks *amazing*. Fresh-cut holly has been artfully arranged down the center, and two silver candelabras with real candles throw a soft gold light around the room. A magnificently bronzed turkey rests on an enormous silver platter at one end, garnished with fresh orange slices and roasted chestnuts, and a large bowl of homemade cranberry sauce sparkles like rubies at the other. Other dishes festoon the table: caramelized Brussels sprouts, balls of sausage stuffing, roast parsnips, bread sauce, glazed carrots. My stomach genuinely gurgles at the sight of it all.

"You must have been cooking for days," I say to Gerry. She scoffs.

"Me? I'm not allowed anywhere *near* the kitchen at Christmas." She indicates Cal with a nod. I turn and see that Cal has donned a beige linen apron with a large stag's head on the front and is carrying a jug of gravy to the table.

Dear God, how I love a man in an apron.

"Untrue," Cal says to Gerry. "I let you peel the sprouts this year."

She smiles. "Oh, and I had to stir something while you went and sorted out Stella's sow," she reminds him.

"Bread sauce. Which you managed to burn," he says under his breath. "And I had to remake." Cal returns to the kitchen while the rest of us take our seats.

"I can barely fry an egg," confides Gerry. "My late husband did all the cooking. Cal learned from him." Cal enters again and sits down at one end of the table beside me. He picks up a bottle of red wine and offers me some.

"Just to be clear, she's lying. She *can't* fry an egg," he says. "She was living on Shreddies when I moved back."

"Shreddies are a perfectly good food," says Gerry staunchly.

Back from where? I wonder. I realize I know virtually nothing about this man, or his history.

"When was that?" I ask.

"Two years ago," says Cal. "Just after Dad died."

"Oh. I'm sorry." I turn to Gerry and offer her a sympathetic glance. She nods and gives a wave of her hand, while Cal continues pouring wine around the table.

"Where were you before that?" I ask, taking a sip of wine.

"London," he says breezily. I nearly spit the wine across the table and his eyebrows shoot up with glee.

London! The rotter!

"Cal did his veterinary training at the Royal College," says Gerry proudly. "Then stayed on to practice in London for several years."

"Where were you based?"

"Clapham, for the first five years," he says. "Then, later, Belsize Park."

South to north. Interesting. I wonder why. Newcomers to London are quick to grow roots, and even quicker to defend their neighborhoods: crossing the river is tantamount to heresy. By now, Gerry has joined Dibber and the others in conversation; Cal and I are left alone at our end of the table and the room instantly feels more intimate.

"Do you miss it?" I ask. "The hurly-burly of the city?"

"Not really, no."

There's a note of challenge in his voice, as if to say: *Should I?*

"I thought I would," he admits. "And was a little surprised when I didn't. But in the end I decided that London's something of a chimera. It's what we project onto it. And often, the picture in our head doesn't quite come together." He takes a sip of wine and once again I wonder about the subtext. There's a large chunk of this puzzle that I'm missing.

I watch as he rolls up his sleeves and picks up a long knife in preparation for carving—at once my mouth begins to water, but it is more the sight of his naked forearms than the turkey that is responsible. Cal sees me staring and smiles a little mischievously. "Dark or light?" he asks quietly. I shoot him a glance; the question feels oddly loaded.

Whichever. Just keep carving!

"Dark, please," I say politely. He nods assent.

"So . . . a *thigh?*" he says suggestively. I glance up at him and the corners of his mouth twitch.

"A thigh would be lovely, thank you," I say demurely. I watch as he carefully slices and deposits a thigh on my plate.

"Help yourself to sides," he says in a low voice, indicating the other dishes. "There's plenty. So don't hold back." He shoots me a glance, then stands up to pass a platter of turkey down the table.

Don't hold back? Am I imagining things? Or is he embarking on some sort of elaborate culinary foreplay here, right in front of the others? I help myself to potatoes and stuffing while he ensures that all the guests have been served turkey, then he sits back down beside me.

"Gravy?" he murmurs, picking up the jug.

"Yes, please," I reply. He pauses, holding the jug out in front of me.

"Shall I . . . *serve* you?" he asks, his voice practically dripping with innuendo. I nearly laugh out loud.

"Please do." I drop my eyes, trying not to smile.

"My pleasure," he murmurs, drizzling gravy slowly but liberally all over my plate in a manner that is almost obscene. Then he picks up the bowl of cranberry sauce. "Cranberry sauce?"

"Yes." My voice cracks slightly. A flush begins to seep slowly upward through my body, spreading to my neck and finally to my face.

"I think cranberry sauce is my favorite part of this meal," he confides quietly, scooping a large dollop onto my plate. "It's the perfect accompaniment. Sweet . . . but tart. Don't you agree?"

I can only nod mutely. He has actually robbed me of speech.

Cal sets the bowl down, then picks up the caramelized sprouts, serving me some. "Sprouts, on the other hand," he continues. "Earthy. Nutty. I like them with just that little bit of crunch. So that the flavor really *bursts* on your tongue when you bite down." He picks up his wineglass and looks at me.

I literally think I will ignite.

Then he raises his glass, his lips curling upward in a smile.

"Bon appétit," he says.

Enjoy.

And I do. It isn't just the sheer fact of his physical presence a few inches away—*I think I can smell his shampoo*—because the meal itself is divine. Food I have disliked for decades, nay an entire lifetime, has suddenly been reborn. Brussels sprouts roasted with garlic and fresh chili are worthy of actual worship, and the bread sauce is so delicious he could have served it alone, like porridge, and I would have been happy.

"As a medic I should probably warn you, that dish contains very little nutritional value," he says, pointing to the bread sauce. I pause, my fork halfway to my mouth.

"Nutrition is overrated," I say.

Cal laughs.

I do not know how I manage to survive the meal. It is simultaneously the most intoxicating and frustrating experience of my life. Cal eats with gusto, as do I—as if we cannot get enough, as if we are *starving*. By the end of the meal I am stuffed to the brim, but still desperately unsated. And I strongly suspect he feels the same. Over the course of ninety minutes I have conversed on all manner of topics with the others (cheese-rolling with Cousin Viv, trends in male facial hair with Dibber, religion and science with the vicar, Brexit with Gerry), but I am barely cognizant of what has been said—by me or anyone else. When Cal finally stands to clear the plates, I leap to my feet and insist on helping.

He does not demur.

Once in the kitchen, our hands laden with plates, we are finally alone. Cal looks at me and I see at once in the glare of the lights that his face is flushed. He dumps his plates on the counter and I do the same, then he turns to me, but in that same instant, Gerry comes bursting through the door. "Don't you dare touch those dishes," she announces loudly. Cal takes a step back from me and turns to her. "I'll do them later," says Gerry in a no-nonsense tone. "You've done enough."

"We're on it, Mum," he says weakly.

Boy, are we! We are so on it! If only she would leave.

"Absolutely not," she says, shaking her head. "Your work is done here. Go sit and relax. Bond with Dibber," she adds emphatically. Cal frowns and Gerry takes him by the shoulders, turns him round, and pushes him back into the dining room. After he's gone, she turns to me and smiles.

"Sorry about the heavy-handed parenting. He really can be stubborn sometimes." She begins rinsing and stacking the plates and I instantly move to her side to help, ever the well-trained guest.

"'Stubborn'?" I ask casually.

Gerry sighs.

"He's barely said three words to Dibber since he arrived," she confides.

"Ah."

"I can see that it's difficult for him. But he needs to understand that people change. *I've* changed. And what was right for me forty years ago isn't necessarily right for me now."

"I see." *Do I see? I really do not see. Does this entire family speak in code?*

"We both need to move on," she says, almost to herself.

Wait. Cal needs to move on? From what? Or, more important, from who?

"I'm sorry, I'm oversharing," she says with a laugh. "Sometimes your children tie you up in knots."

"I think my mother would say the same." *Understatement of the year.*

We carry on rinsing and loading the dishwasher for a moment and I decide to try another tack. "So, Cal moved back here after his father died?" I ask.

"Yes," she says. "It was a difficult time. He and Martin were very close. And while Martin's death wasn't sudden, it was no less . . . difficult. Cal never quite forgave himself for not picking up on the symptoms earlier. Martin had a rare form of bone cancer."

"I see."

"And then there was the Valerie problem." She sighs.

"'Valerie'?"

"Sorry, I thought you knew. Cal's ex-fiancée. She moved down here with him. And it worked out fine, for a time. They set up the practice together."

"What went wrong?" I ask.

Gerry hesitates. "I'm not entirely sure. I think she saw a side of him she hadn't known in London. At least, that's what she claimed. And maybe he realized that there were aspects of himself he'd lost during all those years in the city."

"So she left?"

Gerry nods. "She eventually broke things off and went back to the flat in Belsize Park."

Ah. The North London connection.

"And Cal stayed," I say.

"Yes. It was all very . . . unfortunate."

"How was he afterward?"

"He threw himself into his work. Which was probably the right strategy. And into looking after me. But it was a difficult time. He was still mourning Martin, of course. And missing the dog."

"The dog?"

"Valerie got the dog." She shrugs. "It was more her dog than his, originally. But Cal was very attached to it."

"I see."

Gerry sighs. "Cal's been very attentive this last year," she says hesitantly. As if she doesn't want to be disloyal.

"But it's time to move on," I say.

She looks at me and nods. I see her blink rapidly, then she shakes her head and smiles.

"I'm sorry," she says. "I just want him to be happy. I want us *both* to be happy." She gives a weak laugh, then turns back to the dishes.

"You know what Kant would say?" I ask. Gerry stops and peers at me.

"Immanuel Kant? The philosopher?" she asks. I nod.

"He says it's up to us to make ourselves happy."

She smiles at me, then touches my arm. "I like you," she says outright.

"I like you, too," I say, a little startled. "Thank you for inviting me." She picks up the kettle then and moves to fill it at the tap.

"Oh, that wasn't *my* idea," she says over her shoulder. "It was Cal's."

Cal's? My memory is crystal clear. *Gerry would like to invite you to lunch.*

Just then we hear singing from the other room. Gerry grins and puts the kettle on to boil, then we both return to the table, where we find Dibber strumming a tiny ukulele and singing "Silent Night" to the others. I slide into the seat next to Cal and glance over at him. He seems to be enjoying himself, so I relax a little. Gerry immediately joins in with Dibber, harmonizing, and after another moment both the vicar and Cousin Viv start to sing, too. I wait a moment, then lean over to Cal, until I am barely a few inches away.

"Why aren't you singing?" I whisper.

He grins. "Can't carry a tune," he whispers back.

"Says who?" I reply. He frowns then and gives a little shrug.

Then we both open our mouths and sing. Tunelessly.

We work our way through Dibber's repertoire, by which time it is almost twilight. It has been nearly three hours since I left Peggy and the pups, so I signal to Cal that I must go, and he instantly rises. I thank Gerry and say good-bye to the others. Cal offers to see me out. Outside, the snow has stopped and the evening looks set to be clear and cold. Romulus and Remus are curled up obediently where I left them, and they spring to life like windup toys, watching me expectantly. I hesitate, taking in the winter sunset, and feeling far less certain of Cal than I had while inside. Then I bend down to hitch the dogs to the sulky, while Cal kicks at the snow under his feet. When I'm finished, I rise and turn to him. "Thank you for inviting me," I say a little awkwardly.

He says nothing, merely stares at me, his mouth curled in a half-smile.

"What?" I ask. He shakes his head slowly.

"Everything looks different in the snow," he replies. "Except you."

Then he steps forward and my heart crashes around inside my chest. But as he draws near, we both hear the front door open and Gerry appears framed in the light of the doorway. "Charlie? You forgot your hat!" she calls, holding it aloft. Cal takes a step back and swipes a hand through his hair.

Nooooo.

"I'll fetch it," he murmurs.

OMG, if my lips do not make physical contact with this man soon they will shrivel and drop off.

He trots back up the path to the front door. As he does, I turn to see a car heading our direction on the snowy road, its headlights bearing down upon us. It slows right down as it draws near and suddenly I realize that it's the white van. In the next instant it passes and I peer inside to see the dark-haired man with the enormous mustache at the wheel; our eyes meet and I am certain he recognizes me. As the van pulls away it accelerates, and in that instant I understand where he's going. I glance desperately at Cal, who is now walking toward me with the bobble hat, a lascivious look in his eye.

"I have to go!" I say abruptly, jerking the sulky around so it is facing in the right direction, then jumping inside.

"What?!"

"Sorry! I have to get to the dogs!"

"The dogs are fine—" he starts to say.

"No! They're in danger! I can't explain."

"What?"

"There isn't time." I release the brake, take up the reins, and snap them hard, shouting at the dogs to run. For a split second, the twins look back at me, then instinct kicks in and they set off at a lunge. I grab the sulky to keep from tumbling out and we race off down the lane, leaving Cal openmouthed behind us. The white van has disappeared, but if we hurry we might just catch up with it. I curse my luck! But I cannot leave the dogs at the mercy of Mr. Mustache.

We career down the A road, my heart flailing like a trapped bird inside my chest, until finally we round the last bend in the road before Cozy Canine Cottages. When we do, my worst fears are confirmed as the white van is just pulling out of the driveway. As we approach, Mr. Mustache sees me coming and quickly spins around and speeds off in the opposite direction, his tires squealing. For an instant I do not know what to do—I am torn between checking on the dogs and following him in the sulky. But then I pull hard on the reins and the sulky jerks to a halt.

I race to the door and it is wide open. I am certain I locked it, so he must have either broken in or come through some other part of the house. I dash inside and the first thing I see is Malcolm standing squarely in front of Peggy; he is facing the door, ears back and hackles raised, as if in preparation for a fight and he looks truly menacing.

Good boy! Perhaps he's not a coward, after all.

When Malcolm sees me, his entire posture suddenly relaxes, and he gives a little wag of his tail. I cross over to Peggy, who is panting hard with alarm, and my eyes meet hers. I quickly count the pups, and much to my relief, all eight are there. Peggy looks anxious, but fine; I give her a reassuring pat, then turn to Malcolm and stroke my hand all the way down his massive back. "Well done, Malcolm," I tell him, even though he cannot hear me. "I knew I could count on you." Then I turn round to reassure the others.

That is when I see that Judd is gone.

chapter
22

I am a triple idiot. Here I was, terrified that Peggy and her litter would be stolen, when the most obvious target for thieves at Cozy Canine Cottages was Judd. I bend down to cuddle Slab and Hulk, who are cowering in the corner. "Don't worry," I tell them. "We'll find him." Though I have no idea how. Just then I hear a car door slam outside and Cal's face appears in the window, his angry blue eyes staring in at me. As I stand and cross the room to open it, his brow furrows and I realize that he isn't angry, but frightened. I open the door.

"Are you OK?" he asks anxiously.

I shake my head. "He's taken Judd," I say.

"Who?"

Mr. Mustache!

"The man in the white van that passed us. He's been snooping round the kennels for the past few days. I recognized him."

Cal's eyes widen. "Why didn't you tell me? Which one is Judd, anyway?"

"The Irish setter. He's a triple champion."

Cal hesitates. "Then he'll be worth stealing," he says.

"*How* worth stealing?"

"I'm not an expert, but his stud value could run into six figures."

Six figures! He's a dog! How can that be possible?

"Who's the owner?" he asks.

"Camilla somebody. Scarily posh. And suffers no fools."

"Perfect," he says grimly. "You'd better let her know. Hopefully she's insured." His eyes meet mine and I know we are both thinking the same thing.

Is Jez insured? Lord in heaven, please let Jez be insured!

"Do I have to? Can't I try to find him first?" Cal rolls his eyes.

"Charlie, you can't go messing about with criminals. It could be dangerous. You should ring the police."

"But it's Christmas. The police are hardly going to pull the stops out over a missing dog!"

"Just ring them."

"Fine." I sigh.

"Look, I'm sorry to leave like this, but I've got to get back to Mum and the others. I barely had time to explain. And anyway, I'm due to take Cousin Viv and the vicar home."

"Sure," I say, suddenly disheartened. "You go." He hesitates uncertainly, then reaches out and squeezes my hand.

"Don't worry. He can't have got far. The police will find him."

Cal leaves me to ring the police and promises to return later, once the guests have gone home. But when I call the emergency services I am politely informed that 999 is only for crimes in progress. The fact that Judd is still missing does not count, apparently. *Who knew?* The operator instructs me to ring the Devon and Cornwall nonemergency number instead, and when I do, the officer who answers sounds as if he has drawn the mother of all short straws for working on Christmas Day. The phone call does not go well.

Me: *My dog has been stolen. Well, he's not exactly my dog. I was looking after him for someone else.*

Police: *Madam, are you certain that the owner simply didn't come and fetch their dog?*

Me: *I'm positive. Someone broke into my house! And I saw a suspicious man fleeing the scene!*

Police: *OK. Have you got a description of the man or the vehicle?*

Me: *He has a mustache! A big mustache. Not like . . . a little chevron. More like . . . a walrus.*

Police: (slowly) *A walrus mustache. Is that all? Age? Height? Race?*

Me: *Well, it was dark, so I couldn't really say for sure, but I'm pretty sure he's white. And maybe mid-thirties. Or thereabouts. I've seen him hanging around here before, so I suspect he's local. And he drives a white van.*

Police: *A white van. Not many of those in Devon.*

Hang on! Is he mocking me?

Me: *But the mustache. That could help.*
Police: *I'm afraid we don't keep a criminal database of facial hair.*

He is definitely mocking me!

Me: *What about fingerprints? He broke into my house. Well, it's not my house. Technically, it's my cousin's house.*
Police: *(pause) So you're not the property owner? Is the property owner there right now?*
Me: *Um. No.*
Police: *It would be helpful if I could speak directly to the owner of the property.*
Me: *She's at the North Pole.*
Police: (long pause, weary) *Right.*

OK, given that it's the twenty-fifth of December, this does make me sound like a nutter.

Me: *Couldn't you send someone over to dust for prints?*
Police: (sighs audibly) *I'm afraid that due to the holiday, crimes involving persons are being prioritized over those involving property, which we'll be following up on after Boxing Day. I'm very happy to make a note of your details and an officer will investigate in due course.*
Me: *Crimes involving persons.*

Police: *That's right.*

Me: *But not animals.*

Police: *Animals would be construed as property.*

Me: *But that's ridiculous! Animals are living beings!*

Police: *I'm afraid animals would be construed as property.*

Me: *But he's a triple champion! He's very valuable!*

Police: (pause) *Even valuable property is considered to be property.*

Chattel! The police consider Judd to be no more than chattel! But then I remember that I have a key piece of evidence.

Me: *Hang on! I've got a photo of his car on my phone.*

Police: (dubious) *OK. Is that to say you have the license details?*

I pull out my phone, enlarging the photo, which was taken in the dark, from a distance, with a shaky hand. The number plate is blurry, but I can just about make it out. I peer at it closely: I can definitely discern three out of six digits.

Me: *Mostly . . .*

Police: *Meaning you have a partial number?*

Me: *That's correct.*

Police: *What about the make and model?*

Me: *Um. It was a white van. OK, cars aren't really my thing.*

Police: (sigh) *Madam, could I politely request that you file an online crime report?*

Me: (disbelief) *I'm sorry? What?*

Police: *We have an excellent website with a detailed contact
form. You can log all the details of the crime and someone
will respond within seventy-two hours to follow it up.*

Me: *Are you serious?*

Police: *Completely serious.*

Me: (sighs audibly) *Fine.*

Police: *Happy Christmas. Thank you for ringing Devon and
Cornwall Police.*

O h, the march of progress!
In addition to paying our bills, buying our household
items, ordering takeaway meals, registering to vote, booking a
holiday, or a doctor's appointment, now, when we are victims of a
crime, all we have to do is log on to a website. And instead of in-
teracting with a reassuring human presence, we can quickly and
efficiently interface with a long series of drop-down menus.

After I hang up I feel desolate. Judd could be in danger, or suffering, or even dead. There must be something I can do to find
Mr. Mustache. I squint down at the photograph, trying desperately to identify the license number. Is that a *B* or an *8*? And is the
other character a *G* or a *6*? There can't be that many possibilities.
And if you cross-checked the different combinations with white
vans and geographic locations on the Driver and Vehicle Licens-
ing Agency website, you could probably work it out. The trick
would be accessing the DVLA website.

Which for most people would be impossible.

Although I work in IT, I am not a hacker. Many people assume otherwise. I am more of a systems design person, someone who analyzes organizational needs and devises an IT solution. If you really must know, I'm into data architecture. Just don't ask me to define it. But anyone who works in tech will have come across hackers—and I am no different. They're a very peculiar breed: highly intelligent, endlessly curious, and fascinated by the abstract; they can also absorb countless bits of information quickly and easily, as long as they have total control over that information. But they tend not to rub along well with other humans. Basically, hackers prefer machines to people.

If I sound like a bit of an expert, that's because I have engaged in what Jane Austen might have called *amorous congress* with one. My second university boyfriend (after Felix the film buff) was a guy called Rob. Rob was a classic hacker—he studied electrical engineering but rarely attended class, preferring to spend his days in a darkened room in front of a blinking terminal. I was attracted to him because he was funny, clever, and knew stuff. No matter what topic came up in conversation, Rob always had more information stored in the dark recesses of his cortex than anyone else in the room and, at the tender age of twenty, I found that intoxicating. Rob's brain was like an overactive cricket: it jumped around endlessly, rarely settling in one place for more than a few moments.

Unless he was coding. At those times he operated with total concentration, oblivious to the world around him. Rob could curtain himself off for days at a time if he was working on a project. Naturally, as his girlfriend at the time, I found this deeply annoying. One night when I'd stayed over at his flat, the building's fire alarm went off in the middle of the night. I stumbled blearily out of bed to find Rob at his terminal, completely unaware. I could vaguely smell smoke somewhere in the building, but after remonstrating with him for several minutes, I left him to it and dashed downstairs. As we all huddled outside on the pavement in our dressing gowns, I frantically stopped the firefighters on their way in and explained that my boyfriend had refused to leave. "If I were you, I'd get a new boyfriend," one had grunted, dashing off inside. Eventually, I did.

But we've remained friends (to the extent that Rob *has* friends), though I've not spoken with him in several months. In spite of the fact that it's Christmas, I decide to text him now. Because if anyone can break into the DVLA's database, it's Rob.

Hey. Happy Hols! What you up to?

Right now? Kind of busy.

Doing what?

About to slay a dragon.

I smile. Still the same old Rob.

Minecraft?

Yep.

Are you winning?

Need you ask?

Would you be up for an even more challenging task?

What sort?

An illicit one.

There is a long pause, presumably while Rob is hurling a flamethrower, and then my phone pings.

I'm listening.

Hackers are always up for a challenge—pique their curiosity and you've won. And because they are nonconformists, the more illicit the better, in hacker land. I knew Rob would bite, and a moment later he rings me. I give him all the details and he promises to get to work on it straightaway. Just as soon as he's slain the dragon.

"How long will it take?" I ask.

"Dunno yet. A day?"

"Um. The thing is, the owner is due back tomorrow."

"Then you might need to stall."

Yikes.

The idea of stalling a woman like Camilla Delors makes my blood curdle. But hopefully it won't come to that. I have total faith in Rob.

I pass a restless few hours with the dogs, who remain unsettled and needy. When I take them out to the paddock they bump around my legs like furry toddlers. Nick and Noel are grazing peacefully in the far corner, nibbling the bits of grass peeking out of the snow, but when we enter they trot gracefully over to us, stopping abruptly about ten feet away. I break the thin layer of ice that has formed on top of their water (*whoops*), then fork over some hay, which they chew contentedly, their jaws moving in a clockwise motion. I've brought a few small carrots from the kitchen and I feed them pieces, which they gingerly take from my fingers, staring at me with large glassy eyes. I have to admit they are rather adorable, with sweet, pointy ears and long bushy tails, not unlike those of a fox.

Later, after we're inside, I ring my father on Skype to wish him Happy Christmas, even though I am no longer feeling very festive. When his face pops up on my screen, his expression immediately creases with concern. "Charlie, what's wrong?"

I tell him about Judd and my frustrations with the police. I say nothing about Rob, but my father knows me only too well.

"Charlie, let the police handle it. This man could be ruthless."

"Or he could be just a common dog thief."

"'He who is cruel to animals becomes hard also in his dealings with men.'"

"Um, are you channeling Kant there, Dad?"

"Yes. But I'm in complete accord with him on this point. He was a wise man, Charlie."

"Yes, Dad."

"Have you spoken to your mother?"

"I sent her a text."

"Charlie," he admonishes.

"She's half a galaxy away. Frolicking in the sun. Besides, it's already Boxing Day in Australia."

"Nevertheless, I'm sure she'd appreciate a call."

"Fine. I'll ring her."

My father really is annoyingly reasonable.

An hour later, when I am just beginning to feel peckish, I hear a car door outside and in the next instant Hugo's face looms large at the window. When I open the door, he beams at me expansively. "Happy Christmas!" He holds up a cling film–covered dish. "I brought a cheese plate."

"Thanks. I was just starting to get hungry."

"Actually, it's for the dogs," he confesses, stepping inside. "Malcolm is partial to Stilton," he explains. "How are the alpacas settling in?"

"They aren't."

"Really? They looked very bonny just now." He jerks a thumb toward the paddock.

"Hugo, you need to find somewhere else to keep them. Jez will hit the roof if they're still here when she gets back."

Hugo sighs. "I'm working on it. Give me a few more days."

"How was Christmas with Constance and her family?"

"Fine. Apart from Uncle Claus, who got dressed up as some sort of hairy German devil-goat and then accidentally stabbed himself with a trident. Had to get an ambulance out to the house. And then Constance's mother set fire to her hair when she lit the mulled wine."

"Who lights mulled wine?"

"The entire German nation, apparently. Luckily the paramedics were good with burns as well as wounds. What about you?" He looks around the room, his eyes landing on Peggy. "How was canine Christmas?"

I quickly relate the tale of Judd's theft and Mr. Mustache.

"Crikey! Good thing he didn't steal the alpacas!"

Debatable.

Just then my phone pings with a text message. I am expecting to hear from Cal, but when I look down I see that it's from Rob.

Yo! DVLA laughably easy to permeate.

Seriously? Are you in already?

Yep. Think I broke my own record.

What about the white van?

Have two good prospects.

I'm all ears.

Will send you data in a min.

You're a star.

I'm a bloody constellation.

If you say so.

You owe me.

I consider this for a moment before replying.

Can I pay you in puppies?

"Hugo, I need to borrow your car," I inform him as soon as I put down the phone. He frowns.

"Why?"

"Because the Škoda's dead."

Hugo glances worriedly out the window at his car. "You do realize it's a vintage Ferrari?"

"Fine. *You* can drive."

"Where are we going?"

"To get Judd."

Hugo's eyebrows shoot up with surprise. "Could this be construed as vigilantism?"

"Possibly."

"Is that . . . prudent?"

"Maybe not. But if we don't move quickly, we could lose Judd for good."

"But this mustache chap. He could be dangerous."

"I'm aware of that, Hugo."

Hugo hesitates, frowning. "The thing is, valor was never one of my strong suits. At school I didn't even play contact sports."

"Relax. You're just the getaway driver."

"Let me get this straight: I stay in the car while you confront a dangerous criminal and recover stolen goods all by yourself?" I ponder this for a moment, then lift my chin stubbornly.

"Yes," I reply. *Really?*

"With what, may I ask? Do you have some sort of weapon?"

I hesitate, Valko's voice in my ear: *Guns is better.* I look around the room. There must be something I can use as a weapon. My mind races through the obvious candidates: knives, hammers, crowbars, cricket bats. The thought of carrying any one of these, much less using one, is frankly terrifying.

Then I realize that the perfect weapon is right under our noses.

chapter
23

It takes fifteen minutes, his favorite soft toy (a large, purple turtle) and a generous hunk of Stilton to coax Malcolm away from Peggy and the puppies. The Ferrari is only a two-seater, so Malcolm and I must share the passenger seat. I squeeze myself against the door so that his lanky body can squash in beside mine. He is so hunched over that his muzzle is practically plastered against the windscreen, and his doggy breath is hot and cheesy in my face. "Maybe we should put the top down?" I suggest, even though it is freezing outside.

"Good plan." Hugo hits a button and the soft black top whines, then slowly folds back on itself. In another moment it is safely stowed and the three of us are staring up at the glorious night sky.

It's a superb night for vigilantism.

Luckily we are warmly dressed. Rob has sent me two addresses and we have already looked them up on Google Maps. One is in the village of Little Durnley, approximately eight miles to the south; the other is up on Dartmoor, about fourteen miles north and west. We head for Little Durnley first, hoping to get lucky, and anticipating that the roads on Dartmoor will be harder going with the snow. Our mood as we set out is unreasonably giddy, as if we're on a grand tour rather than a covert and possibly dangerous recovery operation. Hugo begins to sing "White Christmas" and after a moment I join in. He glances over at me. "You're not very musical, are you," he remarks.

The roads are empty and we reach Little Durnley in less than fifteen minutes, by which time I cannot feel my face. We slow down as we enter the village and I direct Hugo. The address we are looking for is just off the high street, half a mile down a side road, and as we approach I spy a white van parked on the street in front of a small row house painted yellow. "There it is," I say excitedly. We pull up alongside and I see large black letters painted on the side of the van.

ROYAL FLUSH PLUMBERS. NEVER RUN TO WASTE! CALL NOW!

Seriously?

"Wrong van," I say with disappointment. Hugo is peering at the house, where an artificial white tree lit with blue lights looms in the front window.

"Just as well," he says. "I don't particularly care for their aesthetics."

We are both half frozen, so we decide to put the top back on for the next leg of the journey. Hugo is forced to change into a lower gear as we head up onto the moor, as the roads here are still covered with snow, but I have to admit he is a skilled driver and the Ferrari handles surprisingly well. Around us the wind howls, occasionally sending up swirling coils of glittering snow, picked out by our headlights like wildly cavorting ghosts. The atmosphere is all very *Wuthering Heights,* and as we drive on in silence, our mood sobers. I track our progress on my phone, and as the blue dot approaches the circled red-dot destination, I feel a strong sense of foreboding. Malcolm, too, seems on edge, his eyes alert in the darkness and his brow creased with quiet alarm.

Suddenly, and without warning, my phone battery dies.

Nooooo. I am a triple idiot.

"Hugo, where's your phone?" I say urgently.

"With Constance."

"Why?!"

"Because she's addicted to Candy Crush."

"Why doesn't she play it on her own phone?" I shout, practically hysterical.

"Because she's a Luddite. And her phone is ancient."

By now we have turned off the main road and are entering the small village of Hexmoor, which sounds vaguely ominous. Hugo slows to a crawl and drives past the village green. Without the aid of modern devices, we are forced to search the old-fashioned way: I peer out the window to the right, Hugo to the left, and Malcolm stares straight ahead with a look of focused intensity, even though he does not know what we are searching for. We loop round the green and turn down a side street, then circle back and try another, but find nothing. We crisscross the tiny village one street at a time, passing rows of silent stone cottages, Christmas trees sparkling in front windows, but we do not see a single white van.

"Are you certain it was this village?" asks Hugo dubiously. My mind flies to the red circle in my mind.

"Yes," I say. *Maybe?*

"It's not here," he says finally, and I detect a note of relief in his voice. Just then I spot a small track leading slightly downhill through a forest on the edge of the village.

"Try there," I say impulsively. Malcolm suddenly stiffens, his spine and ears erect, and as he does my heart begins to thump wildly inside my chest. Hugo bumps the Ferrari down the track carefully, as the snow here is untouched, and suddenly I see something far ahead in the distance—a tiny prefab bungalow with a dirty white van parked in front.

"Stop! That's it!" I say excitedly. Hugo halts the car abruptly, his face suddenly ashen, and switches off the headlights. The lane is surrounded by a dark, scraggly forest of thin trees; the house, and the van are about one hundred meters ahead. "We'll walk from here," I tell him. "You turn the car around so it's facing the right direction. But keep the headlights off."

"OK," he says, hesitantly. As I start to get out, he stops me with a hand on my arm. "Charlie, what's the plan?" he asks pensively. I pause.

The plan?

I realize in that instant that there is no plan. I cannot simply march up to the front door and demand Judd, even with Malcolm's imposing presence at my side.

"Let me go and have a look first," I say finally. "Then I'll come back here and we'll make a plan."

He considers this. "Promise?" he says. "No lone heroics?"

I nod and he releases my arm. I open the car door and slip out into the trees, skidding and sliding through the muddy snow toward the bungalow. Ahead of me the house is silent; there are two front windows, both with curtains drawn, and one of them is lit from within. As I draw near I hear the sound of a television through the thin walls. I circle around the outside of the house to have a look at the rear. There is a small paved area just outside the back door, which opens up into a large unkempt area of scraggly lawn surrounded by bushes and trees. Paw prints of all sizes dot the snow across the entire area. Clearly Judd isn't the only one here.

I am just creeping toward the back door to see if it is locked, when suddenly I hear the sound of dogs barking inside. I freeze. I hear movement, then after another moment an outside light comes on, beaming straight down at me. I dive behind a thick hedge that runs down one side of the lawn and crouch down. At the same time I hear the back door opening. "Out, you lot. All of you," says a male voice loudly.

Mr. Mustache!

I peek through the hedge and see him standing on the rear step, smoking a cigarette. In the next instant a large pack of dogs comes bounding out of the house in a blur. I count five in all: two whippets; one small, white Scottish terrier; a long-eared beagle; and a yellow retriever.

Disappointingly, none of them is Judd.

Where the hell is he?

The dogs instantly scatter around the garden to do their business. I watch through the thick hedge as the beagle slowly works his way toward me, sniffing. Eventually he reaches the hedge, then pauses to lift his leg against it. After he has finished, he stops, raises his nose in my direction and begins to bark repeatedly.

Nooooo. Bad dog!

"Barney! Shut up!" Mr. Mustache shouts from the step. The beagle stops barking, looks at me for a long moment, his nostrils twitching, then whimpers and wanders off to the other side of the garden. Mr. Mustache stubs out his cigarette and goes back inside for a moment, and I am about to sneak back through the woods to the car, when he reappears a moment later with a sixth dog on a lead.

Judd!

He bends down and unclips the lead, and Judd skips down the steps gracefully, like the triple champion he is. He wanders over to the other side of the garden and immediately lifts his leg against a shrub. I am wondering if I can call to him in a loud whisper, when suddenly I hear strange electronic music floating across the lawn, accompanied by a heavy bass and a gravelly male voice.

I'm sexy and I know it . . . I'm sexy and I know—

The music stops just as abruptly as it started.

"Yeah?" Mr. Mustache says into his phone. He turns away for a moment and steps back into the kitchen. Just then Barney the beagle comes back to the hedge, sniffing intently, and circles round the outside until he is standing right in front of me. He growls and I shake my head in horror, raising a finger to my lips *(because all dogs understand the universal sign for* shhhhh*)*, whereupon Barney begins to bark with renewed vigor. In another instant the Scottie comes tearing round the hedge and joins him, growling and then yapping, and within seconds the other four dogs come racing around to join them, including Judd at the rear, who hurls himself right past them, and flings himself onto me, licking my face. I grab hold of his collar and start to pull him away when suddenly I hear Mr. Mustache snarling.

"Oy! What's all that noise! Get back inside! *Now!*"

I yank on Judd and begin to run back through the trees, awkwardly stooping over so that I can hold on to his collar. The other dogs are now in a complete frenzy of excitement; they circle along behind us, barking loudly and snapping at my heels. Mr. Mustache swears, then I hear the back door slam and his footsteps as he runs down the steps. I let go of Judd's collar so I can run faster and shout for him to follow, and all seven of us go racing through the snowy woods, Mr. Mustache somewhere behind us. It's dark and the branches whip across my face as I run, and I am just beginning to wonder if I am heading in the right direction when suddenly I see the blare of headlights come on ahead, and hear Hugo's voice calling anxiously in the distance.

"Charlie?!"

I stumble toward the light, breaking free of the trees and practically launch myself out onto the track, where in the distance I see the silhouette of a man and a small pony in the headlights.

Malcolm!

I sprint the last hundred feet and hear Mr. Mustache in the woods behind me, calling to the dogs. "Barney! Duchess! Ralph! Kitty! Get back here!"

Kitty? What kind of person calls their dog Kitty?

"Charlie!" shouts Hugo. I look up and can just make out Hugo's face, backlit with fear. Next to him, Malcolm stands tall, his head and ears erect, his enormous paws planted squarely in front of him. Suddenly Malcolm begins to bark, louder than I've heard him, woofing over and over in a massive baritone that rolls out across the forest. One by one the other dogs fall away as Judd and I race along toward the headlights. When we reach the car I hurl myself at it, yanking open the door.

"Come on! We've got to go!" I shout, and we grab Judd and Malcolm by their collars and heave them into the Ferrari, squashing their bodies into the middle of the front seat in a jumble of paws, limbs, muzzles, and tails, just as Mr. Mustache breaks free from the forest not fifty yards away.

Hugo fires up the engine, throws the car into reverse and hits the pedal. We scream up the lane backward, the car's headlights picking out Mr. Mustache and his pack of unruly pooches, who now surround him, barking excitedly.

Driving at high speed backward in the dark is possibly the most terrifying thing I have ever done, and I glance over to see Hugo's face tight with concentration, his arms locked against the steering wheel. When we reach the road the Ferrari ejects itself like a missile, flying backward through the air and landing on the icy road with a crash, whereupon it spins like a bottle around on itself. We come to a halt with a screech of tires, and I look over at him.

We are both grinning like fools.

We speed off through the village, leaving Mr. Mustache and his dogs far behind. The drive back across the moor is a raucous affair. We sing carols at the top of our lungs, with Judd on my lap and Malcolm beside me, completely uncaring of the fact that I cannot carry a tune, and work our way through the entire canon by the time we reach the outskirts of Cross Bottomley. But just as we round the last bend before Jez's farm, I spy Cal's blue Volvo parked outside the door. He is standing by the car holding his phone, and as the Ferrari pulls into the driveway, he turns and looks right at me.

I can just make out his furious blue eyes.

chapter
24

On the face of it, this looks quite bad. *We* look quite bad. As Judd, Malcolm, and I come tumbling out of the Ferrari, I can virtually read what Cal is thinking. He may be momentarily relieved to see Judd, but his focus is all on Hugo.

Is this your friend?

My mind frantically gropes for an explanation that will pacify him.

"Cal," I say. But the words do not come.

"You got Judd back," he says, his voice strained.

"Yes."

"On your own? Or . . . with him?" He indicates Hugo and the implication is clear that once again I have chosen Hugo over him.

Nooooo.

Hugo swaggers over to us, full of newfound valor. "Hello, old chap. You missed all the fun."

Cal glances at him, then looks back at me. "I gather," he says.

"Sorry," I say weakly. "I should have rung to let you know. My phone died." I hold up my dead phone. *Damn technology!*

"Glad it worked out," Cal says soberly. He does not look glad.

"Charlie was magnificent," says Hugo proudly. "You should have seen her."

"I'm sure," says Cal. He does not sound even remotely sure.

There is an awkward moment, where I silently will Hugo to take his leave.

"I say we celebrate!" says Hugo brightly. "I've got champagne in the boot."

I turn to Cal. "Would you like to come in?" I ask. He does not look as if he would like to come in.

"I need to get back," he says. He turns to go and I take a step forward and grab hold of his arm.

"Cal." He frowns, looking down at my hand. "It isn't what you think," I say quietly.

Hugo peers at us. "Really?" he asks. "What does he think?"

"Happy Christmas," says Cal quietly.

I watch as he climbs into the Volvo and drives off.

Without so much as a wave.

Hugo insists on cracking open the champagne. And even though I am sad at Cal's departure, a not-so-tiny part of me wouldn't mind celebrating my first successful foray into vigilantism. So we dig out some flutes, pour ourselves a generous measure, stoke up the Rayburn, and flop down on the sofa. I plug my phone into a charger and within a few moments it rings. *Maybe it's Cal?*

I leap up and grab it. "Hi, Mum," I say disappointingly. "Happy Christmas."

"At last! I've been trying to reach you all day!"

Ah well, what with one thing and another.

"Me, too," I lie. "Circuits must have been overloaded. How's Christmas in the Southern Hemisphere?"

"Blistering. My face looks like an overripe tomato. You know how I bloat in the sun."

"I thought you were looking forward to a tropical holiday."

"Was I?" she says wistfully.

"So, I guess you didn't roast a turkey, then."

"Oscar made salmon on the barbie, which is apparently traditional. But it didn't *feel* very Christmassy," she confides in a loud whisper. Irritatingly, I can already detect traces of an affected Australian accent.

"How are the twins?"

"Feral," she snorts. About the time I hit menses my mother began dropping hints about grandchildren. But as soon as she married Richie, who came complete with twin grandsons, she instantly went off the idea. "I swear there's something off-kilter about those boys," she says. "They must have AC/DC."

"ADD?"

"They're out killing things as we speak."

"What sort of things?"

"Birds, insects, rodents. Other people's pets, probably. They've got a small arsenal of weapons: air guns, slingshots, spears. And I don't mind saying they are totally *overindulged* by their parents."

Of course you don't. "Times have changed, I guess."

"I blame whoever coined the term *parenting*," she says with a sigh. "Nouns into verbs is never a good thing."

"True." *At least we can agree on that.*

"How are *you* anyway?" She asks, suddenly remembering her maternal responsibilities. "*How are the headaches?*"

"I'm completely fine now, Mum."

"Good. And Jez?"

"She's terrific," I say jauntily. *This is not a lie; indeed, it is quite likely to be true.*

"You're not overstaying your welcome, are you?"

"No, Mum."

"Good. Is she there?"

"Not right at this moment." *Definitely true.*

"She hasn't left you alone on Christmas, has she?"

"I'm not alone." I glance up at Hugo, who is busy refilling his glass. He holds up the bottle with an enquiring look. "I've got a friend here."

"What sort of friend?" Her voice has suddenly taken on a penetrating quality, not unlike the whine of a mosquito.

"Just a friend. He's staying nearby."

"And does your *friend* have a name?" she asks pointedly. I sigh. *Dear Lord.*

"Here. Why don't you ask him?" I say, handing the phone to Hugo.

They are more than a match for each other, so I leave them to it. I refill my champagne, pull on my coat, and head outside. As I pull the door shut, Hugo looks up at me with a bewildered smile:

I give him a cheery thumbs-up and he nods rather gamely. I cross the yard and enter the paddock. The snow is dense and wet underfoot and glows an eerie white all around me. Nick and Noel are huddled together some fifty meters away, and as I trudge across they stand to attention, their long necks stretching upward. "Hello, lads," I say, stepping gingerly toward them. One of them (*Nick, perhaps?*) cranes his head down toward me and I reach up to scratch the dense fluff atop his head. Noel shuffles forward, eager, too, for attention. I stand there for a few minutes patting them while they make sweet little nickering noises. They may have brains the size of lemons, but their hearts appear to be gargantuan. Nick and Noel have no choice but to live in the moment, so they stick together, take what comes, and aren't afraid to seek affection. Their capacity for trust far outshines my own.

When I go back inside Hugo is just pulling on his coat. "Sorry," I say, indicating the phone.

"You did rather bowl me a googly there. She's quite a card, your mum."

"Queen of Spades."

"She asked me what my intentions were."

Oh God. "What did you say?"

"I told her I intended to pay twice the usual fee. And that your services were exemplary."

I stare at him. "Please tell me you discussed the nature of my services," I say.

Hugo frowns. "Not as such. But she did insist that any daughter of hers was surely worth at least triple the price. And she's right. So you have her to thank for your bonus."

"I'll believe it when I see it," I say.

"I'm a man of my word," he says, struggling to pull on a pair of stiff, brown-and-white-mottled gloves. "From Constance," he says, holding them up. "Python leather. Shockingly expensive, apparently. And very durable. Waterproof, too." He frowns down at them. "I planned to give her something living," he says philosophically. "And she gave me something . . ."

"Deadly?"

He looks up at me and nods.

"Try not to take it personally."

Hugo returns to Constance and her family, and the dogs and I retire. I am feeling fairly wretched, but maybe I can speak to Cal tomorrow and explain. I triple-lock all the doors and decide to sleep on the sofa in the kitchen, just in case Mr. Mustache tries anything else, though I doubt he will. With any luck, Camilla Delors will collect Judd tomorrow afternoon, and I will be finished forever with dog snatchers. Then I remember that I should notify the Devon and Cornwall Police, so once again I ring the nonemergency number, and the same bored officer answers.

Me: *Hello. I rang earlier about a stolen dog?*

Police: (sighs) *Yes, madam. How could we forget?*

Me: *I just want to say that I've recovered him.*

Police: (pause) *Is that to say he was returned to you?*

Me: *Um . . . no. Actually, I went and got him.*

Police: *I see. So you found the dog and asked for him back?*

Me: *Not exactly.*

Police: (pause) *Did you steal him back?*

Me: *Is it stealing, really? If it's yours to begin with?*

Police: (sighs) *Was anyone hurt, madam?*

Me: *No.*

Police: (gruffly) *Devon and Cornwall Police do not endorse acts
of vigilantism.*

Me: *I understand.*

Police: (grudging) *That said—well done.*

Basking in his praise, I give him Mr. Mustache's address and
he promises to dispatch a team of officers to Hexmoor immediately. Apparently, crimes of property can be a priority, after all.

After I hang up I snuggle down on the sofa with Slab. Malcolm
is stretched out on the floor beside Peggy and the puppies, snoring
softly. And Judd and Hulk are curled up happily on the dog bed in
the corner.

Perhaps I really am a failed human, after all.

wake early the next morning to a sharp rap at the door. During
the night, Slab has wormed his way under my armpit, like a giant
hairy teat. I peer across the room in the early morning light and
see two uniformed police staring in at me through the window. I
remove Slab from my armpit and cross to the door, a blanket
wrapped around my shoulders.

Surely it's a bit too early for crimes of property?

"Sorry to disturb, madam," says a tall, attractive female officer
with pale blonde hair tightly pulled back in a chignon. *Who knew*

police could be so chic! "We'd like to ask you some questions about the crime report you filed yesterday?" This woman is all business, though her shorter male colleague looks as if he has only just graduated from police academy: fresh-faced and chubby cheeked, with a startled look in his eyes, as if he shouldn't be trusted with anything more serious than a moving violation. I open the door.

"Of course. Come in." *But, please, no questions until I have some coffee.*

They shuffle into the kitchen while I put a kettle on, and I see their eyes sweep across the room, then flick briefly to each other: *Crazy dog lady.*

Once inside, Blond Officer informs me that Mr. Mustache is now in custody and has given a full confession.

Excellent! Justice prevails!

"But it appears he wasn't working alone," she adds. "He claims that he was hired by the owner."

I turn around, astonished, dropping a teaspoon to the floor with a clatter. "Camilla Delors?" I ask.

She glances down at the small white pad she is carrying and nods. "That would be correct."

"Why would she steal her own dog?" Just as soon as I ask the question, the answer blooms in my mind.

Triple idiot! Insurance!

"Well, that's what we'd like to find out," says Blonde Officer. "When is the dog due to be collected?"

"This afternoon. Two o'clock," I say.

Blonde Officer shoots Baby Officer a look.

"Because we'd like to be here when she does."

A sting operation! Cozy Canine Cottages is going to be the subject of a sting operation! It is all terribly glamorous and exciting. Or at least, it's a teeny-weeny bit glamorous and exciting. Even if one of the officers involved looks as if he would be more happy playing cops and robbers on a playground.

The police leave, promising to return later, and after I have fed and exercised the dogs and the alpacas, I ring Sian to bring her up to date. Her response is typically no-nonsense. "Right. We need to get the whole thing on camera," she says. "It'll be perfect for your YouTube channel."

"I don't *have* a YouTube channel."

"Not yet. Damn! Owen and I would drive out there, but he's got a birthday party later."

"What a shame." *Not.*

"Remember to set the camera up at eye line. And to angle your body slightly away."

"Um . . . why?"

"Because dead-on camera takes are never flattering. And shooting from below makes you look bloated."

"Right." I have no intention of filming the sting operation, nor of launching my own YouTube channel, but there is little use explaining this to Sian. I will simply tell her later that my phone ran out of battery at the crucial moment, which will probably be true anyway.

"By the way, Owen and I stalked the Band of the Household Cavalry on Facebook, and found the ex-girlfriend," Sian says.

"You mean Bonnie?"

"Yep. Does the dishy Danish know she's divorced?"

"No! Really?"

"That's what her Facebook profile says. Her privacy settings are rubbish, by the way."

I smile. *Classic Sian!* Perhaps there's hope for Hugo, after all.

After we hang up, I decide to text Cal, but after several attempts at lengthy apologies and explanations, I delete everything I've written. I lie down on the floor beside Peggy and allow the puppies to scramble over my body like tiny Sherpas scaling Everest. Rudy nuzzles his way to my side and I scoop him onto my chest, where he settles down happily in between my breasts for a snooze. Maybe I will try ringing Cal later, after we have entrapped Camilla Delors. I suspect he would take a very dim view of my involvement in a sting operation.

Valko turns up later and grins at me when I open the door. "Happy Box Day," he declares.

"So it is," I reply. "Where've you been the last few days?"

He blushes. "I am with pigs," he says. *Is that so?*

"Where's Stella?"

"Today, she goes to mother." He shrugs and gives a wave toward the west. "Somewheres." When I tell him about Judd's theft and recovery, he rolls his eyes and chastises me for my failure to get a gun. But when I explain that the police are due later, his eyebrows shoot up.

"Police will come? Here?"

"Yes. What's wrong, Valko? You're not in trouble with them, are you?"

"No," he says forcibly, shaking his head. "I have only . . . small problem. With tax papers." *Ah. Of course he does.*

"Don't worry, they're not due until later."

He offers to take the twins for a walk, which I am only too grateful for, as it gives me time to bathe and dress.

What to wear for a sting operation? In the end, I settle on a stylishly covert combo: thick black leggings and a rather pretty, floaty black tunic that I must have missed earlier in Jez's wardrobe. I brew fresh coffee and am just sitting down to enjoy a cup when I hear a familiar diesel engine in the driveway and look up to see Cal's Volvo pull up outside. Instantly, I am petrified; my hand wobbles as I set the mug down. I creep to the window and watch as he climbs out of the car. Outside it is a brilliantly sunny, crisp winter's day; he is wearing the same plaid shirt and burgundy vest he wore the first time we met, and looks utterly divine. Was that really less than two weeks ago? It feels like decades. I open the door just as he reaches it. In the bright light his eyes are a blazing cobalt blue.

"Hi," he says.

"Hi," I reply.

His gaze flicks beyond me to the kitchen. "Are you alone?"

I hesitate, aware that Valko is due back at some point with the twins. And the dogs are here, of course. "Sort of."

He blinks a few times, which makes him look like a sad owl, and instantly I feel guilty. *Do not trifle with this man.*

"It's just me and the dogs," I explain.

Cal nods, evidently relieved. But he still doesn't smile.

"Do you want to come in?" I ask tentatively.

He steps inside and looks around, taking in the dogs. He still looks worried, the way Malcolm does when one of the puppies cannot find its way to a teat.

"It feels a little crowded in here," he says, turning to face me. "Actually, it's your *life* that feels crowded," he adds. "What with one thing and another." His voice has taken on a more serious edge. It is patently obvious he means Hugo.

"There's room for you," I say hopefully.

He raises an eyebrow. "Is there?"

I nod. He takes a deep breath, then steps a little closer toward me.

"The thing is . . . I'm not very good at sharing," he says.

"You wouldn't have to."

"Are you certain?" he asks.

"Yes."

He nods, and I detect a glimmer of relief in his eyes. He indicates the dogs with a motion of his head.

"What about them?" he asks.

Oh well, them. He would definitely have to share with them.

"I guess we're sort of like a—a package deal," I reply. My voice has dropped so low it is barely above a whisper. He weighs this for a moment.

"Do you ever get time off?"

"Not much. They kind of like having me around," I say and smile.

"They're not the only ones," he replies, which almost makes my knees buckle. "But I guess they did find you first," he says a little grudgingly.

"They'd be willing to share," I say.

He smiles. "What would I need to do to make that happen?"

"I'm . . . not sure."

"Do I need to ask them?"

I shake my head, my face burning. "I don't think that will be necessary."

"So maybe if I just . . . let them watch?" he asks.

What exactly is he suggesting?

"'Watch'?"

He takes another step forward, reaches for me with his amazing forearms, and pulls me to him. And when his lips are finally on mine, his kiss is somehow both utterly electrifying and weirdly comfortable.

Like we've been here before.

At which point, the meter in my brain fizzes and bursts.

I n the end, we do not let them watch. (*The puppies are far too young,* I tell him.) I pull Cal upstairs to the bedroom, where we do not tarry, and he manages to relieve me of my stylishly covert combo in record time. Afterward, I confess to him that Valko is due back anytime, so we return to the kitchen and I brew a fresh pot of coffee. Cal lies on the sofa with Rudy on his chest, while the puppy tugs at his collar, trying to crawl inside his shirt. They look adorable, and Cal is more relaxed than I have ever seen him. I think about the story Gerry told me.

"I'm sorry about your dog," I say. He looks over at me and raises an eyebrow.

Am I fishing? I am definitely fishing.

He shrugs. "Pip was really more her dog than mine," he says. *Her.* It is the first time he has mentioned Valerie outright.

"Why didn't you get another one?" I ask. Cal takes a deep breath and blows it out slowly.

"You know what Freud said about dogs?" he says finally.

I shake my head.

"He said they were incapable of ambivalence. Dogs love their friends and bite their enemies. They don't do both." He pauses for a moment and retrieves Rudy from inside his shirt. "It's only people who mix hate and love."

"OK," I say. "But I'm still not sure why you didn't want another dog."

"Because I'm human. And for a long time, hate and love got muddled up inside me. I didn't think any animal deserved that. Or any human, for that matter." He offers me an apologetic smile.

"And now?"

"Now?" He holds Rudy up in the air, as if he is eyeing up a small melon he might purchase. "Now I think I might be ready," he says. I walk over and sit down beside him, budging him over.

"For a dog or a human?" I ask.

He smiles. "Both," he says. "But not just *any* human," he adds, kissing me.

I kiss him back, and it is just as delicious as the first time. But as I do, a tiny thought worms its way into my brain. This is Jez's kitchen, not mine.

What will happen when she returns?

I have stepped into her life, and rather to my surprise, it fits me like a well-cut suit. One that I will be terribly sad to shed.

And then I stop thinking.

A few minutes later, Valko finally returns from his epic-length walk with the twins. *Bless you, Valko!* He comes into the kitchen and greets Cal, but when I offer him a coffee, he hesitates. "Maybe is better I go," he says uncertainly. "Before police come." Cal turns to me with a raised eyebrow.

"What police?" he says.

chapter

25

Apparently, I forgot to mention the sting operation. As I suspected, Cal is deeply unimpressed. I explain that it is the most benign sting operation *ever*, and will likely be over in seconds. Cal frowns. "But why do the police need to involve *you*? Why don't they just go and arrest her?"

Good point. I hadn't thought to ask. Partly because I wanted to be involved in a sting operation. "Maybe they don't know where she lives," I say. "Anyway, insurance fraud is only white-collar crime. It's practically genteel!"

"You told me she was scary."

"That's because her high heels were intimidating."

"Charlie, don't be fooled. She could be dangerous."

"The police will be here with me," I say, trying my best to placate him. He frowns and folds his gorgeous forearms across his chest. I have to resist the urge to bend down and lick them.

"And so will I," he says.

So it's a party. I am not quite sure how it will work, but apparently we will all be waiting when Camilla Delors arrives later this afternoon. Valko, in spite of his aversion to the authorities, is clearly also intrigued, inventing all kinds of excuses for why he needs to hang about. He cleans out the twins' run, and repairs a broken gutter on one of the outbuildings, while Cal gives each of the puppies a thorough medical exam, pressing his stethoscope to their tiny chests while they squirm in his hand, peddling their little legs in the air. When he finishes, he stands up. "How is Rudy doing?" I ask.

"Not bad. For a runt."

"You do realize that in dog terms that's practically an ethnic slur?"

"It's medical terminology."

"Oh really? What do you call the alpha male with an overinflated sense of importance?" I say with a smile. He reaches out and pulls me to him.

"Predatory," he snarls into my neck.

The police arrive twenty minutes early. By then I've made a large platter of egg salad sandwiches, while Cal looks on with amusement.

See? I can cook, too!

Blonde Officer introduces herself as Sergeant Ursula Strich. *(She definitely should be working for MI5.)* And Baby Officer is

Constable Brian Whinney. The four of us sit down together at the kitchen table to eat our sandwiches. MI5 Ursula eats meticulously, her tongue licking her perfect lips, and I have to kick Cal under the table to prevent him from staring. Valko has stayed behind and is lurking around outside. He has taken Slab, Judd, and Hulk out to the paddock, hoping to watch the proceedings from a distance. At precisely two o'clock, my mobile rings. I glance down. "Unknown number," I say, looking up at MI5 Ursula. She gives me a cautious nod, indicating that I should answer.

"Hello?"

"This is Camilla Delors. I'm just ringing to let you know I've been delayed."

"'Delayed'?" I repeat for the benefit of the others. "How long will you be?"

"I'm not sure yet," she says cautiously. "I trust everything is OK. With the dog?" She is clearly angling for information. Perhaps Mr. Mustache failed to inform her of his failure before he was arrested?

"The dog's fine," I say. There's a moment's hesitation on the other end.

"I see," she says finally. Cleary she does not see. There is another long pause while Camilla Delors works out what to do. "In fact, there's been a slight change of plan," she announces briskly. "I'd like you to hold on to him for a few more days." *What?*

"'A few more days'?" I repeat. Across the table, MI5 Ursula shakes her head emphatically. "I'm sorry, I'm afraid that won't be possible," I say quickly. "I'm going out of town. The dog will have to be collected immediately."

MI5 Ursula gives me the thumbs-up.

Good work! I could be a spy, too!

"I see," Camilla Delors says coldly. "Fine," she snaps. "He'll be collected within the hour."

And with that she rings off.

*O*ne *hour.* Eyebrows lift around the table. We have stowed the police vehicle in one of the outbuildings behind the house, so as not to alert her. Now all we have to do is wait. For the past fifteen minutes, Constable Brian has been looking longingly at the puppies, now he stands up and sidles over to them. "Is it OK to pick one up?" he asks, full of boyish enthusiasm. I crouch down next to Peggy so she doesn't become alarmed, and gently pluck Rudy out of the gaggle of pups swarming her teats, handing him over. Constable Brian returns to his chair and giggles as Rudy crawls up his chest, licking his chin excitedly. Just then I hear a curious *thunk* outside: it chimes deeply with something in my memory, but it takes a moment for my mind to recover it.

A Mercedes! Camilla Delors is already here!

She must have been around the corner when she phoned. I stand up and race to the door, yanking it open, just in time to see Camilla Delors opening the paddock gate, the gray Mercedes sedan parked right beside her, its engine still running. Valko is on the far side of the field, his arms wrapped around one of the alpacas in a full-body hug, and Judd and Hulk are ambling along sniffing the grass about forty feet away.

"It's her!" I say, just as Camilla Delors barks out a command.

Judd raises his head and stares at her, and for a moment he does not move. But then she blows a short, sharp whistle and he obediently runs toward her.

Because he's a triple champion.

Meanwhile MI5 Ursula and Constable Brian have leaped out of their seats and scrambled past me out the door, running flat out toward the paddock. "Valko!" I shout, just as he gleans what is happening and starts to trot across the field from the opposite direction, followed by the alpacas, who clearly think it's some sort of game and go gamboling after him. Camilla Delors glances swiftly in our direction as she grabs Judd's collar, opens the rear door of the Mercedes, and hurls him inside. Then she jumps in the front seat and the car swerves round and blasts out onto the lane, disappearing with a rev of its impeccable engine. Leaving MI5 Ursula and Constable Brian on the driveway behind them.

Within moments they have regrouped and are racing to fetch the police car from the outbuilding. Cal and I watch as the car comes around from behind the house at a clip, pulling out onto the lane with a screech of tires. Then I grab both our coats and hurl one at him. "We've got to follow," I say racing past him. He grabs my arm and yanks me back.

"Charlie!" he shouts. I stop and look back at him.

"What?!" My heart is bashing around inside my chest: in my mind's eye we are already tearing down the road in his car.

"You can't go racing after a police chase!" he says, shaking his head.

Why not?!

The words *reckless* and *irresponsible* echo in my brain.

I stare at him beseechingly, and suddenly this seems far bigger than the sting operation; almost instantly, it feels like a litmus test of our compatibility.

As if our future hangs in the balance.

Cal's eyes cloud over, and for an instant I cannot read him. If he refuses to go, what will it mean? A lifetime of being reined in by my more sensible partner? Is that really what I want?

Suddenly he grabs my hand, snatches his keys off the counter and pulls me out the door. We jump into the Volvo and head off, shouting to Valko to look after the dogs as we pass. Cal puts his foot to the floor and we barrel down the road. I sneak a sly look over at him: his eyes flash with excitement. Clearly, he's not so sensible, after all, I think with glee. And then, somewhat randomly, I hear the voice of Mary Poppins in my ear.

Practically perfect in every way.

chapter

26

We barrel down the A road at an alarming speed, and after a minute we spy the squad car far off in the distance up ahead. We watch as it careers off onto a smaller side road, and do the same once we reach the turn. Immediately we are forced to slow our pace: it's a typical country lane with twists and turns and I glance over at Cal to see him frowning with concentration as he navigates the bends and narrow spaces as fast as he dares.

"Where is she headed?" I ask.

"Who knows? But she must know the area pretty well to take this route."

Suddenly we round a bend and Cal is forced to slam on the brakes. The Volvo skids to a halt and we are both thrown forward against the seat belts. Ahead of us a tractor has just pulled out onto the lane from a side field, towing a trailer filled with sheep. We both exhale and look over at each other, our pulses racing. The tractor trundles slowly up the lane ahead of us, and we are forced to follow at the speed of a donkey. I am practically going bonkers with anticipation, craning my neck to see past it. But the lane is much too narrow and lined with tall hedges on both sides: short of flying, we have little choice but to follow. After about two hundred meters, the tractor veers off onto a muddy side track, and Cal puts his pedal to the floor again, but we are both aware that we've lost valuable time. Within another minute we reach a T-junction and Cal comes to an abrupt halt. I crane my neck to look both ways, but there is no sign of either the Mercedes or the police car.

"Left or right?" he asks. For an instant I wish that Malcolm were here. *Malcolm would definitely know which way to turn.*

"Left!" I say impulsively.

Cal obeys, jerking the wheel to the left and flying off down the road.

I t takes us some time to work out that left was clearly not right. At length we are forced to admit that we have lost the chase. Cal eventually pulls into a country pub called, fittingly, the Lost Lamb, and turns to me. I am obviously disappointed, so he leans over and plants a kiss on my forehead. "Fancy a pint?" he asks. He smiles at me adorably.

"Do you think they'll catch her?" I ask. He nods.

"There are only so many directions she can go. I'm sure they'll call for backup if they need it."

"I guess so," I say with dismay. My career as a spy has been very short-lived indeed. But looking on the bright side, I still have my accomplice. I turn to him and indicate the pub with a sly grin. "Do you think they have rooms?"

They do not have rooms, but we do have a pint *(Sting operations are thirsty work!)* before heading back to Valko and the dogs. We learn afterward that the police finally caught up to Camilla Delors just outside the village of Little Chanter. By then they have radioed for reinforcements and when she reaches the outskirts of the village, three more squad cars are waiting. Apparently, Camilla Delors comports herself with complete dignity, surrendering without a fuss. Later, she insists that it is all part of an elaborate attempt to frame her by a rival breeder.

That night Cal cooks me supper in Jez's kitchen. The dogs and I watch as he rolls up his sleeves and slices shallots and mushrooms; sautés them in butter with bits of leftover turkey; then adds wine, cream, herbs, and freshly grated Parmesan. He serves the sauce over spaghetti, but I could have happily eaten it off his arms. Though I refrain from sharing this with him.

Just as we sit down, Jez rings my mobile, bristling with excitement from her dogsledding trip. After listening to her describe their epic Arctic adventure, I finally tell her about the puppies.

"Oh no! This early?" she exclaims. "I'm going to murder Cal! Does he know?" I look over at Cal, who is smiling slyly at me; he has a bit of cream on his upper lip, which I would quite like to lick.

"He knows."

"Has he been round to check them over?"

"Yes, he's been very attentive." Cal is now rubbing his foot on the inside of my calf, slowly working his way up my leg toward my thigh.

Bad boy!

"Is Peggy OK?"

I glance over at Peggy. She is stretched out on her side with puppies brawling for teat access all around her and seems utterly content.

"Peggy's an old pro," I say.

We could all learn a thing or two from Peggy.

I do not mention Judd or Malcolm or the alpacas, deciding that Jez should not be bothered with minor trivialities during her holiday. Judd has already been placed in a foster home and by the time Jez returns in two days' time, I will ensure that Malcolm and the alpacas have been relocated. But it is a very small village: no doubt she will hear about my escapades in due course.

"What time is your flight due back?" I ask.

And more important, do I have to clean the house?

Jez hesitates. For an instant there's an awkward silence: maybe it's my imagination, but I can almost hear the Arctic winds howling in the background.

"Um. About my return flight," Jez says tentatively.

And the alarm bells start to toll.

epilogue

To ring in the New Year, I make a new list:

Seven Things I've Learned About Dogs

1. They are stalkers. Dogs will follow you to the end of the earth and beyond. But not in a creepy sort of way. In a we-share-everything-so-why-not-the-loo-too sort of way. Which is not as bad as it seems. If truth be told, it is sort of endearing.

2. They smell. Like dogs. Which is also not as bad as it seems. It's kind of like guy-smell: with the right guy, you don't really mind. And dogs are no different from men. In all sorts of ways.

3. They are crazily devoted to us. In fact, men should take a leaf from their book.

4. They prize constancy above all else and will return it in kind. (Perhaps one more leaf for the guys needed here.)

5. They are not afraid to show appreciation. (Definitely a third leaf needed: indeed, all men should be given tails, then sent to wagging classes.)

6. A puppy licking your chin is better than therapy. It is almost better than sex. (It actually *is* better than sex on a bad day. Or bad sex.)

7. In most cases, dogs make better people than people do.

So you might have worked out that Rudy and I are now a team. We've got each other's backs, even though his puppy back is still tiny. In fact, five of the litter have already been spoken for. Valko and Stella have each offered to take one (or rather, a pair, which they intend to raise together on the farm, where Valko has more or less moved in), Dibber wants another, and Constable Brian wants a fourth. So that only leaves three to find homes for.

This morning I have been on the phone negotiating with my insufferable boss, Carl. After considerable time, and not a little posturing on my part (I basically told him I would quit), he has finally agreed to keep me on the Bromley Council project as a consultant, working from Devon. "Look at the bright side," I tell him. "You'll save on desk space. Not to mention loo roll," I add cheekily. He has hived off a distinct bit of data architecture for me to do and I have agreed to come to London once a fortnight for a progress review, and we'll see how it goes.

My flat in Nunhead is currently under construction, which is taking rather longer than anyone anticipated; as it turns out the internal walls and pipes were insulated with asbestos, which is now being painstakingly excised from the entire building. The landlords anticipate that it will be ready later this spring, and the insurance has coughed up a hefty check to cover my interim lodging. *Hooray!*

In the meantime, Jez has postponed her return to the UK for the near future. She and Eloise are still happily canoodling in the tundra and working on a long-term plan. It is not yet clear which one of them will relocate, but they have basically agreed that Viber is no longer a solution if they wish to remain together as a couple. So for now I remain the sole operator of Cozy Canine Cottages, with Slab at my side as overseer and right-hand man. And Peggy reigning over us all.

Except for Cal, who has taken to staying over most nights. Gradually, we are peeling back the layers, exposing a little bit more of ourselves to each other by day—and different bits at night. We have agreed that truth will be our baseline, and with it we have begun the slow but steady construction of trust, brick by measured brick: a process that is at once both terrifying and exhilarating. We are both old enough, and experienced enough, to want our relationship to be built on a rock-solid foundation. No shortcuts will be taken. No asbestos will be used.

And Devon grows on me by the day. I have begun to cherish my early morning walk with the twins. This morning we crunched across frozen fields, slid down muddy slopes, waded through streams, and clambered across fallen logs studded with mossy barnacles. At one point I stood amidst a small grove of Scots pines and just inhaled the stillness. In the space of only a few weeks, breathing has indeed become one of my favorite pastimes.

Who would have guessed?

Sian and Owen came to visit last weekend and I took them for a quick spin in the sulky, which they loved. Afterward Cal cooked us coq au vin, rolling up his sleeves and strapping on a pink pinny that I dug out of a kitchen drawer, while Owen constructed an elaborate fort in the corner out of cushions, and Sian and I quaffed red wine at the table. Over dinner she grilled Cal shamelessly about his past and I learned a thing or two. But I could tell from the glimmer in her gaze that she approved. Afterward, when we were finally alone, she leaned back in her chair and flashed me a satisfied grin, as if her work was done.

"Naught to sixty," she proclaimed.

I gave her a quizzical look.

"Lionel being naught," she added.

This afternoon Cal has gone to his surgery and I have promised Jez I will sort out her invoicing. I have just installed myself at the kitchen table with a stack of correspondence and a liter of coffee, when I hear a car in the drive. I glance out the window to see a familiar dark green Ferrari pull up and in spite of the fact that it is mid-January, the top is down. Hugo wears the giant gold anaconda scarf, and next to him, ramrod straight, sits Malcolm, whose hulking presence Peggy and I have genuinely missed these past few weeks. Malcolm leaps bodily out of the front seat before the engine is even quiet, and within an instant his enormous hazel eyes are peering in at me anxiously through the kitchen door. When I open it, he practically assaults me with affection, trying to scale my body with his ungainly limbs. When he is finished, he hurls himself across the room to where Peggy and the pups are nursing, and sprawls in front of her, like an adoring suitor. Peggy looks pleased in spite of herself, giving a little wag of her tail.

"I had to come," says Hugo with a grin, walking toward the door. "He's been pining terribly."

"Peggy, too, though she refuses to show it."

I pour him a coffee and Hugo sinks down onto the sofa with a sigh. "I've missed this kitchen," he says, looking around.

"You're not going to tell me I'm easy again, are you?"

He appraises me with narrow eyes. "I suspect you're rather more awkward than you appear," he says.

"I certainly hope so."

"How's the local vet?"

"Very local indeed," I say with a grin.

"Bravo."

"And Constance?"

"Constance appears to have gone into purdah. But knowing her, she'll be fine." He takes a sip of coffee. "In actual fact, Malcolm and I spent last weekend in Windsor," he says slyly.

Bonnie!

"And?"

"I wouldn't want to count my chickens. But the early signs are encouraging. Her divorce to the tuba player comes through in a few weeks' time. And I've promised her a short break somewhere fabulous to celebrate."

"How lovely."

"I rather thought I'd bring her here," he adds nonchalantly.

"You want to stay *here*?" I gape at him.

"Don't be ridiculous. I've booked a country hotel nearby. But I was hoping you'd have Malcolm," he says. Relief washes over me.

"I could be persuaded," I say. "For double the fees."

Hugo and Malcolm settle in for the afternoon, as if they never left, and at half past five I hear the familiar rumble of the Volvo outside. Hugo looks up from where he's reading the newspaper. "That would be your knight in shining armor," he says.

"Except I'm not a princess."

He tilts his head at me. "Clearly not," he agrees.

I glance toward the door to see Cal peering in at us with his unreasonably blue eyes. He lets himself in and Hugo jumps to his feet. I have to admit, I'm a little uncertain how Cal will react to Hugo's presence, given the history of our little threesome.

"Hello," says Cal, sweeping us both up with his gaze.

"Hope you don't mind me dropping in," says Hugo nervously.

"Not at all," says Cal. "Are you staying for supper?" He lifts up a bag of groceries he is carrying. Hugo glances over at me quickly and I shrug.

"That would depend on who's cooking," Hugo says cautiously.

"Never trust a woman to do a man's job," says Cal, moving to the counter and starting to unpack the food.

I smile. *Practically perfect in every way.*

acknowledgments

This book would not have been written without the steadying hand of Cordelia Sands, who probably deserves a writing credit but will have to content herself with lashings of gratitude and a hefty gift voucher. Huge thanks as well to my fabulous UK agents Felicity Rubinstein, Juliet Mahony, and Francesca Davies at Lutyens & Rubinstein, and the terrific team at Inkwell in New York: Kim Witherspoon, David Forrer, and Jessica Mileo. I'm also indebted to the supremely talented editorial teams on both sides of the Atlantic who helped guide the dogs home: Clare Hey and Olivia Barber at Orion in the UK, and Margo Lipschultz and Helen Richard at G. P. Putnam's Sons in the US.

Finally, as ever, big thanks to the faithful squad at home: Peter, Theo, Cody, Maddy, and Megan.